RETALIATION

BY L. A. BURCH

BOOK FOUR OF THE MASTERMINDS SERIES

Books by L. A. Burch

The Masterminds Series

Retribution
Beyond Redemption
Reparations
Retaliation

Standalones

Twisted Reprisals
Perfect Melody

Retaliation: 1) To return like for like
2) To get revenge

KDP Publishing
Cover Design: Michelle D. Josey

ISBN: 9798990247260

Special Thanks To

Joshue Noriega

Special thanks to you for allowing me to portray you as Joshue Noriega, Little Capo, in my book.

Special Thanks To

Glendell Nelson
"aka" Fa'ness
Ex-Military

Jackson Smith
"aka" Jack
Security Specialist

Special thanks to you both
for allowing me to
portray you in my book.

L. A. BURCH

RETALIATION

BOOK FOUR OF THE MASTERMINDS SERIES

Prologue

All three of the men who held leadership roles in the World Redemption Agency, were sitting in their HQ, going over the latest reports from their field agents. They all finished about the same time, then leaned back and studied each other. In the clandestine world they dwelled in, trust could get you killed. So, even though they were all technically on the same team, since loyalties were tumultuous at best, they were all cautious.

Reginald Burke, the 44-year-old Head of the WRA, was leading this meeting. They were inside the all-glass observation booth overlooking the WRA Central Control. He had only held the top position for about six months, but he'd already made sweeping changes inside the formally corrupt organization. The problem was, the answer he sought the most, to the most pressing issue, was still eluding him.

Sitting to his right was his uncle, Glendo Burke, the man responsible for unveiling the corruption, and also appointing Reggie as the leader of the WRA. He held the title of Head of Mission Development but, as oldest male Burke, he could take any position he desired, including head of the whole organization. Reggie respected the man, but thought there was something off about his sudden return. It didn't help matters when, nine days after he appeared, revealing he had faked his death 30 years ago, and been living in the shadows ever since, Lucille Drake, Reggie's mother and former Head of the WRA, had been assassinated.

The other occupant at the table was Walter Rogers, who held the newly created position of Head of Internal Investigations. He was a former Army MP, turned SBI Agent and, last year, decided to join the WRA. The 51-year-old had been tasked with, not only getting up to speed on all things WRA, but also finding out who killed Lucille Drake.

His introduction into their world had not been by choice, but Reggie knew he was a man of integrity. He had proven himself smart and capable in everyday life, now it was time to see how he faired in the dog-eat-dog world of spies.

Reggie turned to him first since it was technically his investigation. "Walt, what do you think about these reports? Can they be trusted?"

Walt sighed and said, "I believe they can be trusted, but the problem is, they still don't rule out either of the two main suspects." Leaning forward, he said, "We all know the CIA is capable of anything. The WRA has been working closely with them for over 30 years. They know all the ins and outs of our policies and regulations. Hell, most of our agents are recruited from inside their ranks. There's even a provision in our By-Laws to account for 10% of our staff being CIA informants."

Reggie nodded and said, "I understand that, but taking on the CIA is tantamount to declaring war on the USA. Covertly, we could kick their ass, but we have to have undisputed proof that they're responsible. With that proof, I can go to the President and he'd let us have our war, as long as it stayed undercover." He paused for a second in thought, then asked, "What about the other suspected organization?"

"If I had to put my money up, the Noriega Cartel is where I would place it," said Walter. "With the shutdown of the Prison Contraband Network and the termination of our arms deal with them, the WRA pretty much hung them out to dry. Carlos Noriega is old school. In his mind, when someone makes a promise or agreement, death is the only way to break it. Lucille's death would hurt him in the long run, the threat of the WRA is what kept the other Cartels from opposing him. But his sense of honor would force him to act. And the sting on the game rooms would have been the last straw."

The previous year, Walt had tipped off his boss about the money laundering going on in the game rooms sponsored by the WRA. When the SBI shut them down, the Cartels lost one of the main sources they had of cleaning their dirty money in the US.

Glendo finally spoke up after Walt's last statement. "You were the one who launched the sting on the game rooms," he said, accusingly.

Reggie could tell Walt didn't appreciate Glendo's tone. Walt said, "It was my job to stop criminal activity back then. Plus, you know it wasn't me that launched the investigation. Take it up with your protégé if you have a problem with how everything turned out."

Reggie knocked on the table to bring the attention back to him. "Petty beefs and past decisions have no place at this table. What we need to focus on is finding out who murdered my mother. If either of you need to take a step back, excuse yourself now so we can move forward." The men stared at each other for a few more seconds, then leaned back and turned to him. He told Walt, "Continue with what you were saying."

"Colombia has always been a hotbed for Cartel takeovers. With the WRA backing the Noriegas, it brought stability to the country, but only because everyone who went against us was obliterated. All the Cartels who accepted the situation, Carlos made sure they made money, and their leadership was protected. When Mrs. Drake put a freeze on their agreement, it put the Cartel in a fucked-up position. They needed to unload their drugs, but if they shopped around, word would get out that something was amiss between the Noriega Cartel and the WRA. So, I think Carlos had her killed to make a statement to the other Cartels that he didn't need us anymore. And it worked! None of the opposition has made a move on him."

Reggie nodded again and then glanced towards his uncle. "What do you think?"

"I trained with the CIA, just like most of our leadership," he said, taking a slight dig at Walt. He was the only one in a leadership role with no CIA training. "The guys they have running the show are pussies; they wouldn't risk war with us over the life of one agent. And Paul would be the only reason they had to kill her. The Colombians did it, and all this talk and delay is making us look weak. I told you it was them a week after the murder, nothing I've learned since has changed my mind. Let's go wipe them out and then we can move pass this to help the people this organization was made to help."

Reggie felt both men were right. The Noriega Cartel had thrown a hissy fit because the WRA had taken a temporary step back to deal with another problem. Carlos Noriega had jumped the gun and sent an assassin for the perceived slight. Or at least that's the way they all saw it. The problem was, they still had no proof. And if they were wrong, a lot of people would die for no good reason. He sat in thought before making a decision and sharing it with his team.

"As much as I would like to just blow them off the face of the earth, we still have no solid proof. So, this is what we're gonna do." He laid out his plan and, though his uncle didn't look happy about it, they all agreed it was the best course of action. The three men shook hands and Glendo and Walt left to set their parts of the plan in motion.

Reggie didn't leave because there was one last thing he needed to do before he left one of the most secure rooms in the world: He needed to call his little brother. When Daniel Burke picked up, Reggie said, "Sorry to bother you, Little Bro. I know you're busy planning your wedding. But I'm in a really fucked up predicament, and I need to meet with you, soon."

There was silence on the other end for almost a full minute. Finally, Daniel sighed and asked, "Where and when?"

"Wherever and whenever is convenient for you. But, the sooner the better."

Daniel said, "Come to the house. I've gone over it inch by inch and it's completely secure. I'll be here all day. Just come when you can."

Reggie said, "I'm on my way now. Give me a couple hours."

"Can you tell me what all this is about?" asked Daniel.

"Let's just say, it's about the same reason you felt the need to go over your house, inch by inch," answered Reggie.

Another pause, then Daniel simply said, "See you when you get here." They both hung up and Reggie made his way to the door, hopeful that he was about to get answers, but afraid of what they might be.

Chapter 1

Joshue Noriega, the youngest child of the Cartel Boss, Carlos Alberto Noriega, despised prison with a passion. The cloying mixture of hopelessness and desperation always made him want to gag. It was a good thing he had the privilege of coming and leaving whenever he wanted to. Without that right, he would've probably slit his wrist a long time ago.

Little Capo, as he was known all over Colombia, held one of the most dreaded jobs in the Noriega Cartel: He was the liaison between his father and all the prison Capos in his organization. Under threat of torture and death, all the Wardens allowed him to enter and exit with whatever he wanted so the Cartel could keep control of what belonged to them. He possessed a lot of power because of the information he was trusted with, but the work was long and hard. Most days, he was on the road, traveling from prison to prison, delivering goods and messages that his father didn't trust with anyone else.

At least when he traveled, the 24-year-old did so in style. His father had gifted him a bulletproof, stretched Cadillac ESV with his own personal driver, who was on call 24 hours a day. The man up front was one of the older guys that had started out with Carlos when they worked for the Medellin Cartels. He was tough and definitely a killer, but the twin custom Nighthawks Joshue carried marked him with the same designation. Not to mention, he never went anywhere without his right-hand man, Felipe 'Flip' Dos Santos.

They were finally on their way home after visiting the worst prison in the country, Prison De La Modelo. There, Joshue had been given a piece of urgent information that the messenger said needed an immediate response from Carlos. But everyone's information was urgent. No one ever said that the Boss could get back to them when he had time. Every message was presented to him like it was a life or death warning. But, even he had to admit, the last few messages he received were very important.

Sitting safely in the back of the luxury vehicle, with a UFC fight playing on the 50-inch TV, he looked over at Flip and said, "That was the third warning today about an impending attack from America. We've been getting them for about six months now. Normally, I would write them off as rumors, but the people who said it today have connections in the intelligence community. What do you think I should do?"

Flip was a tried and true shooter. At 25-years-old, only a year older than Joshue himself, Flip had well over a hundred bodies to his name. Six years ago, Flip had been an inmate at Prison De La Modelo when Joshue had made his first trip inside. A rival Cartel member, trying to make a name for himself, had pulled a knife and tried to gut Little Capo. Without hesitation, the gangster, from one of the worst Favelas in Brazil, had saved his life by placing a bullet into the would-be assassin's head.

Little Capo had pulled some strings, a good bit of money had changed hands, and he secured Flip's immediate release. Since then, Flip has been his brother and partner and Joshue rarely made decisions without asking for his input.

Flip shook his head and said, "If you lived in the city where soldiers could blend in and attack at will, I'd say to take it serious. But you guys own your own fucking town. And then, in the middle of that town, you have a fortress that the fucking Colombian Army can't even breach. You know if you tell your father, he'll panic, and we'll be locked inside those walls for God knows how long. I'll be stuck fucking those ugly ass maids while you and Allorah will be on a forced vacation, living it up."

Joshue laughed and said, "I can't not tell my father because you don't want to be stuck with the local pussy. You got to give me something better than that."

"Alright," he said, growing serious. "One thing I know about the Americans is, they are good at covert operations. It's just not possible that three different sources heard about an unspecified Agency coming down here, all at the same time. Now, the Americans are smart, and they do their research. I guarantee that they know about your father's paranoia and his habit to lockdown when he hears about a threat. I don't know if the threat is real, but I do think it's a ploy to get you all in the same area."

Joshue took over the thread of thought. "And if we respond how they think we will, it would be nothing for them to send a drone attack and kill us all at one time."

"Bingo," said Flip. "But you have to question who is coming, and why they would send a warning if it's not to manipulate you?" Flip sat back in the leather seat, his 5-foot 10-inch, medium built body, relaxed. He had no fear of death, so talking about it had no effect on him. Joshue, on the other hand, didn't want to die. The Cartel had serious enemies in America, but not all of them would just kill them outright. He decided to ask one more question before he made up his mind on what to do with the info.

"Do you think it's the WRA?" he asked his best friend.

Before Flip could answer, the SUV swerved violently to the right and something struck one of the back windows. "What the hell?" asked Flip as he righted himself and opened one of the ports to see what was going on. "Un-fucking-believable," he said before wrenching the door open as the vehicle came to a stop.

"Hey! Hold up!" yelled Joshue. But Flip was already jumping out with his gun waving in the air. Not knowing what to expect, he pulled his own gun and cautiously peeked out the door. The sight in front of him was almost comical, nothing at all of what he expected to see.

About ten young boys, ages ranging from 8 to 13, had their hands laced behind their heads, standing with their legs spread wide, while Flip held them at gunpoint. Hulk, their old-school driver, climbed out of the vehicle and added his own gun to the mix. Joshue wanted to laugh and tell them to chill, but both men were acting as if a major offense had just taken place.

"Any one of you fuckers move, I swear, you're gonna die," growled Flip. Some of the boys looked defiant, some looked scared to death. All of them had enough sense not to move as Hulk went down the line checking each of them for weapons. When he confirmed that the thrown rock had been the only weapon at their disposal, Hulk walked back around and stood next to Flip.

The late afternoon sun was still trying its best to broil everything in the area. It was only a couple hours away from disappearing behind the Andes Mountain Range to the northwest of their current location. That would provide a much-needed reprieve for most of Central Colombia. Putting on his shades to cut down on the punishing glare, Joshue was sure no one else involved in this situation was worried about the brightness.

In Spanish, Flip asked the boys if they knew English. All of them either nodded or answered with a confident, "Yes!"

Seemingly picking a boy at random, Flip stepped up to him and asked, "Do you know whose vehicle that is right there?"

The boy was sweating profusely, either from the sun or his nerves. Cutting his eyes over to Little Capo, he said, "Yes."

Backing up a step, Flip asked, "What about the rest of you? All of you know who owns this SUV?" They all answered in some form that they indeed knew whose SUV it was. Flip, fast as lightning, smacked the boy, causing blood to explode out of his mouth. "And yet, one of you little bastards thought it was a good idea to disrespect the Noriega Cartel? You thought you could throw something at a Boss and get away with it?" In quick succession, Flip smacked three more of the boys, forcing all three to the ground.

Joshue took a step away from the SUV where he'd been leaning, with the intention of stopping his friend from terrorizing the kids any further. Hulk caught his eye with a hand signal and motioned for him not to interfere. Reluctantly, he leaned back against the SUV, wishing that he could climb back in and let the cool interior relax his tension-filled body.

"Get up!" Flip shouted at the boys. All defiance was now gone. The boys were whimpering and crying, and none were brave enough, or stupid enough, to stand against Felipe. His reputation for violence was well known in the area.

When the line reformed, Flip asked, "Who threw the rock?" The wind kicking up the dusty terrain was the only sound for about ten seconds. Then Flip cocked his gun. "Who threw the rock?" he softly asked again. More crying and whimpering, but nothing other than that. The sound of the gunshot caused several of the kids to scream, and a dog in the distance to bark in fright.

"That was the only warning shot you'll get," said Flip. "You wanted to act like a man and spit in the face of the Cartel. Act like a man now and stand up for what you did." Again, the kids stayed quiet.

Flip glanced over at Hulk and asked, "Did you see who threw it?"

In his heavily accented English, he said, "Yeah, I see him."

Flip said, "Point him out."

The old-school gangster was nobody's do-boy, but he accepted his new position in life. At 52 years old, Hulk was still a beast. Feared and respected for all the work he'd put in when there was no peace between the Cartels. Working out every day, he was chiseled and fit. A hulk in every sense of the word. Loyal to a T, and ready to do whatever was asked of him, he moved to follow Flip's directive.

Hulk lumbered over, making his way directly to a boy who appeared to be about 12 or 13. Pointing, he said, "Is this one." Urine immediately streamed down the boy's legs, but he stood still, probably too afraid to run.

Patting him on the back, Flip told Hulk, "Good man. Now go ahead and wait in the vehicle." Hulk nodded and made his way back to the driver's seat, giving the children the evil eye for their disrespect.

Flip scanned the gathered boys with a smile on his face. Finally, he said, "As Colombians, every one of you should have a healthy dose of respect for the Cartels. By the time you can talk, your parents should have made you understand what that respect needs to look like. Obviously, your parents failed. The soft teaching style didn't work. So now, I have to teach all of you the hard way."

Joshue watched as the pistol began its elevation. As if his body and mind were submerged in molasses, he was too slow to react. Flip lined the barrel up with the kid's forehead, remorselessly pulling the trigger.

His screamed, "NO!" was more an expression of disbelief than any thought that he could actually stop the bullet. All Joshue was left to do was watch as the other children fell to their knees, begging in terror, thinking they would die next.

Flip placed his gun back in its holster and said, "The next time this happens, all of you will die. Don't fuck with the Cartel." With that, he left the kids cradling the body of their friend and made his way back to the SUV.

Joshue was numb. Of course, in the heat of battle, he'd seen children die as collateral damage. In this part of the world, it was a common sight. But seeing the ruthlessness of someone he called brother, up close and personal, it caused his stomach to turn over. He took one last glance at the traumatized children, then climbed in beside Flip.

Hulk pulled away from the scene as soon as his door closed. Yes, this was Colombia, the world's largest producer of cocaine. Yes, the local governor over their department was as corrupt as most of the Cartel Bosses. But killing a child in cold blood, no matter what the reason, was still frowned upon. Not to mention, they knew nothing about the kid. He could end up being a relative of a Cartel member or a government official. It was best that they didn't dally around, and make it back to their home base as soon as possible.

Villavicencio, the town owned by the Noriega Cartel, was still about 20 minutes away. Joshue couldn't even look at his friend as the anger built up inside of him. He loved Flip like a brother, but the bullshit he'd just done was as cruel as it was reckless. This one act could bring down the Colombian Military or rival Cartels on their heads. And this at a time when they possibly had a serious threat to worry about.

Reading his friend like a book, Flip said, "I know you're mad and you think I crossed the line. But if you still want to achieve that goal we talked about, you have to take that emotional shit and purge it from your soul."

Joshue looked at his compadre, opened his mouth to make a rash comment, but checked himself. Finally, after thinking it over, he settled for, "A child threw a rock. A fucking rock, Felipe! Smack him around, threaten him with worse. But at the end of the day, you just jeopardized all of us over a child throwing a rock!" He was steaming mad and showing it with every shouted word. But Flip was calm, cool, and collected. Sitting and taking the reprimand on the chin.

Nodding slowly, Flip glanced off into space like he was seeing a scene farther away than the inside of the Cadillac. After a minute of motionless thought, he turned to Joshue and said, "Let me tell you a story, something that happened in my youth. And you tell me if I overreacted, or just did what, really, you should have done. It happened 15 years ago…"

Brazil has always been known for three things: Poverty, corruption, and beautiful women. For 10-year-old Felipe, poverty and corruption were part of his everyday life. The only women that he saw on a regular basis were his mother, grandmother, and the whores who roamed his home town. To him, they were all beautiful, but in their own way.

Felipe wasn't in a gang like the American idea of the word, but his crew consisted of 18 boys who would kill or die for each other in a second. The love ran deep. All of their families were close and looked out for the boys who were not actually their relatives. Nothing was off limits in making sure that everyone in their circle had food, shelter, and protection from all outsiders.

It was common for ten of the boys to leave on weeks-long missions in an effort to supply everyone's needs. On one such occasion, Felipe and seven other members of the crew were left behind to maintain the safety of their village. They all had guns and none would hesitate to use them. Most of the older crews stayed away from their area because of how coldhearted the kids were said to be.

Then, one day, a pack of rivals, hearing that most of them were gone on a mission, decided to put the crew in its place. Twenty or so teenage boys infiltrated their territory, tied them up, one by one, and relocated them to a field on the outskirts of town. After they had all been beaten and abused in unspeakable ways, the band of rivals made their way back to the town to complete their debauchery.

While the eight boys were tied to trees, unable to render aid, the teenagers robbed and brutalized everyone they came across. Felipe cried and cried as he heard the screams and pleas for mercy. For two days this went on, with most of the town's men lying dead in the streets, and the women being terrorized.

With the sun setting on the second day, the teens, gleeful and proud of what they'd done, returned and freed the boys. They marched them through the destruction until they came to the small square in the center of town. There, a man waited to give them a message. With shock, Felipe realized that he knew the man. It was his mother's brother, an uncle he hadn't seen in years.

In deference to their relation, his uncle killed all the other boys, but left him alive. He told him that his little gang had robbed one of his warehouses and killed a bunch of his whores. To pay back the debt, he was coming to their territory and taking their women to replace his dead whores. With that, his uncle and the teens loaded their captives into a bus, then left him surrounded by the bodies of his seven brothers.

The first thing he did, after regaining his composure, was run all the way to his home where the nightmare continued. Both his mother and grandmother had been tortured and murdered by his uncle's gang. He had no more tears. The pain was still there, but all it did was harden his heart even more than it had already been. Before he buried the mangled bodies of his loved ones, he made a vow to them: No matter what he had to do, he would get vengeance on the ones responsible for these heinous acts.

The rest of the crew returned a few days later, having heard through underground connections what had happened. He tried his best to rally the boys into seeking revenge against the other gang. They all declined saying that they were too small a crew to go after a faction that was so great in numbers and power. The boys eventually left to find new homes with the survivors of the attack.

But not Felipe. He stayed in his desolate hometown and trained himself to be a killer. Over the next five years, he killed as many members of his uncle's gang as he could. Finally, at 17-years-old, he got the opportunity he'd been dreaming of.

Sitting in a well-known whorehouse, right outside of Rio, Felipe was waiting to see the local Boss about a bodyguard position that had just opened up. One of the women had just come to retrieve him when his uncle stepped in the door of the dimly lit establishment. Felipe froze, thinking that he must be hallucinating, but one of the lights touched the man's face and all doubt faded away. His uncle didn't even recognize him as he picked out his woman and made his way up the steps.

Felipe sat outside the building for hours, and when his uncle emerged, he followed him to a house about five miles away. The darkness, by now, was Felipe's home. He could move in silence, blending into any environment. He crept up to one of the front windows, didn't see anyone in the living room, so he continued his trek around the house.

He found his uncle relaxing on the back porch, smoking a cigar. Felipe got within ten feet of the man before he was alerted to a presence. But it was too late. Seeing a man pointing a gun at his head, he settled back in the chair and took a long pull on the cigar.

Felipe asked, "Do you know who I am?"

His uncle shrugged. "Does it matter?"

Shrugging himself, Felipe said, "No, I guess it doesn't," and shot his uncle in the face.

He spent the next six months on the run from the law, as well as his uncle's gang. Finally realizing that, if he stayed in Brazil he would die, Felipe made his way to Colombia. Broke and without many options, he attempted to rob a bank, which landed him in prison. Bad for him, but good for Joshue. That journey is what led him to being there to kill his would-be assassin.

Flip said, "Technically, I should have killed all those kids, but they weren't as far gone as my crew. That was the mistake my uncle made; he left me alive. But the point was to tell you what happens when you allow children to have no fear of your organization. Those kids grow up. And without those hard lessons being taught to them early, they mature into adults who don't know their place." Tapping his head, he finished with, "A rock today, a bullet tomorrow."

Joshue sat and absorbed the lesson. Six years they'd been by each other's side, and this was the first time Felipe had opened up about his past. That's what helped Joshue understand that Flip was right. Little Capo had big plans, and if they worked out how he predicted they would, he couldn't afford to be soft. Even towards little kids.

Reaching over, he put his fist out for his friend to tap. Leaning back, he nodded and said, "I got you now. I understand." Then they both went quiet, Joshue forgetting all about the very serious threat from the unspecified American Intelligence Agency.

Chapter 2

Supposedly, it was a full moon, but the thick cloud cover obscured even a hint of light from breaching its curtain. The headlights of the transport van illuminated the road ahead, but it only seemed to make the passing foliage on each side of them darker. About a quarter mile back, the follow car, containing two US Marshalls, had its own lights shining bright. The drivers shifted the distance between the two vehicles at random times so any attackers would have to guess when to strike.

Fully shackled and secured in the back of the prison van, Tremayne Michaels, AKA Delmas Burke, could only estimate what time it was. He knew it had to have been about 1:00am when they left the Wake County Detention Center. The captain on duty had told his drivers to step on it because he wanted them to reach Rock Hill, South Carolina before the sun came up. At 10:00am Delmas would have his first appearance for the quadruple murder of a group of gangbangers the previous year. Even though he'd been locked up at the time of the murders, he told police that he'd ordered the hit.

Six months he'd sat in Solitary Confinement, confessing to crime after crime, until Wake County was forced by a federal judge to take him to South Carolina. After his court date there, he would go to Florida, Georgia, Alabama, and Missouri to face other murder changes. He hoped the journey wouldn't make it that far, but you never know. He could end up on the road for the next ten years of his life.

His transporters for the first leg of his voyage were both 20-year veteran Sheriff's Deputies. They'd warned him that he would be the first to die if anything happened while on the road. They were stone-faced, hard-bodied men and they thought they were capable of carrying out their threat.

What they didn't understand was that, even fully shackled, Delmas could kill both of them without breaking a sweat. They were trained to kill in self-defense. Delmas, on the other hand, was born and bred to be a killer of killers. The police could do everything right, but you couldn't defend against something you've never encountered.

Eyes laser sharp, and constantly looking at his surroundings, a mile-marker in the headlights caught his attention. It meant nothing on its own, so he needed to keep his eyes on the next few they passed. The deputy in the passenger seat was using his visor mirror to keep Delmas in his view. So, even as the second and third mile-marker confirmed his suspicion, he remained stoic and indifferent to the world outside the van.

The fourth mile-marker didn't contain the dots like the previous three, and Delmas started to think he'd imagined the whole thing. They were only a few miles into South Carolina; had only been on the road a few hours. It was foolish to think that his helpers would set up to break him out on the first trip. The trek to Florida would be long and full of desolate roads, perfect for setting up an ambush. Delmas told himself to be patient and focus his mind on the long haul.

Then the fifth marker appeared, and the van, inside and out, went quiet as, instantly, all the power cut off.

"What the hell?" asked the driver as he tried to maneuver the dead vehicle over to the side of the road. Finally rolling to a stop on the grassy shoulder, he looked at his partner and said, "This is it! Load up and put a gun on that son of a bitch!" They both strapped their weapons back to their armor-clad bodies, and the passenger put a shotgun up to the grill separating them from their prisoner.

Delmas knew the law-abiding officer wouldn't just shoot him, so he smiled and decided to test the waters a little. "I hope both of you told your wives and children you love them. You won't get another chance."

The deputy holding the gun on him said, “Shut the fuck up, you piece of shit! You better believe that, if I die, I’m taking you with me.”

The driver had been frantically trying to use the radio and his cell phone to call for help. Neither device seemed to be giving him the desired outcome. He said, “Coms are down and all signals are blocked.” Finally showing a bit of fear, he turned to his partner and said, “We’re sitting ducks out here! What are we supposed to do?”

The passenger remained calm. “We follow protocol. People know where we are. When they can’t reach us, they’ll come looking. We’re in a bulletproof vehicle, and I got a gun on the prize. Don’t worry, we’re as safe as we can be.” As he finished the statement, a huge explosion in the distance didn’t speak well for the Marshalls in the follow car. Both officers now looked worried. It was a big difference between bulletproof and bombproof.

“Damn!” Delmas said with a laugh. Shaking his head, he said, “Shit just got real. You both realize this is your last day on earth. If you need to pray and accept Jesus in your life, better do it now.”

Almost growling, the cop holding the gun said, “Shut the fuck up before I shoot you in the face!”

Shrugging, Delmas asked, “And then what? Right now, me being in the van with you is the only reason you’re still breathing. Shoot me and you’re essentially committing suicide.” Both of the officers had families. No one wanted their spouse getting that early morning visit telling them the life they’ve lived is over.

The driver was anxiously going back and forth from the ignition switch to his phone. Slamming the phone on the dash, he looked over and said, “Fuck this shit, Mike! Let’s let him go and live to fight another day!”

“Sounds like a good idea to me,” proclaimed Delmas.

“SHUT UP!” screamed Mike. Turning to his partner, he said, “Listen Sam, we’re not some piss-in-your-pants-at-the-first-sign-of-trouble rookies. Our bullets kill too. All we have to do is hold the fort down until backup arrives. Just keep your head on a swivel and we'll be back home before you know it." Not looking convinced, Sam turned to keep an eye on his side of the road.

They sat in silent darkness for about five minutes before anything else happened. No movement one second, the next, the van was surrounded by armored soldiers with weapons of mass destruction pointed at the front. All the warriors were dressed in black tactical gear with mask covering their faces. One detached himself from the rest and pointed a pistol at the driver's head.

Through the mask, Delmas heard the man say, "No one has to die. Just open the doors, lower your weapons, and allow us to walk away with Mr. Michaels."

Mike yelled from the passenger seat, "Fuck you! And I'm not negotiating. Any of you fuckers try anything and your buddy gets the first bullet!"

Another guy separated himself and stepped up to the passenger window, pointing his own gun. The man at the driver's window said, "This is your last chance to comply. We don't want to kill you for doing your job. And Mike," he said drawing the attention of the more aggressive guard. "Your wife, Dianne, and your two children, Mike Jr. age 14 and Jessica age 10, will also die if we have to do this the hard way."

Turning to the driver, he said, "Sam, you're all your kids have left, but I'll put both your little boys in wheelchairs for the rest of their lives. You know what happens to handicap kids in foster care? Make the right choice, Sam."

This was how people in the clandestine world operated. Nothing was left to chance. Backup plans had backup plans. Delmas had no doubt that both of these officers' families were in eminent danger. These guys wouldn't hesitate to kill or maim women or children.

In movies, this would be the time the bad guy said the wrong thing and the hero would kill him, content to die in a blaze of glory. In real life, Delmas knew to keep his mouth shut so the cops could see how hopeless their situation was. There was no need to rub it in and cause one or both officers to do something stupid. What the men were deciding now was if the life of a scumbag murderer, the fucking Prison Guard Killer, was more important than the lives of their loved ones. Undoubtably, they would conclude that family had to be their number one priority.

The officers looked at each other and nodded. They lowered their weapons, opened their doors, and raised their hands, waiting for further instructions. The soldiers reached in and collected all their weapons, their phones, and the keys. Then told them to stay still or die.

The leader, or at least Delmas assumed he was the leader because he'd done most of the talking, took the keys and moved to unlock the back door of the van. He climbed inside, squeezed into the back, and spent the next minute releasing Delmas from all his restraints. When he finished, both men exited the vehicle as another van, this one black, screeched to a stop in front of them. The leader looked at Delmas and said, "We need to get a move on. We have a plane idling on a runway about a mile from her. Someone will be waiting for you on the other end of the flight."

Delmas nodded and said, "Very good. I just have to do one thing and then we can go." He asked the man for the rifle he had slung across his back and the man handed it over without comment. Delmas took the two steps needed to come level with the officers in the vehicle. Both looked at him with their hands raised, but it was Sam who found the courage to speak.

"We complied. You don't have to kill us. Lock us in the back and you'll be long gone before help arrives." Mike didn't even try to beg, he already knew what was coming.

All the jokes and smiles were gone as Delmas asked the officers one question: “What’s my name?”

Sam stuttered as he said, “Tremayne Michaels.”

Mike dropped his head and said, “He means the other one, Sam.”

Looking confused, Sam said, “The other one? I don’t…” Then understanding dawned in his eyes. Under his breath, he said, “The Prison Guard Killer.”

Bringing the automatic weapon up, the PGK, at least according to the world, said, “Exactly,” before pulling the trigger and filling the two bodies with dozens of holes. When the clip was empty, complete silence ruled. He looked around at the gathered soldiers before handing the gun back to the leader. “Alright,” said Delmas. “Let’s go.”

Five soldiers loaded into the black van with Delmas as the rest of them stayed behind to clean up the mess. Within a couple of minutes, the van was parked next to a sleek, white jet with absolutely no markings on the outside. The leader, sitting in the passenger seat, looked back and said, “Good luck. Your benefactor will meet you wherever the plane lands.” He handed Delmas a 9mm Glock and turned, signifying the end of the exchange. Delmas took one last look around, nodded at the still masked men, and exited the van.

No sooner had his feet hit the ground, the van pulled off and a female flight attendant stepped to the door at the top of the steps. With a brilliant smile plastered across her stunning, dark-chocolate colored face, she said, “Good morning, Mr. Burke. We are cleared for takeoff as soon as you board.” Hearing his real name threw him for a bit, but it limited who the person could be behind his rescue. Shrugging, he climbed the stairs and walked pass the flight attendant, who hit the button to retract the steps.

He took in the opulent décor at a glance and sat in the forward most seat with the Glock still naked in his hand. The woman ignored it as she turned and said, “Buckle up. And before you ask, I have no idea where we are going or how long it's going to take. The cockpit door is locked and I haven't even seen the pilot." She said all this while buckling into her own seat as the plane rocketed down the runway before taking off.

As they started to ascend, Delmas asked, "Who are you and how do you know who I am?"

"My name is Amira and I work for NetJets, the company that owns the plane. I know your name because my boss handed me an envelope with $20,000, a note containing your name, and directions on what I needed to do. Basically, feed you, fuck you, or anything else you want to do until the plane lands. Then, keep my mouth shut about the whole state of affairs."

She was about 5'6", slim but curvy, and extremely attractive. The dark blue uniform molded to her body in a way that reminded him just how long he'd been locked up. But his mind was on more important things than his dick right now.

The plane leveled out and the seatbelt sign turned off. He unbuckled and stood up, saying, "Although you make a very tempting offer, I need food, a shower, and clothes." Thinking for a second, he said, "And a cellphone or computer."

Standing up herself, she pointed to the back and said, "Bedroom is back there. There's a suitcase on the bed, but I don't know what's in it. By the time you get out of the shower, I'll have a meal ready for you." He nodded, turned and entered the backroom.

More luxury was laid out before him, but Delmas had been around it his whole life. So, it had little effect. Opening the suitcase, it narrowed the field down a little more on who could be behind all this. The tactical pants and t-shirt were black and exactly his size. The phone and laptop were the same make and model he'd used before being locked up. Deciding to get clean before he started his research, he kicked off his shoes, stripped out of the orange jumpsuit he'd left the detention center wearing, removed his underwear and socks, and padded naked to the bathroom.

While he washed, he thought. The note he'd received right after his uncle visited him in jail said that if he confessed his sins, he'd be set free. A long time ago, someone he knew had received the same message and, after they'd confessed to a bunch of murders, people had helped him escape. A lot of people in his circle knew the story, so there was really no telling who was helping him now. Fuck it, he thought while drying off, he wasn't gonna wreck his brain trying to figure it out. He'd find out whenever he got off the plane.

Walking back into the bedroom, he ignored the sharp, feminine inhale in response to his nudity. He hadn't eaten anything since last night because he'd known the officers wouldn't give him access to a bathroom until they reached their destination. In response to the loaded down, hoagie style sandwich and French fries, waiting on a food cart next to the bed, he didn't care how he looked. All he wanted to do was eat, get dressed, and start the research he needed to begin his mission.

Clearing her throat, Amira asked, "Are you sure I can't help you with anything else?"

In between bites, he looked over and caught her staring at his lower region. Then her eyes traveled up and locked with his. He said, "I know I'm probably missing out on one of the best experiences of my life, but I really have a lot of work to do. Maybe another time." She seemed satisfied with his answer and inclined her head before turning and leaving him alone.

He polished off the food, got dressed in the clothes provided him, and then turned on the cellphone and laptop. Based on the latest intel he'd received, which was from his uncle last year, the Agency he worked for didn't have a clue who had killed their leader. To some, that was all Lucille Drake was; the leader of the World Redemption Agency. But to Delmas Burke, it was a bit more personal. She was also his mother.

So, his research was simple; he needed to access the WRA network and see if anyone had been named responsible. If not, then he needed to know who had been cleared, and who was still a suspect. Pulling up the dark web access point into the WRA underground server, he was somewhat surprised to learn his codes still worked. He wouldn't have to waste time trying to hack in. Knowing the process, he probably had 15 minutes before his presence was discovered and he was kicked out. With that in mind, he bent low and got to work.

18 minutes and 30 seconds later, the computer's internal hardware started frying as one of the WRA antihacking technicians forcefully expelled him from their network. He didn't delude himself for a minute, they had known the second he'd escaped from custody. And heads would roll when they found out no one had disabled his login codes.

Delmas wasn't a complete computer geek like some members of his family, but he knew how to find information. The time he'd stolen on the WRA network had given him a ton of material he needed. Now, he was ready to take a few steps forward in his mission of revenge.

Next, he used the phone to access the regular internet and learn some facts about his targets. After seeing what the WRA had compiled on all the possible suspects, there was really only one group that could be responsible. It only took a couple hours to put together a plan that was sure to get him the truth. Just in time too, a loud ding proceeded an announcement for all passengers to return to their seats and prepare for landing.

The window next to his reacquired seat showed a beautiful landscape from a bird's eye view. The fact that it was still dark affirmed his belief that they'd been traveling west. But even without that affirmation, he recognized the

City of Angels spread out below them as the plane continued its descent.

Of course, they didn't head for LAX, the pilot aimed for a semi-lit airstrip a little north of LA. He took that as a sign of fate as this put him almost exactly where he needed to be. After the plane touched down, it taxied to a stop next to a pair of all-black Mercedes-Benz G63 AMGs. It wasn't the Savage Edition he was so fond of, but it was further proof that the person behind his escape was close to him. While he unbuckled, the attendant got up, opened the side door, and pressed the button for the stairs to extend down.

With a bright smile, she said, "It was a pleasure flying with you, Mr. Burke. I do hope I get another chance to travel with you in the future."

He shrugged noncommittal and said, "You never know," before exiting the plane. As soon as he stepped down, the steps retracted, the door closed, and the flying machine slowly started to roll to the end of the runway. He watched as it turned around and sat idle, waiting for the vehicles to get out of the way so it could take off.

The backdoor to one of the Benz's was propped open, so he made his way over to the vehicle. Peeking into the interior, with the Glock's comforting weight in his grip, he looked into the eyes of someone who was neither friend nor foe. Though this act pushed him closer into the category of the former. The man didn't smile or extend a hand, he just waited to see what Delmas would do.

Finally, Delmas climbed into the back of the vehicle, the Benz pulling off as soon as his door closed. Seconds later, behind them, the plane rocketed down the airstrip and lifted off to destinations unknown. Delmas glanced around the dark interior and noticed two things that were out of the ordinary. First, there was a partition separating them from the driver's compartment. Second, the man sitting to his right had a cane clutched in-between his legs. The partition didn't really bother him because he didn't care who was driving. The cane, on the other hand, was very interesting.

"What's the story with the cane?" he finally asked.

In the same menacing voice he used to terrorize clandestine agents all over the world, he said, "Had a run in with your fucking brother."

Delmas chuckled and asked, "Which one?"

With a mild look of irritation, he said, "The only one who could have forced me to use a cane."

Nodding, he said, "You mean Reggie." When the man nodded, he said, "I guess you haven't run into Daniel lately or you wouldn't be so confident that only one of them could hurt you. I can assure you, he's nothing like he used to be."

The man didn't answer, he just pushed a button over his head and said, "Pull over up here." Within seconds, the SUV slowed and pulled into a small turnoff. Out the back window, Delmas watched as the identical vehicle pulled over behind them. His rescuer looked over at him and said, "Everything you'll need is in the SUV behind us. It's yours, do with it what you please. The phone you have is secure and the number saved in speed dial will contact me. Good luck and call if you need anything else."

Delmas cocked his head and asked, "How do you know what I'm planning to do, and what I'll need to do it?"

The man shrugged and said, "You're a Burke, it's in your DNA to seek vengeance." They stared at each other for a long minute before Delmas nodded and opened the door to leave. With one foot out, he turned back and searched the man's face.

"Why?" he asked him, knowing no further explanation was needed.

Once again, the man shrugged. "What else could I do? There was no way I could leave my cousin to a fate that I once avoided."

"Humph," Delmas said on a nod. "No, I guess you couldn't," he said to The Author before getting out and heading to the second SUV.

The driver of the second SUV exited with a mask covering his face and took the seat that Delmas had just vacated. Shutting himself inside the vehicle, he watched as the other Benz performed a U-turn and headed towards LA. The Author obviously knew at least the first step he planned to take. He'd even driven him the first few miles in the right direction. He didn't have too much farther to go, so he took his time as he headed north towards his first target.

He'd learned as a little boy that there was no such thing as a fair fight. A declaration was not needed to declare war on a foe. Walking up to your enemy in broad daylight was sometimes a fool's move. It was better to carry out all the necessary strikes under the cover of darkness. So, when the light gleamed, it would reveal the aftermath of a battle your adversary didn't even know he was engaged in. This was the motto of the Burkes. That's why, if you aimed at one, you had better pray that shot hit them all. Because, even if only one of them were left alive, well, vengeance might belong to the Lord, but it very well might be packaged in the form of a 200-pound, bald, black man with a gun pointed directly at your head.

Chapter 3

The light Phenom 100 jet landed on the small airstrip without a hitch and taxied to within feet of the idling, twilight-purple, Rolls-Royce Ghost Black Badge. The plane cost the WRA about $5.5 Million. The car added another $500,000. That kind of money was nothing to sneeze at, but with Reggie now at the helm, the $1 Trillion mark for the Agency was just around the corner.

The WRA Head Honcho stood up and stretched before finishing off the last of his MaCallan single malt scotch whiskey. Since the bottle ran about $9,000, that last sip cost approximately $100. He glanced at his Rose-Gold, Jacob & Co. Bugatti Chiron watch and saw that they were right on time. Like clockwork, he thought. Anything dealing with the WRA, Reggie's goal was to make it as reliable and dependable as possible.

He exited the jet after throwing on his Versace jacket and shouldering his supply bag. A young female agent, who had been shot in the shoulder last year, jumped out of the Rolls-Royce and handed him the keys. She smiled, putting him in the mind of Nia Long, then stepped to the side so he could enter. He asked, "How are you liking your new post, Ms. Moore?"

Meka gave him a fast nod and said, "Oh! It's beautiful here. But, um, I wouldn't mind a little more action. You know," she hurried to say, "I just want to prove myself worthy of the second chance."

Meka Moore was a rising star in the WRA. With a genius level IQ, and aptitude scores off the charts, it was only a matter of time before she moved into a supervisory position. She was beautiful, resourceful, and a well of untapped potential. After last year's debacle of a mission, where her team was executed for branching off on its own, she had escaped the same fate because of Reggie's intervention. While her arm healed, Reggie had given her a cushy job guarding one of the WRA's luxury safehouses. It seemed that she was now ready to get back to work.

Reggie paused and studied her for a minute. He wasn't sure, but he might be able to find a role for her on his current mission. Making up his mind, he said, "Alright. After you and the pilot store the plane, make your way over to the auxiliary safehouse. I'll be staying at the main one like we planned. I can't make any promises, but I might call on you to aid me in my mission. Is that okay with you?"

Her eyes flamed with joy, but she kept it professional. "Yes, Sir!" Flashing those pearly whites, she added, "I'll be ready when you call." He gave her one more nod and then slid into the driver's seat and pulled away. He chuckled when he saw her doing a little happy dance in the rearview mirror.

He sobered pretty quickly when he thought once again on the conversation he'd had at Daniel's compound. Just like always, Daniel was ten steps ahead of the WRA leadership. It surprised him that Walt had actually been the first one to figure it out, but Daniel had always told them how much of an asset he was.

The problem now was, what was he supposed to do with the knowledge? He hated relying on others, but it seemed he didn't have a choice this time around. Driving the 30 minutes to the safehouse, Reggie let his mind replay the meeting he'd had with his younger brother.

It still amazed him every time he pulled up in front of Daniel's Charlotte compound and the gate actually opened. Even before the last four years of all-out war, Daniel had been drifting away from the family. Reggie now knew it was because their uncle had been feeding Daniel stories about their mother being a murderer and a traitor.

Rounding the last curve of the driveway, Daniel's Mega-Mansion came into view. Reggie could see Daniel sitting on his top step with his adopted daughter, Gabby, sitting beside him. He pulled his Aston Martin V12 Vantage parallel with them, cut the engine, then hopped out to join them.

Daniel, Reginald's younger brother by five years, was dressed in his customary, all-black gear. Gabby, on the other hand, was wearing ash-blue jeans, a pink Chanel shirt, and a pair of pink Nike Air-Max tennis shoes. Reggie said, "What's going on, little bro?" Turning, he added, "Hi, Gabby!"

She inclined her head so she could look down her nose at him, then said, "Hi." All he could do was shake his head. Gabby hadn't warmed up to the rest of her father's family. To punctuate the point, she kissed Daniel loudly on his bald head and said, "I got homework. See you later. Love you." She was almost to the door when Daniel stopped her with a word.

"GABBY!" he exclaimed.

With slumped shoulders, she turned back around and said, "Bye, Uncle Reggie! Hope you have a nice rest of the night." Reggie could only chuckle at the false salutation before she disappeared into the gigantic house.

Daniel shrugged and said, "She'll come around. Just don't give up on her. That's what she expects you to do, but if you do, she'll hate you forever."

Sitting down next to his younger brother, Reggie said, "With what she's been through, I don't hold the attitude against her. She's yours, so I love her. I'll keep doing my best to show her that."

In their youth, love was shown as a reward for following orders or completing a task. Their sister, Kashonda, after she had kids, was the first one to show them how children were meant to be treated. Reggie, Delmas, and Daniel loved their nieces dearly. At times, they had to be tough on the girls so they knew how to survive this bleak world. Other times, they just needed to show love to a vulnerable family member. Gabby was no different. Reggie would kill or die to keep her safe. It didn't matter one bit that they didn't share blood.

Daniel looked over at him and asked, “So, what is this all about?”

Reggie, knowing his brother wouldn’t ask unless the area was secure, dove right in. “Something isn’t right with Uncle Glendo. I mean, on the surface, he hasn’t done anything wrong. But, when you look at everything as its own event, the story just doesn’t add up.” He expected Daniel to jump up and defend his mentor. He didn’t. Reggie said, “And you don’t seem surprised by my accusation one bit.”

Daniel pulled out his phone, tapped a few buttons, and handed it to Reggie. All he said was, “Read this,” before he went quiet.

He read the file, scrolling through page after page, with growing dismay. The truth was right here in black and white. The man pretending to be Glendo Burke was actually his twin brother, Ronald Burke. Reggie glanced over at Daniel and asked, “Is this legitimate?”

Daniel nodded and said, “Keep reading.”

The file was very detailed. It explained how Willie James Burke, Reggie’s grandfather, had found out his wife was pregnant with twins, but told her to keep it quiet. Having more than adequate medical training, he delivered the twins himself at their home. Glendo was raised with the Burke family, while Ronald was sent to New York to live with cousins.

Willie kept in constant contact with his son, making sure he had the same training as his siblings. Eventually, Ronald was old enough, and trained enough, that Willie started sending him out on missions. Several times, he was sent as backup for his brothers, who had no idea that he was there, or even existed. Then, like smoke, he disappeared.

The last notation in the file revealed that Ronald had one child, a son by the name of Wilford Sealy. Reggie handed the phone back and laughed. After a beat, they were both laughing. It was just to relieve the tremendous amount of stress they were under, but it felt good to laugh with his brother.

When they both had control of themselves, Reggie recognized how tired he was. When was the WRA gonna be purged of all corruption? That was the question that made him so weary.

"The Author is our cousin?" asked Reggie.

"Yeah," Daniel replied.

"How long have you known this?"

"A better question would be, how it took us so long to find the information?" Daniel retorted. "Walt, not even a month on the job, found this file in the family archives. He's not that good of an actor, so I know you've seen the animosity he has for Uncle Ronald."

"You mean Walt found the file?" he asked incredulously. At Daniel's nod, he sighed in frustration and asked, "What can we do?"

Daniel shrugged. "The By-Laws are clear. There's not much we can do. He's still a Burke, it's right there in the file. The only way to legally remove him would be a challenge from one of us. Then, all he would do is appoint one of us to be his champion and make it a fight to the death. So basically, he is within his legal rights to come in and take over like he did, regardless of what name he's trying to use."

Reggie looked sideways at his brother. "You said 'legally remove.' You said it that way for a reason. So, what illegal ways can we use to remove him?"

Daniel looked up at the moon and stars that were illuminating the cool night. He said, "I've always been told that I'm the smartest. The best at everything I did. Always placed in competition with the whole world. It took me a while to realize that this way of thinking was by design. It was to keep me focused on what is most important in our domain."

Standing up, he said, "This man tricked me. I can't even blame it on the fact that I was young, he still had me up until

Walt found this file." Looking at Reggie, he added, "But mom knew what was going on."

Reggie jerked back in surprise. "How do you figure that? I don't think she would have sat back and did nothing knowing she had a long-lost brother out there who could blindside her at any time."

"That's the point, Reg! She didn't sit back. Walt said he found that file on an auxiliary server that hadn't been accessed but a few times in the last twenty years. Mom hid that file because she didn't want any of us to ever stumble on it and learn the truth. By my actions, I must have tipped my hand that I'd found something related to the subject. She just didn't know that, instead of using his real name, Ronald decided to take over the identity of his twin. Glendo, being my favorite uncle, I was willing and ready to believe everything he said.

"He filled my head with lies, because he couldn't risk me leaking to mom that he'd resurfaced. Mom would have sent assassins for him the second she knew, because the By-Laws are clearly on his side. There was nothing stopping him from showing up and taking over the WRA except for our strength as a unit. Think of it like this: If this stranger pops up and tells us to exile Mom on his word alone, would we have done it? By-Laws be damned, we would have killed his ass!"

Reggie was confused. "But why would he need our permission to exile or kill Mom in the first place? He was in the right! He could have reassigned, exiled, or killed her for what she did to their brothers!"

Shaking his head, Daniel said, "You still don't get it!" Pulling his phone out again, he said, "Read this."

It was another file of length and, by the end, Reggie was sitting with tears coursing down his face. Finally, he looked up, but it was Daniel who spoke. "Yeah, Reg. Mom was innocent. Ronald was the one who killed all the Burke men."

The second file was the investigation done by Lucille Drake that outlined the fact that, when Uncle Calvin and

Uncle David were killed, Ronald had been their shadow agent. Where the first file ended with his disappearance, this one listed everything he'd done after that point.

The first item on the list, the murder of his own father and the remaining cousins he'd grown up with. It was painfully clear that he was trying to erase any trace of his existence. But he hadn't stopped with that goal being realized.

Obviously, with Willie dead, his wife having died of cancer years before, Ronald was free from discovery, but had no way of cashing in on his name. The investigation found that he had introduced himself to his brothers, one by one, but explained his need for secrecy. Telling them he was on a deep cover mission sanctioned by their father, to protect the WRA from American Counter-Intelligence. Then, in a bid to get what he really wanted, the WRA, he embarked on a journey to kill them all.

Daniel said, "Uncle Glen wasn't killed by Paul, but Paul was his shadow agent that night. He witnessed him being shot but, when he explained what he saw to mom, she swore him to secrecy. They identified the body as belonging to Uncle Glen, and confirmed the killer was Ronald. Later that same year, Ronald was in a plane crash, and the report was that there were no survivors. Clearly, there was at least one.

"But he was badly hurt, it took years for him to recover. That crash actually saved his life because it made Mom believe he was truly dead. Lucille Drake was still a Burke woman so, because the body was never recovered, she built up the WRA and her family to withstand his return. If it wasn't for me falling for his tricks, the WRA would have been too strong for him to try his takeover. We would still be a cohesive unit and Mom would still be alive."

Reggie shook his head. "It's not your fault. If we have to blame anyone, besides Ronald himself, it has to be Mom. If she had told us all this instead of keeping it a secret, then we could have taken him out and that would have been that. Now, he's pretty much untouchable."

"Yeah," said Daniel. "To WRA personnel."

Reggie smiled and said, "Oh yeah! The By-Laws only apply to WRA agents."

"That's why I turned the job offer down in the first place. I didn't want to live under the By-Laws. After this was revealed, it's a lucky break, but it's one I intend to exploit," said Daniel.

"Alright, so what's the plan?" asked Reggie.

"You're WRA, I can't tell you or he could accuse you of plotting and order your death," said Daniel. "Let's do this the smart way. There's no doubt that he used someone to assassinate Mom. The suspect list is still the same. Whichever one it was still has to pay for what they did, so you focus on that. You leave Uncle Ronald to me." They stood staring at each other until Daniel said, "Trust me, Reggie. I will do what needs to be done."

The brothers hugged and Reggie left the conversation at that. Within the hour, he was in the sky on his way to take care of his part in the dilemma.

Pulling up to the safehouse in the mountainous city of Bogota, Reggie knew he needed sleep. The mission would be hard enough for him to do on his own without him falling asleep in the middle of it. Just as he was exiting the car, he got a text from his sister Kashonda. He read the message, leaned on the car, and sighed with exhaustion. Of course, Delmas had escaped while he'd been in the air headed to Colombia.

He sent a text back to Kashonda asking where he was now, and she replied, 'GONE!' He dialed Daniel's number; the phone was answered on the first ring.

Daniel said, "I'm fast, but you have to give me more than eight hours!"

"No," said Reggie. "I was calling because of Delmas."

"Oh! Well, he's already out of state so I don't think it's a problem."

"Wait! So, you know where he is?"

"Of course!" said Daniel. "He's in California. Right outside of LA."

"How do you know that? Kashonda doesn't even know!" Their sister was the Head of Intelligence for the WRA.

"The same way I know you're in Bogota, standing outside one of the WRA safehouses."

Reggie stayed silent for a full minute, his hand absently rubbing his chest, remembering the projectile his brother shot him with. Then he said, "You little son of a bitch!"

Daniel laughed. "Yeah, I love you too, Brother." Then he hung up.

Delmas and the Cartel would have to wait until tomorrow, thought Reggie. He walked to the front door of the luxury house, stumbled into the living room, and wanted to fall face first on the couch. Instead, he leaned on the wall, put in the code to reset the alarm, then made his way to the bedroom. Fully clothed, he fell on the bed and was out before he knew it. Safe and secure in the knowledge that his little brother was protecting his six.

CHAPTER 4

The 42-year-old Delmas Burke watched her from the Pacific Ocean with less than 50 yards separating them. This was her nightly routine. With an hour of sunlight remaining in the day, she would exit the huge, oceanside mansion with a pitcher full of margarita mix, make her way down to the private beach, and lay out on a lounge chair waiting for the sunset. The seven days he'd been watching her had been full of whimsical decisions that took her all over Southern California. But this part never changed. She would lay and drink and watch the sky until darkness consumed her private oasis in Ventura, California.

On the first evening he followed her here, he couldn't help but notice how exquisite she was. The clothes she wore during her numerous outings were expensive, but designed to not attract too much attention. It was a good thing because, the mixed African and European bombshell already drew many admirers. Her caramel complexion and her extremely curly hair that always cascaded around her shapely shoulders drew stares from men and women alike. But, laid out on her own private beach, with armed security making sure she was not disturbed, she displayed no such inhibitions.

The two-piece swimsuits she donned for every beach visit were colorful, sexy, and framed her long, toned body to perfection. Even though the breeze coming off the water was comfortable, her skin always responded to the blazing sun by becoming dewy and luminous. Studying her guards, Delmas concluded that they were all top-notch, or either gay. Not one of them let his eyes deviate from the job at hand to roam over the tantalizing image of Allorah Noriega.

Tonight, things wouldn't end with Allorah watching the sunset and then retiring to her three-story glass mansion. This night, she would realize that the Cartel life wasn't all about the glitter and the gold. And she would also find out that there were bigger and badder things out there than the infamous Noriega Cartel. Yes, she had come a long way from her humble beginnings in South Central, LA. But after tonight, she might wish she would have stayed there.

Finally, after the sun had disappeared over the horizon, she sat up and stretched her arms to the sky. Her head rolled on her shoulders and she arched her back sensually. When she stood up, the view from where he lay would put most models and actresses to shame. There were so many opportunities in the world for a woman with her attributes, he couldn't understand why she decided to become the wife of a Cartel Boss. If things went according to plan, he would ask her. If they didn't, she would die, and the answer wouldn't matter anyway.

As she walked up the stairs toward her landscaped property, the guards started their last full sweep of the night. They had patrols that would stay diligent, but these would be the last offensive moves they would make. He put the SCUBA mask back in place over his mouth, and drifted back farther into the ocean. Some of the guards would actually strip down and dive in to make sure nobody was lurking in the surf. The high-powered searchlights on top of the house would scan the whole area all night until the sun reappeared.

The setup was excellent. Not only would the measures deter most people from even trying, but it would catch 99% of anyone else who made an attempt. It was good for him that he fell into the remaining 1%. He used to bypass systems like this when he was a preteen. Swimming back up to the shoreline once all the rounds were complete, he removed all his underwater gear and prepared himself for the first leg of his mission.

To begin, he activated a device designed by the WRA research department that fried every electrical device in a quarter mile radius. All lights, cellphones, TV's, and security systems, along with their cameras, instantly became inoperable. The house went dark as Delmas put on his night vision shades and watched the security team scramble about trying to figure out what was going on.

Next, he pulled out a truly silent gun that shot subsonic bullets, both provided by The Author, and advanced towards the house. His brothers would have used knockout rounds, or some other form of non-lethal ammunition, but he wasn't fucking around with these people. Making sure his armor was secured and all his gear was strapped tight, he let his instincts take over and went hunting.

On the beach, a guard was walking towards his position from both directions. Leveling the gun, he dropped both of them in under two seconds with head shots. Because the searchlights and radios were disabled, security personnel were running around yelling, making it easy for him to drop three more without changing positions.

One of the guys who saw his coworker fall, screamed, "Active shooter! Active shooter! Man down! I repeat, MAN DOWN!" Delmas ended his screams with a bullet between his eyes.

Finally realizing that running around screaming in the dark might not be a good idea, the guards quieted down, trying to ascertain where the attacks were coming from. Shaking his head, Delmas crept up on three more and executed them, the crashing waves cancelled out any noise he may have made.

By his calculations, that left three more men in the house, one on each floor, and two more on the roof. Backtracking to the shoreline, he walked over to his discarded bag and removed the rifle from its waterproof case. This weapon was not silenced, so he needed to take out the guys on the roof before he turned his attention to the guards inside the glass structure.

The first man was always the easiest to kill in situations like this. They had the high ground and they would have high-powered weapons of their own. The men would feel safe, which led to two very dangerous attitudes: Comfortable and reckless. Standing up and using his scope to survey the roofline, these guards didn't disappoint. Both of them were peering over the side, trying in vain to see if they could help their comrades.

Lining up, the first shot struck the nearest guard center mass, launching him backwards out of sight. Before he could pick off the second one, he dove behind one of the searchlights and Delmas didn't have an angle to flush him out. No matter, the idiots in the house thought the darkness was protecting them. Since the guard on the first floor was standing at the glass wall peering out, it only took Delmas a few seconds to take him out of the picture.

The breaking glass had the desired effect; the other two guards reacted as if the threat was now inside the house. The man on the second floor posted up in position to defend the stairs and Delmas put a bullet in the side of his head while he laid on the floor.

Movement on the roof captured his attention before he could target the third-floor guard. The man was attempting to find his location, using his rifle scope to scan the area. Delmas moved to line up his own shot and knew from the abrupt movement of the other rifle when the shooter had spotted him. He clicked over to a three round burst and squeezed the trigger twice to send six projectiles flying at his would be killer. The gun clattered to the rooftop, but Delmas wasn't sure if he'd hit him or not. The guard could be playing hurt so he would be left alive. If that was the case, he would regret that decision shortly.

Turning back to look for the third-floor guard, he saw that the man had descended the steps to check on his coworker. The guard tried to stay low, but there was really no place to hide. His best bet would have been to run for the front door, the stones making up that side of the house would have offered him some form of protection. But really dedicated guards didn't run. Plus, if the Cartel found out that he had fled the scene, leaving his protectee behind, he would die anyway. And Cartel deaths, for things like cowardice, tended to be more brutal than the bullet to the head Delmas was prepared to offer him.

Anyway, the motive behind his movements became clear seconds later when he yelled something over his shoulder. Allorah, wearing blue jeans and a black t-shirt, dashed out of her third-floor room, descending the steps as fast as she could. She was almost within arm's reach of the guard when the bullet struck his head and he toppled over like a downed tree. She paused for maybe a second, then her sneaker-clad feet poured on the speed in her attempt to escape.

Delmas stowed the rifle back in its case after scanning the roof one more time, then took off at a light jog to meet Allorah on the other side of the house. She was doing what any sane person would be doing: Trying to find a way to stay alive. He would give her the chance but, alive or dead, she would serve her purpose.

So many people stumbled into his world and died as collateral damage. It was yet to be seen if he could apply that philosophy to her or not. Rounding the side of the house, he stopped and watched as she jumped from car to car, trying to get one of them to carry her away from peril.

Seeing the small Beretta clutched in her hand, he yelled, "HEY!" before ducking behind the stone wall. As expected, she sent a barrage of bullets his way, not really aiming, but hoping to get lucky with a stray shot.

Even under duress, she showed that she was clever. The act of screaming and sending shot after shot into the wall would have convinced a less trained man that his target was out of control, and out of bullets when she stopped firing. But Allorah wasn't in the panic she was trying to portray. She had left one bullet in the nine-shot pistol. So, if he made the mistake of stepping out into her view, it would be the last mistake he made.

Delmas knew all the games, and he knew all the moves to outthink an opponent. Since his gun was silent, he couldn't trick her with the sound of a gunshot, but he could force her body to react to a perceived threat. He backed up and aimed carefully before putting a round into the gas tank of the Porsche parked at the curb. The explosion, though not as big as the movies made them out to be, was quite impressive. It caused Allorah to tense and send her last bullet flying off into the night.

Stepping out with his gun raised, he finally came face to face with his target. Knowing time was running out, as he could hear sirens in the distance, he said, "I have no intention of hurting you, but I will if you deviate from any instruction I give you." Stepping over to the grass, he said, "Follow the path back down to the beach because we have to get out of here."

She let the empty gun fall from her fingers, and with a look of total aloofness spread across her face, she eased her way forward to do his bidding. As soon as she was level with him, he kicked her left leg out from under her, causing her to lose balance, and he swung her to the grass, facedown. He'd dealt with Cartel women in the past; he knew there was no way she had left her home with only the one weapon.

If he had more time, he would have just told her to strip, but he didn't. So, he would have to manually remove what he could. The gun tucked along her back waistline was soon tucked into his own. The switch blade in her pocket, he removed and tossed to the side. The baby .380 at her ankle, he unholstered and shoved into his pocket.

Turning her over, he discovered a knife hidden in her cleavage, and another running down her thigh. When he searched her curls, his fingers brushed a tiny transmitter that he left in place. His device had fried all its circuitry but he wanted her to have a false sense of hope. She might cooperate more if she thought an army was coming to rescue her at any second.

Standing up, he extended his hand to help her up and she took it, lumbering to her feet. He asked, "Did I hurt you?"

She shook her head no, so he directed her to continue walking in front of him to the beach. Almost as an afterthought, when they walked pass the edge of the house, Delmas removed two phosphorous grenades from a pack strapped to his thigh and tossed them both inside. The kitchen immediately turned into a hellscape upon detonation. Allorah stopped and gaped at her home, but he shrugged and said, “Won’t need any of it if you are dead. Now, get moving!”

He maneuvered her over to his gear and collected it all before leading her down the beach, ditching the confiscated weapons along the way. They were about a half mile away when he turned back and saw all the emergency lights around the burning structure. The young woman just trudged along without complaint.

Her acceptance wouldn’t last long. She would be a fighter because her lifestyle dictated her to be. But a pretty face wouldn’t garner any sympathy from him. He would placate at first, then he would endure her inevitable rebellion, until he couldn’t. When he reached that point, he would put a bullet into her skull and move on with what he had to do.

At the two-mile mark, he could see flashlights coming up behind them in the darkness. They had been walking in the surf with him hoping the shifting sands would obliterate their shoe prints. Their walk would only take another three minutes, but if the followers got too close, he would kill them and go about his business.

This mission could not fail. Because, even though he was no longer an official WRA agent, the Burke family name was nevertheless at stake. He would kill any and every one to make sure the legacy of that name was never tarnished.

With the pursuers still a half mile back, they arrived at the steps that would take them to the stashed Benz. He prodded her in the back to make her hurry, and they climbed up to another oceanside mansion, but this one was vacant. They jogged around to the front of the abode and he hurriedly ran over and snatched the SUV's backdoor open. He said, "Get in!" and she climbed in without a word.

He then told her, "Scoot over to the middle and put your seatbelt on." When she complied, he reached under the seat and pulled out a set of shackles that were attached to a bolt in the floor. He snapped a link onto each one of her legs, then reached in and stretched her right arm along the length of the seat. He revealed another cuff that was bolted into the side of the vehicle and secured that arm before slamming the door and running to the other side.

Opening the backdoor, he repeated the process with her left arm, closed the door, and then hopped into the driver's seat. He took a few seconds to glance back and make sure his captive couldn't move, then drove off the property, heading back towards LA.

Emergency vehicles were flying by them at regular intervals; every cop in the area probably alerted to the 14 dead bodies he'd left behind. The whole criminal world of Southern California would be in chaos when word got out that Allorah Noriega had been kidnapped. Not only would her husband and his Cartel buddies be on a warpath, but her father held the rank of Godfather for one of the biggest Blood sets in the area. Delmas had nowhere near the backing he would have had as a WRA agent, but he wasn't worried. By the time all the players figured out what was going on, his mission would be complete and he would disappear like an early morning Spring fog.

Slowing down after a brief ten-minute drive, he turned the SUV onto a dirt-packed road that led down to a small, single-story dwelling on the beach. This wasn't anything like the area they'd just left; there wasn't much sand, and there certainly wasn't any landscaping. The "beach" was mostly rocks and grass, but the views still made the property cost in the millions. Anyway, there was privacy, and that was pretty much all he needed. No one but The Author knew where he was, and he wasn't planning on staying any longer than he had to.

He stopped parallel to the front door, cut the engine, and exited the vehicle. While his prisoner was secured in the back, he walked over to the house, opened the flimsy front door that wouldn't stand up to a 10-year-old's kick, and did a cursory inspection to make sure everything was like he'd left it. Then he returned to the Benz, opened the backdoor, and stared in at his captive.

She was being damn cool about the situation she was in. Not one question or demand had slid pass her plump, tantalizing lips. He didn't know if this was her real personality, or if she was buoyed by the presence of the tracker he'd left in her hair. If it was the later, he wondered how she would respond when she found out it was useless. Not that it mattered, whatever reaction she showed, he would handle it, whether it required light discipline or an end to her life.

They were hidden from the street by a couple of well-placed shrubs, but he still needed to get her inside, asap. He reached in and unlocked her right hand with the handcuff key. Then he handed it to her and said, "Use it to free yourself, then slowly exit the vehicle."

Once again, she followed instructions without comment, and handed him the key back when her feet hit the ground. He took it and side stepped, keeping a few paces between them as they walked into the house. She didn't try to kick the door closed on him or run off, she just walked inside and stopped when he told her to.

The place was spartan to say the least. One wide open space, with the living room doubling as the bedroom. Straight back was the kitchen area, then the sliding glass door that led out to a patio. The bathroom was a windowless cube off to the left of the front room. The only furniture was two full-size beds, set up like a hotel room in the front, and a folding table and two chairs placed in the center of the kitchen. There was a microwave, a refrigerator, and a trash can. Nothing more. This wasn't a vacation home, this was a structure built for exactly what he was using it for: To hold a prisoner. He wondered how many captives The Author had kept in this place.

Staying behind her after he closed and locked the door, he allowed her a few seconds to peruse her surroundings. Then he said, "Turn around and face me." She turned with her arms wrapped defensively around her mid-section. Her luminous, brown eyes bore into his with the intensity of someone who knew eventually their positions of power would reverse. She had witnessed his ruthlessness in the killing of her 14 guards, but she really thought her station made her untouchable. It was time to shake her up and make her see she wasn't as in control as she thought.

Delmas said, "It's been an extremely long week watching you cavort around on that beach every evening in those sexy swimsuits. It reminded me of just how long I've been in that prison cell before I escaped. So, tomorrow I'll have some very important questions for you. In the meantime," he said, pulling his gun out once again and chambering a round. "I'm gonna need you to strip all the way down and get on that bed over there."

When he pointed the gun at her knee, real panic showed in her eyes. Something else he learned from his spy-filled family; the threat of death wasn't always the most effective threat. Making your captive think that they'll be disfigured and helpless usually got the desired result. Not many wanted to die, but to some, that was preferred over being unable to fight or run if the chance presented itself.

Looking into his eyes and seeing not one shred of sympathy, she did the only thing she could think of to stay healthy and whole. With tears falling down her face, she reached and pulled the black t-shirt over her head. Within a minute, she was standing naked in front of him, her eyes imploring him not to go through with this degradation.

Nodding in satisfaction, he said, “Now, get on the bed. Lay face up.”

A touch of anger entered her eyes at the humiliation, but she did what she was told. Once she was horizontal, he smiled and said, “Now we can get down to the fun part.” With that being said, she looked up in horror, trembling as he took his first step towards where she was laid out, completely at his mercy.

Chapter 5

Seven days they'd been on lockdown, and Joshue had no one to blame but himself. Flip was pissed because he couldn't go out and sniff up something new. And Joshue was mad because he couldn't fly in Allorah to share the lockdown with him. His dad was taking his paranoia to a whole new level. Everyone was suspect. Within minutes of being told about the possible American threat, Carlos had put a stop to all incoming and outgoing traffic to and from the compound.

His two older brothers, Christian and Juan, wouldn't even talk to him because they felt that they'd gotten caught up in his bullshit. At least they still had access to their wives, thought Joshue. Both of his siblings still lived in their father's house with their families. It seemed that he was the only one who wanted to make his own mark on the world.

Christian Raul Noriega, oldest son of the Cartel Boss, was 32-years-old, and almost as wide as he was tall. He was a real asshole to the people he felt wouldn't hurt him, but a coward when dealing with anyone he perceived as a threat.

Carlos had concluded, around the time Christian turned 14, that he could never be the one to take over the mantle as Boss. He just didn't have it in him to be a powerful and fair decision maker.

Juan Carlos Noriega was 29-years-old, and as different from Christian as two people could possibly be. He was only 5'7" tall, thin, and had a curly afro that made people think he was fun and lovable. But neither of those traits could be applied to him.

He was ruthless. A bona fide killer. A merciless jackal whose sole mission in life was to make everyone afraid of the Noriega Cartel. He and their father butted heads on every aspect of the operation. All Juan was waiting for was Carlos to die so he could restore the Cartel back to its former glory.

The only good thing about the lockdown, as far as Joshue could see, was the place that served as their prison. The razor-wire topped, 15-foot wall might from the outside look daunting. But once you get pass it, the inside was luxuriousness unmatched except by the richest people in the world.

Mediterranean in style, the three-story, sun-drenched abode was surrounded by rolling, green lawns, immaculate landscaping, a par-three golf course, several man-made fishing ponds, and miniature bungalows spread all over the property. Encompassing over a hundred acres, the protective walls also hid a tennis pavilion, an official-sized soccer field, and three full basketball courts. Everything was tended by a professional staff that knew any mistakes could lead to their untimely demise.

Walking inside the 18-bedroom, 20-bathroom home, with its soaring ceilings, has left many visitors speechless. The huge crystal chandeliers, sparkling like diamonds in the entry hall. The marble floors, gleaming and spotless, making it seem offensive to even walk on them. Twin spiral staircases, mirrored at four different entrances, made it a regal event to ascend to the upper floors. Multiple brick and granite fireplaces, adding just a bit of coziness to the otherwise staunch interior. But the grander was only for shock and awe, geared towards showcasing the Cartel's wealth. Once you really got into the heart of the residence, that's when the true magnificence kicked in.

Two heated pools. A 16-seat movie theater. Ballrooms. Libraries. A full gym, with every machine imaginable, occupying its own underground level. A sauna attached to each bathroom. Three full-sized gourmet kitchens, each with its own access to the 4000-bottle wine cellar. A six-lane bowling alley. Four different game rooms, all containing multiple 100-inch TVs. Numerous balconies jutted from the bedrooms on the upper floors. And a dedicated glass elevator that glided to a stop at the top of a transparent tower, producing panoramic views of the Andes Mountains, and the Meta River that flowed through their land.

The warehouse-style building that held the Cartel's motor pool also contained suites overtop where the live-in butlers and maids resided. To cut down the effects of the summer heat and blazing sun, scores of Granddaddy Oaks were scattered about, providing people with some much-needed shade. Everything exquisite. Everything perfect. But yet, all still their prison. At least until Carlos said otherwise.

After a two-hour workout, followed by 20 minutes in the sauna, and a 15-minute shower, Joshue was ready to turn in for the night. Sliding his 5'9", 180-pound body between the silk sheets, he sighed, thinking he better check in on Allorah before falling asleep. They'd been arguing the last few days because she wanted to come be with him. It didn't matter how many times he explained that the lockdown was not his call, she still felt like he could do something about it. Deciding to get it over with, he reached for his phone and dialed the number of the love of his life.

It was only 10:30pm in Ventura, so it puzzled him when she didn't answer the phone. But maybe that was for the best. She liked to drink while watching the majestic sunsets over the Pacific. And when she drank, only two things would settle her down: A good fight or a good fuck. Since only one of those things was possible at the moment, it was better to just call her again in the morning. Placing his phone on the nightstand, he got comfortable and went to sleep.

After a week of no sex, it was no surprise that his dreams were erotic in nature. Allorah, with her head thrown back, pulling on his long, dark hair as he devoured her burning core, was a sight that could keep him going for hours. Her caramel skin and shimmering eyes glowing with sweat and desire. Those juicy, pink lips emitting the most sensual moans. That delicious scent drifting from her body, awakening a primal need in him to proclaim that she belonged to him and him alone. He had just positioned himself to take what she was willingly offering, when the dream changed.

Her hand shot up and clamped onto his mouth with amazing strength. He shook his head and tried to pull back, but he couldn't break her unyielding grip. Some part of his brain yelled, "Wake up, idiot!" and his eyes flew open to the sight of a man, dressed all in black, standing over him. Instinct being what it is, he started to fight.

Flip whispered, "It's me, motherfucker! Calm down!" His power was absolute as he held Joshue immobile with a hand on his chest. "I gotta get you to the suite!"

That statement caused Joshue to freeze and look up at his friend. Flip moved his hands off of him, but said, "We have to stay quiet. Someone has breached the wall and is killing people."

Jerking up and hurrying to dress, Joshue asked, "Who's been killed?"

Shaking his head, Flip said, "A few guards along the river. The guard at the entrance to the pool house. We have no idea who it is or how many because, after the cameras picked up the initial kills, all our power went down."

Joshue looked around for the first time and noticed that everything was dark. The moon was shining so bright into his room, he'd thought a light was on. He finished getting dressed, grabbed his phone and twin Nighthawks, then said, "Let's go!"

Flip led the way over to the door and peeked around the jamb, making sure the hallway was clear for his charge. He glanced back at Joshue and gave one nod before he creeped out with his gun held high. Little Capo, knowing Flip knew what he was doing, walked confidently, but silently, behind him.

Normally, in the case of an intruder, a horn would be blaring, and red strobe lights would activate. None of that was happening as the two men crept down the massive second floor hallway to the underground protection suite.

Joshue wondered if everyone else had already made it. He opened his mouth to ask when Flip threw his fist up, signaling him to stop.

The stairs were around the corner and directly to their right. Flip gazed around the edge and quickly pulled his head back. He flattened himself along the wall and directed Joshue to do the same. They remained like that, hidden by the darkness and their stillness, until Joshue wanted to scream from anxiety.

He wasn't exactly scared, but the adrenaline making his heart thunder was also making him antsy. Just when he felt he couldn't take it anymore, Flip took a long, lingering look and then gestured for Joshue to move out.

They trotted down the steps with the moonlight streaming in the enormous windows. When they hit the bottom, they turned left to head towards the library under the steps. Joshue wanted to ask Flip what he had seen that caused him to pull back earlier, but they were moving fast now. Once they entered the library, Joshue took over the lead and walked over to the special bookcase. He removed the set of books that hid the control panel, entered his access code, and a small click let them know the passageway had opened.

Flip kept his gun pointed at the door as Joshue guided the bookcase, on its well-oiled hinges, until it was wide enough for them to slip through. The darkness was absolute, but they were safe now. Both men pulled out their cellphones and used its flashlight to illuminate their path. As they walked, Joshue asked questions.

"What did you see on the steps?"

Flip glanced over at him but kept moving towards their destination. "There was a drone hovering in the entryway. At least it looked like a drone. It was small and seemed to be scanning the area for people or movement or something. I've never seen anything like it so I didn't want to take a chance it would attack us."

Joshue nodded and asked, "Did everyone else make it in?"

Flip shrugged. "I don't know, they're not my concern. I work for you and my job is to keep you safe." His voice was very matter-of-fact, but betrayed his feelings for the rest of the Noriegas. "I got enough on my plate trying to keep your ass out of trouble," he added.

Nobody else in the family trusted the young Brazilian. They said his intervention to save Joshue's life had been too perfect, too precise. They felt that he was a plant from one of the other Cartels, and he'd end up killing them all in their sleep. At first, Flip had tried to convince them he was loyal to Joshue and the Noriega Cartel. But, once the attitudes towards him persisted, he started to show them the same animosity they showed him. Without fear, he treated everyone except Joshue with a disdain that bordered on disrespect.

The two men turned a final corner and arrived at the narrow stone steps that led down to the safety suite. Really, it was a bomb shelter done up Cartel style. Room enough to sleep ten comfortably, the upscale area was more like a Presidential Suite at the Ritz than a bunker. But the safety measures were top of the line.

Reinforced concrete and steel enclosed the entire perimeter, ceiling and floor included. An arsenal was available to anyone who could gain access. And a dedicated generator, with enough fuel to live lavishly for up to a year, provided all the electricity they'd need to stay sane. At the bottom of the 40 steps, Joshue entered a different code into the glowing access panel, and turned the knob on the solid steel door.

The first thing that hit him was the cold air that floated out of the door. Joshue and Flip entered and secured the door, instantly becoming aware of the raised voices drifting down the hall. The argument was heated; the combatants sounded ready to trade blows. Recognizing the voices of

Carlos and Juan, they glanced at each other and shook their heads. As they slowly advanced, this is what they heard:

Juan: “What the fuck do you mean, you forbid it? I’m not a fucking coward!”

Carlos: “Do what you’ve been told for once in your life! We need to stay safe!”

Juan: “No! We need to be out there giving whoever breached our walls hell!”

Carlos: “That’s what we have soldiers for. Let them earn their keep.”

Juan: “Twenty minutes! That’s all I’m giving you! After that, I’m out of here. I’m sick of you trying to control my life. Don’t you get it? We’re not children anymore!”

When Joshue turned into the living room, Juan was storming off to one of the bedrooms. His father, Carlos, watched his middle son until he disappeared, and then sighed in defeat.

Joshue said, “Dad.” Carlos looked up in relief as Joshue asked, “Did everyone make it safely inside? Where’s Christian?”

“Oh! Thank God!” Carlos exclaimed as he rushed over and embraced his youngest son. Stepping back, but still holding onto his shoulders, Carlos said, “Yeah, everyone made it in. Christian is in the back room trying to calm down his wife and kids. Juan is here for the time being, but he’s chomping at the bit to get out there and fight.” Almost as an afterthought, the Cartel Boss looked at Flip and gave him a slight nod. Flip didn’t return the gesture.

As Carlos explained how the rest of the family had braved the darkness and unknown to make it to the suite, Joshue took a second to examine his father. The 53-year-old, Carlos Alberto Noriega, fit the Hollywood image of a Cartel Boss to a T. From his cleanshaven face, to his slicked-back, salt and pepper hair, the man exuded power and grace.

But as all great men do, he has weaknesses. His love of beautiful and bountiful women is the reason why his wife, mother to his children, left the bunch of them and is now living happily in New York City.

Carlos wrapped an arm around his son's shoulder and led him over to one of the plush couches. With a thick, white robe draped around his body, he threw his 5'10", 220-pound frame down like he had the weight of the world on his shoulders. He said, "I'm glad now that we took heed to those warnings. If all of you hadn't been here, it would have been easy for them to pick us off one by one."

Joshue asked, "Do you know who it is?"

Shaking his head, Carlos said, "I don't know for sure, but I bet it's the WRA. It definitely isn't a rival Cartel because we would have seen and heard them before they reached the town. No, I'm not 100% positive, but I'd give ten to one odds it's the WRA."

Flip asked, "Why do you think it's them? Why not the CIA or DEA?"

Joshue could tell his father didn't want to include Felipe in the conversation, so he answered the question, but kept his eyes on his son. "They would have had to notify our governor, or at least the President, either of which would have notified me or one of my Capos. Plus, they have rules that dictate their actions. They would have had to request a surrender before they just started killing people."

They sat in silence for a bit before Joshue asked, "Does the WRA have a reason to come after us?"

That was the question that had plagued the family for the past six months. They had all been questioned on the topic of Lucille Drake's death. They all denied involvement, but they all knew no one would admit it if they had been involved. Joshue could only say that he himself didn't have anything to do with the murder. All other certainties weren't certain in the least.

Carlos had just opened his mouth to answer when Christian and Juan stepped in from the back. "Yeah, Dad," said Juan. "Does the WRA have reason to come at us?"

The Cartel Boss gritted his teeth and shook his head. "You know what, Juan? I'm really getting sick of you!" Jumping to his feet and squaring up to his son, Carlos said, "I know what you want, and over my dead body is the only way you'll get it. Anytime you feel you've got the balls to take what's mine, give it a try! I'll bury your little smug ass right alongside the others who have tried!"

Christian and Joshue wedged in between the two head-strung men and separated them before a fight could break out. They were both still talking shit, only falling silent when the lights flickered then died.

The generator had shut down. The air conditioner had turned off and Joshue was straining to hear the tiniest sound. Someone cocked a pistol to his right, which was where Juan had been before the lights went out. He knew it wasn't Flip because his gun would have already been locked and loaded at the first sign of trouble.

Something buzzed near his ear, sounding like a bee or some other flying bug. A slight sting on his arm had him swinging wildly to prevent any other attacks. He heard a body hit the floor nearby. Then another. And another. He felt a hand grab his arm almost simultaneously with a disconnect between his mind and body. He didn't lose consciousness, but he sagged to the floor, feeling the pain of the fall, but not able to do a thing about it.

As sudden as they had gone off, the lights flicked back on to reveal a man, dressed in black, standing over them. He sported a calm expression as he looked from one slumped body to the next. Methodically, he bent down and searched each of them, taking any and all weapons, phones, and keys he found. The man stored everything in a backpack that had been strapped to his body, then pulled out a bag containing thick flex cuffs.

Joshue was trying to get a better look at the man, and when it was his turn to be secured, he met his captor eye to eye. His breath froze in his lungs as their gazes connected and he recognized the new Head of the WRA, Reginald Burke.

At that instant, Joshue saw death. This wasn't gonna be another interrogation or inquiry. If the legendary killer was here himself, someone was going to die. In a showcase of power that sent shockwaves of fear coursing through his body, Reggie picked them up, one by one, and deposited them on the couches like they weighed as much as a loaf of bread.

He moved one of the recliners over so he could face them, then pulled out a gun with one hand and a wicked looking blade with the other. Kicking his feet up, he leaned back, and closed his eyes as if preparing to take a nap.

No sound could be heard except the labored breathing of his family. Joshue didn't hear the kids crying or the women complaining, so they must be immobile just like the rest of them. This was what he and Flip had been afraid of. The WRA had used their own procedures and protocols to corral them all into one space. This one man now had the power to fell the formidable and infamous Noriega Cartel.

A thump sounded to his right, drawing him back into the present. He couldn't see what made the sound, but the WRA Boss stood up and stretched, then walked in that direction. He heard Reggie say, "It will be uncomfortable for a minute, just stay still and let it work its way out of your system." A series of thumps issued in rapid succession and then a pain-filled moan escaped into the air.

Reggie laughed. "My little brother developed a pain free version; I used that on the women and children. But I figured you tough Cartel men could handle a little pain."

One after the other, they went through the sequence of motions. First Christian, then his father. By the time it reached Flip, Joshue knew it was determined by your size how fast the drug released you. When it hit him, he wanted to cry out from the pain. It felt as if someone was trying to remove his skin with a cheese grater. The process only lasted about 30 seconds, but it felt like an eternity. Then it vanished, as if he had imagined the whole experience.

Once Juan went through it, gritting his teeth until the pain subsided, Reggie eyed each of them before starting his speech. "I don't think it was a whole-family thing, but one of you knows what happened to my mother. Well," he said looking up at the ceiling, "all of you know what happened, but one of you is responsible. Because I don't know which one of you it is, I'm gonna have to treat all of you like you're guilty. Unless one of you wants to confess and spare your relatives the upcoming events?"

Joshue looked at each of his family members and knew that all of them wouldn't be alive an hour from now. Christian looked terrified, while Carlos looked annoyed. Flip and Juan seemed incensed, probably watching for the one mistake that they could exploit.

None of them would confess to anything, especially not in front of the rest of them. He tried to school his own features to look as innocent as possible. Reggie didn't act as if he expected anything different than what he got. But Joshue didn't expect his next move.

Reggie shrugged, tucked the gun behind his back, strolled over to Christian, and plunged the knife hilt-deep into his leg. Blood sprayed everywhere as Joshue's oldest brother screamed and tried to lunge away. Reggie placed his massive forearm across the big man's neck, pulled the knife out and plunged it in again.

Christian's mouth gaped open in a silent plea. He convulsed, then his whole body seemed to sag in on itself. Reggie pulled the knife free, wiped the bloody blade on the injured man's t-shirt, and then looked over at Carlos.

Reggie asked, "Got something you want to tell me?" Carlos just looked at the man and slowly shook his head. The super-agent shrugged again and took a step towards the Cartel Boss.

Juan jumped up and yelled, "You touch my father and you're a dead man!" His voice was full of promised violence, but it only seemed to amuse Reggie.

He laughed without humor and asked, "And who's going to kill me? You?" Reggie looked him up and down, clearly not impressed with what he saw. He said, "I'll tell you what. How about I give you the knife, I set my gun over in the kitchen, and you can have your chance to kill me?"

Juan gave his nastiest smile. "Now we're talking. Let's go, big man!" Standing in front of his brother, the matchup didn't seem fair. Reggie was tall and thick of body. He looked like a giant compared to his short, thin brother.

"NO!" shouted Carlos. "No!" Joshue turned to see a pained expression on his father's face. "He doesn't know what he's saying, Mr. Burke. None of us had anything to do with Lucille's death. If you came for your pound of flesh, so be it. But don't kill my sons."

"Fuck that!" said Juan. "You secret-agent motherfuckers and your gadgets. Using tricks and drugs to weaken your opponents. I bet you've never fought anyone straight up. You keep your gun and your knife, just let my hands free and let's see what you got!"

Reggie chuckled and focused on Carlos. "How old is the little guy now? 29? 30? He's a man now, Carlos, let him make his own decisions." Carlos exhaled and Joshue had the impression that he was giving up on the situation.

The WRA Boss turned to Juan and said, "Turn around so I can cut the ties." Juan followed the directive and Reggie eased over and used the knife to free his hands. Juan turned around to face him, but Reggie was already walking to the kitchen area, where he laid his gun on the counter. Then he strolled back over, Juan rubbing his hands together in anticipation.

Reggie smiled and tossed the knife at Juan's feet. He said, "Trust me, you'll need it. I'll try my best to not kill you, but

I'm gonna teach you some respect." He turned briefly and looked at Joshue. "Don't worry, I'll give you a shot next."

Joshue's stomach plummeted to his feet. He didn't want a shot. He didn't want any parts of the WRA, period. But Juan didn't feel that way. With a full-on belly laugh, he said, "You underestimate us. We're not as stupid as you think. See, I might not be able to take you by myself, but who said this has to be a one on one fight?"

Faster than Joshue had ever seen him move, Juan bent down and scooped the knife from the floor. At the same time, Flip lunged to his feet and turned just in time for Juan to cut his cuffs. Then the two men turned to face a smiling Reggie.

Juan gave the WRA man a huge smile of his own. He said, "Still feeling confident?"

Reggie reached in his pocket and pulled out a pair of black shades. Slipping them on his face, he said, "Yeah, I am. But since you changed the rules, I feel intitled to do the same thing." After a brief pause, he yelled, "LIGHTS!" and they were once again plunged into darkness.

Chapter 6

Delmas was energized by the restful sleep he'd received the previous night, as well as the bright sun streaming down on his body. From his cell in Wake County, he'd never felt the sun. So, every day since his escape, he'd been soaking up as much of the invigorating rays as possible.

He was sitting on the patio, watching the rolling waves, and listening to the ocean's calming effect. It brought back memories of family excursions to Myrtle Beach that his mother insisted they take every year. It used to bother him that she never went with them, but his mother knew that the trips would bring their family closer.

A silent tear stirred and traveled down his face in remembrance of his mom. So many people misunderstood her and judged her based off of their misguided assumptions. Even most of her family thought she was nothing but a heartless monster.

The secrets were to blame, ultimately. It had led others to see her actions as selfish instead of the sacrifices she'd made daily. At one point, he'd begged her to expose everything to his siblings, but she shot him down. So, he did what he always did: He played his role, followed orders, and watched his family be destroyed from the inside out.

Standing up, he stretched in his black sweatpants and t-shirt. It didn't matter what her faults were, she was still his mother. As her son, it was his duty to avenge here death. Turning to go back inside the small house, it was time to start the next part of his plan.

Walking through the kitchen, he looked to his left at the first bed, and came eye to eye with a very naked, very angry, Allorah Noriega. The bed had been stripped, so there was nothing she could use to hide her body. The chain around her ankle rattled as she curled up into the fetal position and ignored him.

"Stop trying to look so victimized. Here," he said, tossing the key to the lock so she could free herself. Slowly, she looked at the key, then at him. Eventually, her common sense kicked in, and she worked the key until she was unbound.

She swung her feet off the bed and glanced over to her clothes, still in the pile where she'd left them the previous night. He extended his arm in invitation and she scrambled over to get dressed.

With her clothes on, he could tell she was regaining her confidence. Last night, when he'd told her to strip and get on the bed, the fear and humiliation had been real. Her immediate thought had been that she was about to be brutalized. But Burke men had integrity. Mind games were one thing, but a rapist he was not. He had used her fear to petrify her until he could secure her to the bed. Then, he had fallen gratefully into his own. It had been some of the best sleep he'd had in years.

Allorah was trying her best to stare him down with her icy glare, but her back and forth shuffle only made her look ridiculous. He pointed to his right and said, "Bathroom is over there." With as much dignity as she could muster, she hurried over to the door, opened it, and slammed it closed behind her.

He shook his head as he turned back to the kitchen to make them a light breakfast of toast and orange juice. He heard the small shower turn on a few minutes later as he sat patiently waiting for her return. After 15 minutes passed, he sighed and stood up, walked over to the door, and knocked politely.

"Allorah, you have 60 seconds to come out or I'm coming in to get you. I promise, you won't like the results. Don't make this harder than what it already has to be." 90 seconds passed with the shower still running and the door closed. Shaking his head, he stepped back and kicked the door open.

Like a warrior princess making her last stand, she screamed a battle cry and hurled a plastic cup filled with, from the smell of it, urine. He dodged it and she used the distraction to lower her head and charge at his midsection. He sidestepped and gave her a slight nudge in the back that sent her careening into the kitchen table and chairs. She issued a grunt of pain as she crashed to the floor, splayed on her stomach in the concoction of toast, orange juice, and piss.

There she laid, eventually rolling over and looked up at him with pitiful eyes. He turned and marched into the bathroom, ripping the shower curtain from its rod. Facing her, he pointed and said, “Get your stupid ass in the shower. I’m not talking to you with you smelling like a sewer.”

She sat up and then staggered to her feet, looking around at the mess she’d made. He walked back into the kitchen and said, “Matter of fact, clean this shit up first. I don’t know why I expected you to act like a lady instead of the savage you clearly are.”

Her eyes flashed with anger. “So, I’m the savage?” she asked with her first words spoken to him. Her voice, even filled with angst, was melodic and just as beautiful as the rest of her. He didn’t think she would appreciate his observation, so he kept it quiet.

Now that the well was open, so to speak, she seemed to have a lot more to get off her chest. “Am I the one who came to your home, killed everyone in sight, blew up your car, and then burned your house down? Did I kidnap you and force you to strip, like some pervert stalker? And then you bully me, assault me, and have the audacity to call me a savage! I’m not cleaning up shit! You don’t like the smell, you clean it up yourself! Like I’m supposed to be thankful for some damn toast and orange juice. FUCK YOU!”

When she spiraled back down, Delmas just couldn’t help himself. He titled his head back and roared with laughter. By the time he got it all out, he was leaning on the refrigerator, tears coursing down his face. Damn, she had spunk, he thought, wiping his face. He had to admit that he was actually enjoying himself. The young woman reminded him of Ann when she was younger. Of course, Ann Grace, his former lover, was degrees more attractive and desirable than Allorah, his taste running more toward elegance than young sexpot. But, that inner spark was in them both.

Enjoyment or not, he couldn't let her defiance go unpunished. He sobered up and said, "While that was fun and exciting, I'm serious. Neither of us are used to living in squalor, and the surroundings we occupy now are bad enough. I'll help you, but I'm not sitting in here smelling your piss all day. So, we clean, then you'll shower, and then we'll get to your punishment for behaving like a child."

Allorah wanted to rant and rave, he could see it in her body language. But she was also dreading this punishment he spoke of. In the end, her shoulders slumped and she asked, "Where are the cleaning supplies?" before they both tackled the destroyed kitchen.

None of the furniture was broken, just scattered about and upturned. After they finished, Allorah marched into the bathroom while Delmas strolled out onto the patio to enjoy the Southern California weather.

The ocean soothed him, acting as a balm for his tortured thoughts. But he couldn't melt into the healing atmosphere fully because he had to keep one eye on the kitchen so the Cartel wife wouldn't escape.

This time, when she emerged, her dewy body was wrapped in the gigantic robe he'd left hanging on the door for her. Concealed as she was, with her bare toes winking with each step, she looked younger than her 23 years. She was melancholy and had the look of a child waiting to be scolded. To ease her mind, he said, "Come on out. It's scenic, but definitely not up to par with your usual view."

Cautiously, she eased through the opening and slunk over to the chair opposite him. He glanced over and saw that she wasn't looking towards the view at all. Her luminous eyes were staring right at him.

He leaned back and said, "I know you didn't ask for this, but in a way, you did. You could have been anything you wanted to be. Why would you choose to marry into the Cartel?"

She did look at the waves then. Her body language clearly said that she wasn't gonna answer, probably because it was none of his business. "Look," he said. "No harm, no foul. I'm not gonna punish you, but don't let it happen again. I told you from the beginning that I would only hurt you if you disobeyed. Just chill out and this will all be over soon. Now, since you destroyed breakfast, I didn't get a chance to eat. Are you hungry?"

Finally turning towards him, their eyes made brief contact before she lowered hers and nodded. He stood up and gestured for her to go back inside when, softly, she asked, "What did they do to you?"

He sat back down, not willing to play games by acting like he didn't understand the question. "How much do you know about their activities?"

She said, "Everything. Joshue doesn't keep anything from me."

He marveled at her naivety, but kept his face neutral to let her keep her illusions. He said, "Well, this should be easy then. Do you know about their deal with the American government Agency?"

She nodded. "Not the name of the organization, but I'm aware of the deal. Pretty much, this organization was the only customer the Cartel had. All of their drugs went to them, and in return, they got money and guns. Whoever these people were, they kept the Cartel safe and free to operate however they wanted."

Delmas cocked his head. "Why do you speak of them in the past tense?"

"Well, about six months ago, something went wrong. Obviously, I don't know the details of what happened, but whatever it was, it impacted the whole Cartel and all of its operations. The entire leadership has been in a panic and there's been a lot of infighting. My guess, they tried to cheat the Agency and they were cut off."

He squinted in thought before he shrugged and stood up again. "I don't communicate well on an empty stomach," he lied to her. "Let's eat and then we can pick this conversation back up."

They entered the kitchen and Delmas closed the door behind them. After watching her sit down, he leaned on the counter and said, "Allorah, I really don't want to hurt you. Don't pull anymore of those stupid stunts and you'll leave in the same condition you arrived. Okay?"

She actually seemed to think about it before she gave him probably the most honest answer a captive could give. "I can't promise you that I won't try to escape, because I can't trust your word. But, as long as you don't try to bully and humiliate me again, I'll try not to be too much trouble." Throwing her arms wide, she said, "That's the best I can give you right now."

He chuckled and shook his head before saying, "Allorah, I like you. I think we understand each other, and we'll get along just fine from now on." With that, he turned around and made his second batch of toast in as many hours. All the while, sporting a small, stealthy smile on his handsome face.

At the same time Delmas and Allorah were sitting down for their second breakfast, there was a drama being played out inside an oddity in Southern California. While everyone else living in the land of dreams wanted everyone else they encountered to think their lives were glamorous, the people in this house wanted the complete opposite. Most of the inhabitants were millionaires, waiting to retire to some foreign, glorious locale. For anyone passing by the two-story home, they would see a rickety structure in bad need of repair. No one would guess its condition was by design, a strategy to hide the true wealth enclosed inside its walls.

Two young, black males stood outside the second-floor suite, arguing quietly about who was gonna knock on the door. There really was no need to whisper, they were sure the three people inside couldn't hear them over all the noise they themselves were making. The shouts of, "OH! GOD!" and, "OH! YES!" coupled with the erotic sounds of flesh on flesh and moaning, clearly told the two men that any interruption wouldn't be welcome. But somebody had to tell the man inside what was going on.

"Man, I don't even know the chick! It will be better coming from you," said the guy on the left.

"Fuck that!" his companion responded. "I outrank you and I'm giving you a direct order to tell the OG what's going on."

Shaking his head, the guy said, "Rank and orders don't mean shit if he kills whoever disturbs him! I tell you what, violate me later because I'm out of here." He spun on his heels and hightailed it back down to the first floor.

"G-Baby! G-Baby! Get back here! I'm gonna kill your ass!" the man left at the door whispered loudly. "SHIT!" he exclaimed when it became clear he was on his own. The sounds of pleasure behind the door were still going strong. He said a silent prayer, looking up towards whatever higher power was willing to help him, before he gave the door three hard raps.

The people inside ignored him. In fact, it sounded as if the women were screaming louder in an attempt to drown out the knocking. This time the guy pounded the door with the side of his fist until everything went quiet inside the room. Tentatively, the man said, "OG?"

"Yo! What the fuck do you want? You can't tell I'm busy?"

Swallowing the lump in his throat, he said, "Big Homie, this is Zero!"

"I know who the fuck it is! You couldn't wait until…" After a brief mumbled conversation on the inside, the OG said, "Open the fucking door! Got me yelling and shit."

Zero pushed the door open to the sight of his OG, Tano Jackson, still slow stroking a big booty white chick from the back, while pressing her face down into the crotch of his girlfriend.

Zero could still see the white girl's tongue moving between Ciera's thighs, but Ciera was scowling at the door just as hard as Tano. Finally, after becoming mesmerized by the sight of the two beautiful women, Zero shook his head to clear out the cobwebs, and faced his OG.

"Listen, I don't have all the details, but some bad shit went down last night." The sight of the pale body, trembling and undulating in extasy, distracted him for a bit.

Ciera sucked her teeth and said, "Stop acting like you aint never seen tits and ass before! What the fuck happened?" Finished with her climax, the white girl lowered her head once again to the feast spread out before her.

Zero, turning to leave, said, "It involves that chick ya'll grew up with. I'll holla at you when…"

"Hold up!" Tano said, finally stopping his in and out motion. "What's going on with Allorah?"

Zero looked at him once again and said, "The beach house in Ventura got hit last night."

"What you mean 'hit'? You talking the police or a rival?" demanded Tano.

"Nah, Gang. This definitely wasn't the police. From the report on the news, last night, a neighbor called in what they thought was gunshots and an explosion. By the time the cops got there, the house was burning down and bodies were all over the place."

"What did they say about Allorah?" asked Ciera.

"Nothing. They just said there were no survivors at the scene."

Tano and Ciera glanced at each other, then Tano said, "Little Homie, give us a minute. I'll be out to speak to you in a bit." Zero nodded, took one last look at the naked women, and closed the door.

He knew that his set had a strong connection to the Noriega Cartel. Tano and Little Capo, as Joshue Noriega was known, were like brothers. Zero knew that Tano had actually introduced Joshue to his wife, Allorah. He also knew that Allorah's dad was the leader of his Blood Set.

At first, the whole Gang had been against the union. Particularly because of the lifestyle connected with the Cartels. Of course, the Gang lifestyle wasn't too much better, but their rivals wouldn't hunt down a female, non-member and kill them just for spite. For the Cartels, on the other hand, those kinds of actions are what they thrived on.

The reality was, Allorah's dad had allowed the marriage, but had warned Joshue that, if anything happened to his baby girl, every Blood in the world would instantly become enemies of the Noriega Cartel. Zero had only met the girl a few times, but she was very close to Tano and Ciera. All he could do was hope that the girl was okay.

Tano exited the room with the white girl walking in front of him. He turned her around, grabbed two handfuls of her delicious, healthy ass, and tongued her down. When he released her, she had a dazed look on her face, and her body leaned heavily on his. He said, "You did good, Megan. Come back tonight and we'll continue where we left off." She nodded dumbly and walked off down the stairs, her juicy ass bouncing in her yoga pants.

Both men watched until she was out of sight, because to do otherwise was impossible. Then Tano got down to business. "Have you sent anybody out there to see what's up?" he asked Zero.

"Yeah, and the police are all over it. Called one of our LAPD connections, but all he could say was they found a total of 14 bodies. None had been IDed as of 20 minutes ago."

Ciera chose that moment to join them in the hall. Zero tried to stay focused, but the image of the white girl between her splayed, reddish-yellow thighs, and her perfect breasts pointing towards the ceiling, made his mouth go dry. Tano's girl was BAD. Her hazel eyes, small, straight nose, and short, light-brown hair put him in the mind of the girl from TLC. But her Gangsta was undeniable. She was Gang just like the rest of them, and would kill you just as fast as any man in their set.

She said, "Fill me in on what's going on with my girl," and he repeated what he'd just told Tano. She nodded after he finished and said, "We need to find out if she's one of the 14 bodies. What's the next step?" she asked, looking at Tano.

"One thing is certain: We can't let the GF find out about this from the news. Zero, I need info, fast. Send out everyone we don't need for security and see what they can dig up. 30 minutes from now, I need to call her dad, and I can't tell him we don't know shit."

Zero nodded and headed down the steps, leaving Tano and Ciera still standing on the landing. He immediately pulled his phone out and started issuing orders. Everyone he passed as he headed to the backyard, he signaled for them to follow him. Tano had hundreds of soldiers under his command; Zero thought they might need all of them.

When he hung up the phone, he looked around at the 15 hardened gangbangers that stood at attention, awaiting his orders. These men would kill the President if he said that's what Tano wanted. He said, "Tano has a mission for us all. Right now, rank means nothing, we all need to hit the pavement as hard as possible. We have 27 minutes to gather everything we can on what happened to the GF's daughter.

Take this seriously and hit up every connect you can. What we dig up will mean the difference between us all laying up with our women tonight, or preparing to go to war with the Noriega Cartel."

Chapter 7

Through the earpiece that functioned as a two-way communicator, Reggie was able to send and receive information from Meka Moore, who was still at the safehouse. After the lights turned off, she informed him that the security above ground was still searching, and reinforcements from the city had arrived. His exit would need a diversion, and she was prepared to deliver a big one.

Burkes were excellent at reading people and predicting what they were going to do next. With his night vision shades, developed by his cousin and WRA inventor, LaCora Clay, firmly on his face, he watched Juan hand the knife to Felipe, then take off for the kitchen while Flip cut Joshue loose. Since the space was wide open, Juan made it to the gun sitting on the counter in record time. Then he snatched a drawer open and pulled out the flashlight.

Reggie smiled and closed his eyes as Juan flicked the power button, and the flashlight exploded in his hand.

"AHHH!" he screamed, dropping the gun and grasping his mangled hand. "You son of a bitch! I'm gonna kill you for this!" Reggie calmly walked over and delivered a right-hand hook to his chin that silenced his tirade and laid him flat on his face.

After Flip had freed his Boss, he circled around behind Carlos and stood as if preparing to defend him. But Reggie didn't think that was his intention. He hustled back over to the living area and pulled Carlos from the couch just as Felipe brought the knife arching down. It embedded directly where the Cartel Boss's chest would have been.

Interesting, thought Reggie, lunging over the laid-out Carlos and grabbing the knife. With a flick of his wrist, he sent the blade flying at the retreating Felipe. A smile lit his face as he heard the satisfying thud of impact. The Brazilian crashed to the floor with the knife handle the only visible part sticking out of his left shoulder. Reggie was impressed that the man didn't cry out. Instead, he made several unsuccessful attempts to retrieve the weapon, then jumped up and tried to make good on his escape.

Reggie didn't care if the kid got away, so he let him go. Christian was still on the couch, blubbering from the pain of his wounds. Juan was still unconscious, and Carlos continued to lay on the floor. Joshue, even though he was free, hadn't made a move to fight or flee. Reggie said, "Lights!" once more, then removed his shades as the room illuminated.

Meka said, "Felipe never exited the suite. Be careful because he's lurking around somewhere. Since the only camera is in the common area, I can't tell which room he's hiding in. Chances are, he's going for the arsenal." He nodded to acknowledge her message, then reached down and helped Carlos back to the couch.

That strike by Felipe was unexpected, Reggie admitted. He knew the Noriegas and the Brazilian didn't like each other, he hadn't known it had progressed to murder. He wasn't in the business of sharing info with potential enemies, so he filed the action away for later use. Sitting down in the chair he'd first sat in, his gaze volleyed back and forth from Carlos to Joshue. Neither man said anything, so he decided to get the conversation going.

"Our two organizations have been working together, prosperously, for a long time. That partnership died along with Lucille Drake. Now, let's not kid ourselves here. I can wipe you and your Cartel cronies off the map in less than 24 hours. But, I'm giving you all an opportunity to turn over the ones responsible, then the rest of you can go about your lives."

Carlos, with his hands still secured behind his back, said, "Mr. Burke, I swear to you, no one in my organization would move against the WRA! Like you said, this has hurt us a lot more that you all, at least financially. It wouldn't make sense for my Cartel to bite the hand that's been feeding us."

Reggie nodded, conceding that the Cartel Boss had a point. "On the surface, it would seem ludicrous for you to murder our leader. But your family isn't operating as a unit. Everyone has their own goals and motivations. Like your son, Juan," he said, pointing to the not-moving man. "We both know that he wants to take over, but if he kills you himself, the other Cartels will band together and annihilate him. So, wouldn't it make sense for him to kill Mrs. Drake and hope that we came after you for a little retaliation?

"Then, you have your other son, Joshue." Hearing his name, he sat up straighter, ready to defend himself.

"He enjoys the money and status that the Cartel life affords him, but he hates the violence and brutality he is forced to allocate out. With you no longer in the picture, Juan would take over, Little Capo could retire to one of his beachfront properties, and enjoy life with his beautiful bride. And I don't think I have to point out how his right-hand man feels about all of you."

Joshue turned to his father and said, "I've never made a secret of my disdain for unnecessary violence, but I have never gone against anything you have decreed. All families have their internal problems, but conspiring on the level he is hinting at, goes beyond mere tribulations. I don't have any ambitions that would necessitate your death. I'm an errand boy. I'm content with that, and don't have to resort to murder if I want out. You've said as much to me in the past."

Reggie could tell that Carlos believed his son. He asked, "And what about Felipe?" just to see what each of them would say.

Joshue said, "Flip is my friend, brother, and employee. He has no reason to want my father dead."

Reggie turned to Carlos. "Felipe and I don't like each other, but my animosity developed because I think he will get my son killed with his recklessness. I don't think our mutual dislike has reached the point of murder."

Reggie wanted to laugh out loud at the naivety of such a powerful, older man. But he understood that power tended to create a distortion between the one with the power, and the rest of society who didn't. In his world, he was the only one who decided who lived and who died. That attitude is what makes him such an easy target for the true alpha predators roaming the earth.

"Well," he said, standing up. "Carlos, I'm giving you 48 hours to turn over the person or persons responsible for this act." He held up his hand to stop the objection the man was poised to make. "You of all people should know that I don't operate off of assumptions. If I'm here, it's for a reason. You're supposed to be the only one with the authority to make decisions of this magnitude, but I'm giving you the benefit of the doubt. Fair warning: If you can't figure it out your way, then I'll figure it out mine. Do you understand me?"

Carlos considered him for a second, but he never got to give his answer. Darkness consumed the whole area as Meka shouted, "Move! Move! Felipe just turned the corner with a machine gun!"

She didn't have to worry. Reggie had seen the guy step into the room and was already scrambling across the floor to a new location. He slipped the night vision shades over his eyes, and watched as Felipe sprayed the whole area where he'd been standing. When the gun clicked empty, he released the clip, slammed a new one home, and continued to hose down the vacated seat.

Then, everything went quiet. Well, not quite. Compared to the deafening cacophony of automatic gunfire, what he was hearing wasn't that significant. But, on another level, the gasping coming from his left spoke volumes.

Where Felipe had failed with the knife, from the looks of it, he had succeeded with the gun. From his position on the floor, Reggie could see that Carlos had been struck in the chest area a dozen times. This was no mistake. This was a heated rivalry settled by a kid who would do anything to win. Even sadder than that was the fact that Christian had also paid with his life. The sins of the father coming to bear on his oldest child.

But something about the boy's dedication to kill Carlos spoke to his suspicious nature. Maybe this was more than just a beef being settled. It might even have something to do with the reason he was there. If you were worried that a coconspirator would cave under pressure, the best thing to do was kill them. Something to think about at a later date.

"Joshue!" yelled Flip. "Joshue! You alright?"

Little Capo hadn't been near his father or Reggie, so he sat up, uninjured, and said, "Yeah. Did you get him?"

"I think so," he replied. "I know I caught him by surprise."

Reggie watched as Flip kept his gun at shoulder level and cocked his head in an attempt to hear the slightest movement. It was a futile endeavor. A herd of buffalo could come through and the man wouldn't know. His ears would be ringing for another ten minutes, at least. After pulling out the modified gun, Reggie lined up his shot and sent the projectile flying straight towards his target's chest.

The only response was a sharp intake of breath before the body slumped. Reggie padded over with silent steps, dragged the limp body to his chest, and yelled, "LIGHTS!" once more. Another gasp issued in response to him and his victim being revealed.

Reggie said, "Lower your weapon or your brother and Boss is going to die."

The motionless body of Joshue was now being used as a shield, preventing Flip from firing his weapon. When he still hesitated to comply, Reggie placed his real gun, not the one that shoots knockout rounds, to Joshue's head. The Brazilian exhaled loudly and dropped the automatic gun to the carpet.

Standing at 6'3", and blessed with a 240-pound, supremely powerful body, Reggie could hold the 180-pound man for days. But now that he'd accomplished what he wanted, which was Flip not having a gun pointed at him, he lined his barrel up with Felipe's face and let Joshue crumple to the floor.

"Put your fucking hands all the way up! Stretch them out!" Reggie demanded. With a smirk on his face, Flip raised his hands and stayed still. Reggie walked over to him and removed two handguns and two knives, then pulled out the knife that was still imbedded in his shoulder. He tossed all of it over to the side and pushed the man down on his knees.

Pulling out the tranq gun, he put a round in Juan's back, just to make sure he was really out of commission, then pulled out three heavy-duty flex cuffs. The first one, he looped around Flip's neck and made it snug enough so that it wouldn't come off. Then he placed one around his wrist as tight as he could get it without cutting into the man's skin. He used the last one to secure Flip's hands to the back of his neck. A well-placed kick to his ass tilted him forward until his face mashed into the carpet.

Putting all his weight into it, Reggie dug his knee into his back and said, "You even think about moving, I'll tighten this flex cuff and watch as you choke to death. I'll tell you now, that tough guy act isn't gonna work on me. Mostly, because I know that's exactly what it is, an act. I know the real you. Maybe it's time Joshue learns the truth, too."

"Fuck you!" Flip growled before Reggie sprang up and walked over to Joshue.

Little Capo didn't like the tranq any better than the bee sting. He was fighting the drug with everything he had. Reggie reached into his pack, removed the tweezers, and plucked the small mound off the man's chest. They all sat in silence until Joshue jerked up, looking at Reggie with wide eyes. Then his eyes tracked pass Reggie, and the look that crossed his face probably mirrored the one Reggie had given when he'd witnessed his mother being murdered feet from where he stood.

"Oh God! No, no, no! Flip! What the fuck did you do?" Little Capo leapt to his feet and rushed over to the obviously beyond-help bodies of his father and oldest brother. No tears, but the devastation was clear. He tangled his hands in his long maim, pulled with what appeared to be monstrous strength, and screamed out his pain.

Flip said, "It was an accident, Bro! The darkness threw my aim off. I was trying to kill this fucker. I'm sorry, Joshue!"

The young man stared at his family, then spun on Reggie with a snarl. "You did this! It doesn't matter who pulled the trigger, you and your bullshit caused this. We told you that we didn't kill your mother, Mr. Burke! Your unwillingness to see the facts for what they are has brought us to this point."

Reggie considered him, then said, "Sit down, Joshue." When the Colombian continued to stand, belligerently staring at him, Reggie sighed and said, "Right now, your pain is all mental. Emotional. Unless you want to add physical pain to the mix, sit the fuck down!" Almost like he was coming out of a trance, Joshue's whole body shook, then he walked over and lowered himself on the other couch.

Heading over to the kitchen, Reggie grabbed another chair, since the one he'd been using was shredded to bits. He slammed it down in front of Little Capo and took a seat, making sure Flip was still in his view.

"Listen to me," he said, drawing the other man's attention. "You and Juan are still alive, and the deaths of Christian and Carlos don't excuse this family's culpability. You have 48 hours to give up the culprits or you all die. Do I make myself clear?"

Joshue let his eyes roam over to his deceased family members. Reggie had to wave his hand in front of his face to bring him back to the situation.

Finally, Joshue said, "I understand you, but like we've been telling you from the get go, no one here is responsible. You either acted on some bad intel or you're fishing. There are no answers here."

Reggie sat back and said, "You really think you know the people around you? Very rarely does a person tell you a whole truth when those truths will make that person look bad." He gestured to Flip and decided to shake up Little Capo's nice and orderly world.

"You know that we have all of your vehicles and phones bugged. I listened to that little fairy tale that your brother over there spun for you last week. I'll just use this example to show how people will lie to make themselves look a certain way."

"Fuck you, motherfucker!" yelled Felipe. "You don't know shit about me!" He was smart enough not to move while he let them know how he felt about Reggie's announcement. The two men ignored him while he went on with the story.

"15 years ago, the village Flip was living in was attacked by an organization with ties to my own. He was truthful about the little gang he belonged to and how they were caught while most of their members were away on a mission. The rest of the story was completely fabricated to make him look more favorable than the truth would have."

"He's lying, Joshue! Don't listen to his bullshit! Remember, they are always playing these types of games with people!"

Reggie said, "If you don't want to hear the truth, Joshue, I'll leave it where it is now. The choice is yours." Joshue glanced at his father and brother, then gave a slight nod for Reggie to continue.

"Felipe, in a word, is a coward. But a coward's bullet is just as deadly as anyone else's. When his uncle's people caught his crew, they were never taken to any trees and tied up. The teens took them straight to the town square where his uncle waited. Pluto, his uncle, named after the god of death, immediately separated his nephew from the others. He told him that, for his family to survive the encounter, the other boys needed to die by his hand."

All was quiet in the room, but Meka was steadily feeding him information on the guard's movements. "That is why I say," Reggie continued, "that a coward's bullet is just as deadly. When Flip should have sacrificed himself for his crew, taking out as many of the enemy as possible in the process, instead, he mowed down his comrades, similar to the way he just killed your family.

"When the rest of the crew returned home, they found that, the family members that hadn't been kidnapped by Pluto, were dead. They begged Flip to help them seek vengeance, but he had already struck another deal with his uncle's crew. So, he led the boys on their revenge mission, which was a setup that cost all of them their lives.

"Pluto took Flip in after that and helped him develop into an uncaring, killing machine. His mother and grandmother live in a massive mansion in Brazil, paid for by his Uncle Pluto, who is very much still alive."

Hearing this last comment, Joshue's whole upper body jolted in surprise. "Yes," said Reggie. "Felipe Dos Santos is full of shit. He never killed his uncle. Flip was kicked out of the organization because he failed to carry out a mission in Rio."

"He's fucking lying, Bro! My family is dead. I killed my uncle!"

"The real reason he fled Brazil was because, after he was banished, he picked up some work as a bodyguard in a whorehouse. One of his uncle's Generals came in one day and started talking shit about how far he had fallen. It turned physical and Flip ended up killing the man.

"There were so many people trying to kill him, he finally decided to leave. Joshue, I don't think Flip had anything to do with my mother's death, but I want you to understand that people have secrets. The people you think you know the most, they're the ones that want to keep their lives hidden. They start to rely on seeing themselves through the eyes of the people around them. Mostly, because they can't stand to look at themselves."

Both Joshue and Flip were quiet now. Reggie felt it was a perfect time to leave. Standing up again, he said, "48 hours. That's all I'm giving you." Tossing a package on the floor, he added, "The women and children are unconscious. Follow the instructions on the bag and make sure you give them the correct dose to wake them."

He walked over to Juan and removed the mass from the hole in his shirt. "Give him about five minutes and he'll be able to move. Get him to a hospital quick or he's gonna lose that hand." He strolled confidently pass Joshue and Flip, then stopped at the entrance to the hallway. "If I were you, I'd stay down here for a bit longer. And, um, sorry about you family and the house," he said before dashing to the exit.

Closing the door behind him, he told Meka. "I'm at the bottom of the steps. Go ahead and do your thing." The ten attack drones delivered their deadly payload to clear the way for him. He was too far underground to hear it, but he could feel the vibrations of the artillery hitting the structure. After what just happened to Carlos and Christian, he hated to pile the destruction of their familial home on top of it. But no way was he going to fight it out with a hundred Cartel loyalist just to spare some feelings. Two minutes later, Meka gave the all clear and he headed back to the surface.

Whole walls were missing. He hurried because the structure looked as if it could cave in on itself any moment. He made it outside, looking around at all the dead and destroyed, but not feeling a thing in response. This was the life he inherited. The only life he knew. Emotions kept you going, but the wrong ones could get you killed. His mission to restore the WRA was far from complete. And, sad but true, this wouldn't be the last scene of death he left behind before it was all said and done.

Making it back to the Meta River, he recalled the submersible to the shoreline. He entered and began the ten-mile trek back to where he'd left his vehicle outside the city limits.

Neither him nor Meka, with all their technical advances, picked up the man with eyes on Reggie until he was out of sight. Then, like smoke, he faded away, ready to give his report to his Master.

Chapter 8

Ciera Winds, all 5-foot, 125 pounds of beautifully built redbone, stood between the two ranking members on scene, waiting for the last few members to trickle in. Tano leaned his shredded, 6'3" body against the wall, while Zero posted up with his arms crossed in front of his chest. The second that the last soldier sat down, Zero said, "Let's hear it. What did you all find out?"

Their security personnel had already swept the backyard to make sure no bugs were present, and each member had been checked as they entered the house. Anyone trying to capture their conversation with long-range recorders would only hear static because of the noise distributors placed around the property. This was how Gang business was discussed. No one would ever have the opportunity to collect evidence of a conspiracy involving the leaders.

A dark-skinned guy with dreads raised his hand and Tano said, "What you got, Kampaign?"

In his deep baritone, he said, "The bitch, um, I mean chick, Allorah, wasn't found at the scene. All the bodies have been identified as those belonging to her bodyguards. My source didn't know anything more than that her body wasn't part of the 14 found, and the police are treating this like a kidnapping."

Everyone present was dressed in black, white, red, or some combination of those colors. But no one wore bandanas or sagged or looked like gang members in the slightest. All were in their 20s or 30s, most had college degrees, and all were about making money. This wasn't a gathering of foot soldiers, the ones the movies loved to portray as ignorant and prone to violence at the smallest provocation, but a meeting of men and women who got shit done. No one's sources would be questioned at this point. Under penalty of death, every word had already been checked and confirmed before it was presented to the leadership.

Ciera nodded in her black, Nike jogging suit, and said, "That's good news. At least we don't have to tell the GF his daughter is dead."

Another dark-skinned guy with dreads, sitting in the back, raised his hand. Zero nodded and he stood up and said, "All of the men were killed with only two guns, and investigators say that it was most likely one shooter. 13 of the 14 were killed with single shots placed with precision and skill. The other was hit multiple times, but only because the victim was trying to hide behind a spotlight."

As soon as he sat down, a female member raised her hand. Tano said, "Good intel, Fa'ness." Then signaled for the thick, super intelligent Satavia to proceed.

"I don't know how any of this fits, but all the electronics in the area were fried. I'm not talking about in the fire, I'm talking about before it even started. This includes the cameras that were nowhere near the house, and even the electrical systems in the cars parked on the road. My source thinks there was some kind of EMP device used so the alarm would disable and no one could call for help."

When she sat, everyone looked around in silence, probably wondering what in the world they were dealing with. None of them had ever heard of the Cartels using EMPs, but this had to have been Cartel business. Ciera nodded when the next hand shot into the air. This was the person who normally had the best intel, and for good reason.

The brown-skinned man, with his piercing eyes and clean-cut looks, was a lawyer assigned to the DA's office in Los Angela's county. Garcel Christian had been groomed since he was a toddler to be exactly what he was: Smart, ruthless, and cunning. He was a chameleon, able to thrive in any habitat they needed him to infiltrate.

He said, "I couldn't get a copy of the video, and it didn't show much, anyway. A house, almost two and a half miles away from the scene, has a motion activated camera pointing towards the beach. It caught sight of a man leading Allorah around to the front of the home. The cops searched the vacant structure and determined that no one had been inside for months.

"About three minutes after that, another camera picked up a black Mercedes Benz G Wagon driving from the direction of the fire, the only vehicle for 30 minutes, before or after the explosion, that wasn't of an official capacity. The thing is, there is a lot of property in that area, but all roads take you to a choke point about 15 minutes from the Noriega house. The cameras at that intersection never picked up the Benz leaving the area.

"As we speak, the police are going door to door, but it's still a long shot. Ventura doesn't have the capabilities, or the manpower, of LA. It could take weeks before they find anything. By then, Allorah could be moved or dead."

Zero asked, "Couldn't the guy have stashed the Benz somewhere and just switched to another vehicle?"

Garcel nodded. "That's why they are focusing their search on the vehicle and not a certain suspect. The police hope to find it and use other cameras in the area to figure out what the other vehicle looks like, if it even exists. They're also hopeful that the guy feels safe enough, and is stupid enough, to just stay in the area and they can catch him by surprise. Maybe make him do something out of desperation."

Tano scoffed. "You're not gonna catch someone by surprise after they just kidnapped the wife of a Cartel Capo. But this is good news. I mean, not good, but it's something I can tell the GF." Looking around, he asked, "Anybody got anything else? Everything is relevant. You never know when the smallest detail could make the difference." He was just about to call the meeting adjourned when a hand from the middle of the pack went up.

One of their newest recruits, a Blood member for decades, but a new addition to their ranks, stood up. Charles Kelly, a

Blood from North Carolina, and the richest of them all, said, "Before I left the East Coast, there were rumors floating around about a secret organization that had these super-soldiers trained in all kinds of warfare. One of the loudest murmurs was about the demise of a Crip Set called the Big Rollin Crips. Sources said that one guy, using drones and other gadgets, killed a hundred of them on his own.

"The part that might be related to this is that, the Noriega Cartel was said to be connected to some secret organization here in the States. About six months ago, as we all heard, the Cartel started having problems. We might want to put somebody on this thread to see if we're involving ourselves in something that will make us a target of this organization."

Tano said, "Reach out to your people on the East Coast and ask if they've heard anything else on the matter. Hopefully, we, or the police, can find Allorah and we can let the Cartel burn in hell. But if that's not an option, then we need all the info we can get. Right now, we need to…"

"OG!" one of the security men ran from the house. Tano knew it had to be something important, the man was risking his life by interrupting.

"What is it?" asked Tano.

"The Noriega Cartel was hit in Colombia last night! It's all over the news!"

Tano adjourned the meeting and everyone flocked to the living room where the TV was showing video of what appeared to be a warzone. They all stared, transfixed, as a reporter relayed the relevant information on the attack.

The severe looking brunette said, "The sheer magnitude of this attack has authorities up in arms looking for answers. Villavicencio, a small city in Central Colombia, population of 360,000 souls, has been devastated by the loss of life. Witnesses say that an explosion earlier in the night brought the townspeople to the compound owned by the alleged Cartel Boss, Carlos Alberto Noriega. While they were attempting to figure out what was going on, drones came from every direction and destroyed everything in sight.

"The last official body count was 87 people, and the rescue efforts are still underway for those trapped inside the structure. With the amount of people missing, representatives from the Department expect the total body count to reach well into the hundreds. We will now cut to an interview of a survivor recorded moments ago."

Tano, Zero, and Ciera glanced at each other with trepidation as a haggard and dirty old man flashed on the screen. In broken English, he said, "My sons go to help the family inside, and I watch from outside the walls. Next thing, there are robots in the sky, shooting down inside the walls. I can hear screams and shouts, then nothing. No sounds. Machines fly away and then house collapse. So many people, dead. My sons, dead." The video continued to roll as the man broke down in tears.

The reporter came back. "This is being investigated as a Cartel war, but it is still in its early stages. We will keep you updated as we receive more information on this horrific event in Colombia. Please continue to pray for this community."

Tano walked up and hit the mute button, then turned to his people. "This shit is the real deal. Charles," he said to the former NC Blood. "I need that info as soon as you can get it. After what we just saw, your theory doesn't seem so farfetched anymore. Everyone else, I want you hitting that area between LA and Ventura with everyone we got. Get all the soldiers, but I want nothing less than groups of three. I don't need some dumbass stumbling into them, getting killed, and alerting the guy in the process.

"No matter what we have to do, finding Allorah Noriega is now our main objective. Money is of no concern, but discretion is paramount. Be silent and be invisible. Once she is located, contact one of our leaders so we can coordinate our efforts and do this the right way." Giving his soldiers a salute, he said, "You're all dismissed. And, good luck." Within seconds, Tano, Zero, and Ciera were the only ones left in the house.

Tano looked at Ciera and Zero, seeing two people who would kill or die for him. Their loyalty and love were things he never had to question. They had all been in some perilous situations in the past, but he had a feeling that this encounter would be different. He sat on the couch for a moment, deep in thought, before he lifted his head to deliver his decision.

"Listen, I want both of you to go to our secondary safehouse and coordinate everything from there."

"But OG, we need to…" started Zero.

"No! My brother, this isn't a debate. I'm giving you a direct order that I expect you to follow." Standing up, he said, "That shit Charles was talking about with the Crips, I remember those rumors. At one location, 50 plus members got smoked. And only one body didn't look as if it was from natural causes.

"At the next site, it was just like what we just watched on the report a minute ago. Drones came out of nowhere and shot the shit out of everything that moved. Another double-digit body count. We're dealing with some next level shit. I'm not letting my line die out for this bullshit. You guys met Allorah through me, and I'm gonna be the one on the frontlines to bring her home.

"But, I can't do that without knowing our power structure will still be in place. I'm not sidelining you guys, I'm putting competent people I know I can trust in a pivotal role, so maybe we can survive this. You understand what I'm saying?" They both nodded, so Tano pulled out his phone.

"I'm already late for my daily," he said, referring to the daily call he was supposed to make to their leader. "Let me reach out to him and then we can do what we need to do." He dialed the number and, three rings later, the phone was answered, but the line remained silent.

"Yo! Hello? You on here, Bro?"

"Why the fuck you late, Blood?" asked the GF.

"Well, we ran into a situation and…"

"So, my fucking daughter getting kidnapped is a fucking situation!" roared their leader.

Swallowing his own anger, Tano said, "I've been gathering intel and putting a plan in motion to get her back. I didn't want to call you without…"

"Who in the hell gave you decision making powers? You don't decide when to tell me what the fuck is going on with my seed! The second you heard…"

"Listen here, motherfucker!" Tano yelled, finally losing his cool. "This shit isn't on me! I'm not the one responsible for keeping up with your daughter. But I got the whole hood out looking for Allorah and the fucker who took her. Everything else is on hold until we find them.

"Now, I understand you're mad as hell, I love Allorah like a sister. But, what's not going to happen is you talking to me like I'm a fucking Scrap! I been getting Bloody for a long time, and you not gonna disrespect me, Gang! So, I'm going out to find my sister. You do whatever the fuck you have to do!" Then Tano hung up and turned back to his people.

Zero said, "Yo, Blood. You know he can DP you for that? The GF is hurting…"

"Fuck him," Tano said, cutting Zero off. "I grew up with that girl." Glancing at Ciera, he stated, "We grew up with that girl. That fool was nowhere around for most of her life. But to me, she is bigger that Blood. I'm gonna do what I have to do, and he'll do the same. After she is home, if he wants smoke, then we'll settle it like Gangstas."

Ciera reached and touched his arm with a brief caress. "Go get your family, Love. Me and Zero will head to the Spot so everything goes smoothly." Kissing him on the lips, she added, "One war at a time, but if the GF wants it after this is done, then I guess we'll all be getting new ranks," she said with confidence. Zero nodded in agreement and Tano saluted them both, then made his way to the garage.

Living in an outwardly ugly home was one thing, but driving around in a hoopty was another. Climbing into his bloodred Chevy Corvette Z06, he cranked it to life and let the power flow from its engine into his soul. He rocketed down the driveway and turned towards Ventura. He had no idea if he would live to see another sunrise, but if he had to give up his life to save someone he loved, he would make sure to take the man who kidnapped his sister with him.

Chapter 9

Delmas ended the call and turned to look at Allorah. "I have to leave for a bit, but I won't be gone too long. In the meantime, I'm sorry, I have to secure you to the bed. Do you have to use the bathroom before I go?"

They were sitting out on the patio, enjoying the weather, as Delmas gathered the rest of the data he needed on the Noriega Cartel. All morning he'd been getting alerts on what happened in Colombia. Someone had beaten him to the punch and attacked his target. This complicated things, but didn't change his overall objective in the least.

The style of attack spoke of a WRA hit, and he found himself hoping that it had failed. On one level, dead was dead, and vengeance for his mother would be achieved. On another level, maybe a little higher than the first, was his need to extinguish the perpetrator his way. The Burke way. The way that would send a message to the rest of the world not to fuck with the Burkes.

Allorah stood up and stretched her long, toned body, now encased in her recently dried, but badly wrinkled, clothes. She smiled her most innocent smile and asked, "If I promise not to run, will you trust me to stay out here?"

He chuckled and stood up himself. "I don't trust you when I'm sitting right next to you."

With a twinkle in her eye, she asked, "Is it me you don't trust, or is it yourself?"

This was the new tactic she was employing. Super nice, super innocent, with a little bit of flirtiness thrown in to keep him off track. He would bet that she'd never had a problem bending men to her will. He would play along because it was harmless at this point, but he was prepared to put her back in her place if it got out of hand.

Amused, he said, "Oh! It's definitely you I don't trust. Now, I really have to go. Use the bathroom so I don't ever have to smell your piss again, and let's get this done." She gave him a sexy pout, spun on her bare feet, and marched over to the bathroom.

Five minutes later, she came out and walked straight over to the bed. Laying down, she said, “I could use a nap anyway. Don’t hurry back, but when you do return, can you bring some real food? Pizza or chicken or something that will fill me up. I’m tired of fruit and bread.”

He locked the cuff around her ankle, checked to make sure the whole setup was secured, and said, “I’ll see what I can do.” Then he walked out the door, jumped in the SUV, and pulled off.

He wasn’t going far, just a quick five-minute drive to meet his benefactor. The Author wanted to talk. Delmas figured he owed the man at least some conversation. He acknowledged he would still be in some stuffy ass jail cell if it wasn’t for him. He followed the directions and turned into the driveway of a hillside mansion before pulling the Benz in the garage.

Wilford Sealy, The Author, was already there, sitting inside the gloomy interior, waiting for him. As soon as he stepped out of the vehicle, The Author said, “Take everything out that you’ll need because you have to switch to this one.”

He indicated a Rolls-Royce Cullinan, finished in a stunning midnight blue, and, without question, Delmas started the transfer.

After he completed the task, he turned to his older cousin and asked, “What did you want to talk about?”

“Allorah Noriega is the daughter of a high-ranking Blood in one of the biggest and most powerful sets in LA. They have people and a lot of money and they’re using both to try and get her back.”

Delmas shrugged. “I don’t step into things without knowing all the details. This isn’t news to me.” Shaking his head, he said, “The second I start to worry about a bunch of gangbangers, it's time for me to retire. What I'm worried about is what's going on in Colombia."

"I'll get to that," Wilford said, impatiently. "What you need to do is take my warnings seriously. There is no WRA to back you up. No satellites or drones to cover your six. You've relied on these things for so long that you're making silly mistakes without them."

"What the hell are you talking about? What mistakes?" demanded Delmas.

"They know the vehicle you used and they already tracked you to the area your currently staying in."

"What! How?" asked Delmas.

"The unoccupied house where you stashed the SUV during your assault has a camera that you neglected to disable. I gave you the black box, but you didn't activate it again after you left the house. A couple of miles after you got in the vehicle, another camera picked you up driving towards LA. Then, and here's the part where you really fucked up, all the roads around here are dead ends or loops that lead right back to the main road. When the SUV didn't turn up on any of the exit cameras, they knew it was still in this area."

Delmas felt shame. He was doing sloppy work, and without the man pointing it out, he would have been ignorant of the fact. Having the WRA behind him since day one had led to him being lackadaisical about security and prep work. Normally, lower members in his department would do all the mundane stuff, and he would focus on the big picture. It gave him a deeper respect for the other Burkes who did these jobs all the time, flawlessly.

The Author said, "I'll get rid of the Benz and, since the police have already been up here to search this area, if need be, you can bring her here for a short time. But, I'm telling you, this is terrain untraveled for you. No one will help if you find yourself in a jam. Reggie stripped me of so many of my assets, I've done pretty much all I can do for you."

"I appreciate the help and I got it from here. I'll be careful and tighten the fuck up because, this is a mission that I can't afford to fail." Switching topics, Delmas asked, "What's your dad's plan? If it involves taking over the Agency, I want in. Those bastards threw me to the wolves and I want some get back."

Shaking his head, Wilford said, "He's had to take a few steps back because of some suspicious activities between your brothers. He was sure he had Daniel fooled, but now he's not so convinced. The plan was for Daniel to come aboard and take over your job. Ronald can't figure out why he deviated."

"It could be because of Alisha and Gabby," Delmas offered. "I can honestly say that they have his undivided attention for the time being."

"Yeah, well, until my father is sure all threats to his position are neutralized, he will be playing the role of Glendo Burke." Cocking his head, he asked, "How did you find out, anyway?"

Delmas cocked his head in thought. He studied his cousin, trying to find some ulterior motive behind the question. After weighing the pros and cons, he found no reason not to be totally honest with the man.

"My mom was showing a lot of interest in you when you were captured in Texas. Your skillset was impressive and Reggie was pushing to save you and bring you in. When my mother put so much effort into her refusal, it made me suspicious. I did a search of your name in every database I could access and got a hit on a hidden file that had been locked for years.

"It took me weeks to crack it, as hacking isn't one of my specialties, but when I did, I found the whole story. About you, your dad, the death of my other uncles, and the story of my grandparents. I didn't know my mother was the one who hid the file until I approached her with the discovery. She swore me to secrecy, said the family wasn't ready to deal with it yet. But, we thought Ronald was dead until last year. Well, at least I know I did."

Wilford seemed to think over his answer, probably trying to detect any deception in his words. Shrugging, he finally said, "Well, I only hear from him when he can get a message out securely. He had no idea how invasive the surveillance was inside the HQ. You guys literally have 25 dedicated agents who do nothing except try to expose espionage."

Old habits die hard, but Delmas figured his cousin was lying about everything except the danger Delmas himself was in. Neither Ronald nor his son were true Burkes in his eyes. He would stay informed, insinuate himself in their plans if he could, then kill them both if they thought he would stand by and let them take over his grandfather's legacy.

Not giving anything away, Delmas shrugged and said, "Policy is policy. With Reggie at the helm, every Bi-Law in the book will be followed to the letter. Now, what do you know about what happened in Colombia?"

"Fucking Reggie is what happened," The Author said with total disdain. "He's been in Colombia since the night you escaped. He was supposed to be down there to figure out if they were the ones who hit your mother. I've tapped every source I have and nobody knows what's going on."

"Are the Noriegas still alive?" asked Delmas.

Wilford shook his head. "No one's seen or heard from them and authorities are still pulling bodies out of the wreckage. Everyone knows about the security suite they have under their compound, but word on whether it's still intact hasn't filtered out yet. I do know Reggie made it out alright, but he's being very tight lipped on the whole situation. He hasn't reported anything to anyone. Just another thing that makes Ronald uneasy about what your brothers know."

Steering him back on topic, Delmas asked, "Who's helping Reggie?"

Waving his hand as if the question wasn't important, Wilford said, "None of the top agents. Just the local caretaker of one of the WRA safehouses." Delmas had no idea who that could be. Most of the time the WRA would assign injured agents to guard the hundreds of safehouses they had spread out all over the world.

"So, what are you getting into next?" he asked the serial killer. Delmas felt that he'd gotten all the info he could out of the man, and it was time to go. But it never hurt to see what type of lies someone would tell you.

The Author stood up, took a few test hops on his bad leg, and said, "It's time for me to get back in the game. I've healed up enough where I can start practicing again."

"Practicing?" asked Delmas, confused.

Laughing, he said, "Killing. Murder. You know, serial killer shit. I don't have to pretend to be civilized like the rest of you. I think I'll go somewhere quiet, where crime is scarce, and brush up on my skills." After a moment, he added, "After you're done here, if you're still alive, you can join me. It's always good to release those demons."

Backing away from the deranged psychopath, Delmas said, "No thanks. I'm exercising my demons with this mission. After I finish, I think I'll take a vacation somewhere with beautiful weather and laws that can be bent for the right price. I still have a couple Billion Dollars stashed for a rainy day. Let me know where you end up and I'll reimburse you for all this."

The Author gave one of his signature sadistic smiles, shook his head, and said, "You are your mother's son. You'll find out where I've been by following the bodies. See you around, Cousin," he said in dismissal.

Delmas climbed into the Rolls-Royce, never taking his eyes off of the ex-WRA hitman until he was driving back down the long path towards the main road. "Sick motherfucker," he murmured to himself. The Burkes were a family of killers, none of them could deny that. But Wilford enjoyed it too much. If he was sure the man had outlived any future usefulness, he'd turn the SUV around and end the fucker now.

Forcing his mind back to a productive tract, he wondered if the Noriegas were still alive. From the looks of their property, he didn't give them a good chance. Heading back to the ocean-side property, he decided to let Allorah go if the men were in fact dead. Her role was only to be bait to draw out the Cartel when the time was right. Once he got his hands on a couple of them, he would discover the truth. Now, depending on what his brother had done, he might never know for certain if they got the people responsible.

There really wasn't much he could do until he found out the diagnosis on the Cartel men, so he let his mind rest while he cruised back to the house. He did think about going to get Allorah her pizza or chicken, but thought that would send the wrong message. He wasn't her friend. He wasn't supposed to care if her food was to her liking. Shaking his head, he wondered why he pictured how disappointed she would be with his decision.

Pulling up to the front, he turned the engine off, looked around carefully, but didn't see anything out of the ordinary. Even so, something didn't feel right. The Author said that the police were out searching, but on the drive over, he hadn't seen hide nor hair of a single one. Was the man lying about that also, or had the authorities found their target and were waiting to spring their trap?

Grabbing his bag, he pulled his gun and tucked it beside his leg. The windows on the Rolls were blacked out, so he could see out into the bright afternoon sun, but no one could see inside. By the way the heavy vehicle handled, he could tell it was armored. None of that would help him in the least once he exited the SUV.

Surveying. Scanning. He'd been sitting inside for ten minutes and hadn't seen a thing move. That would be telling in itself if they were in a more populated area. One thing that was a benefit to the house's location, no sniper could get a clear shot at him. The hedges would make a clear sight line impossible. His senses weren't picking up on any particular threat, more like a warning to take extra precaution. Deciding to test the waters, he opened his door about a foot, but stayed seated for the time being.

No smells that spoke to his predatory mind of imminent danger. No sounds other than the distant rolling of the ocean. No cars zooming by. No birds chirping happily. He didn't know what to make of the alarm flowing in his veins, but he needed to figure it out one way or another. Slamming the car door, he cranked the engine to life. Mashing the gas, he roared around the loop, but stopped the vehicle before reaching the street.

Anyone out there would have had to respond to that. Whether the Cartel, gang, or police, someone would have tried to strike before he got away. Still not willing to ignore his feeling, he reversed back to his original parking spot, grabbed all the gear in the SUV, and hightailed it into the house.

Immediately after crossing the threshold, he slammed and locked the door, dropped everything except his gun, and did a quick walk-through of the entire house. Allorah, sensing something was wrong, stayed quiet and still, watching him like he'd lost his mind.

He posted up along the side of the backdoor after clearing the inside. Nothing looked disturbed in the back. Shaking his head, he rushed back to the front and peeked out of the window. Didn't see a thing. A less trained man would have brushed the feeling to the side as silly, but he knew what he felt was real. Dropping his gun hand to his side, he turned and studied Allorah.

"If you saw something, or did something, let me know now. I can promise you this; a lot of people, including you, will die if they try to breach this house."

"I haven't seen anything," she stated. "I've been sleep. Just woke up when I heard you drive up."

He saw it in her eyes. She was lying. Raising the pistol, he stalked towards her. "Tell me the truth, Allorah!" he roared. "What did you do?"

"Nothing!" she screamed back. "You're acting crazy!"

He shot. It was just a warning that missed her by a mile, but she reared back and screamed in terror. "Talk, you stupid bitch!"

Pointing shakily, her face hidden behind her hands, she said, "A man at the back door. Said I was safe now. They have the house surrounded."

"Was it your people, or the police?"

She shook her head. "Not the Cartel. I don't know…" A sound at the back of the house cut her short.

He heard the boom and had time to turn towards the glass door, but that was it. The door shattered and the canister bounced off the kitchen table, landed about three feet behind him, exploded, filling the small dwelling with smoke. Delmas lunged for one of the bags he'd left by the door, grabbed it, then hunkered down between the two beds.

He pulled out a gas mask, slipped it over his face and, with hate-filled eyes, watched as Allorah choked on the noxious fog. Now he could hear it: Walkie talkies and men yelling to coordinate the attack. His hands worked frantically to organize the things he pulled from the bag. When everything was in place, he said her name once to draw her attention. "Allorah!"

It was muffled, but she heard him none the less. She pulled her face from the pillow to look at him, but recoiled when she saw the gun pointed in her direction. He said, "You picked the wrong team, but I'm gonna give you one chance to live. Put this on."

The item he handed her didn't fit the situation, especially since she was still coughing from the smoke. But, she used them as directed, sporting a small frown as nothing seemed to happen.

After a minute, he signaled for her to remove the item. He said, “Let’s go. We don’t have much time.”

He unlocked the shackle and gathered as much as he could carry, leaving behind everything that wasn’t absolutely necessary. He jerked the front door open and she followed close behind. Only after he stored the baggage did he notice that she was no longer by his side. Turning quickly, he saw her still stuck at the front door, staring out at the disturbing scene.

Shaking his head, he marched over and grabbed her arm, dragged her to the Rolls, and all but tossed her inside. He circled the vehicle and jumped in so they could make good on their escape.

But Allorah was in a daze. Her eyes never left the carnage as they drove away. Bodies littered the ground. All those officers, none moving, none appeared alive.

She reached up and touched the tracking device still secreted in her hair. If this was the fate she was drawing her people into, she needed to rethink her position. As stealthy as possible, she reached up and crushed it between her fingers.

Of course, he saw it, but he understood what she was thinking, so he let it be for the time being. Let her feel the hopelessness of her situation. Maybe it will keep her calm and complacent until he no longer needed her.

He headed towards the house that he’d just left minutes ago. It was the only option he had left at this point. He prayed The Author was gone and they’d have the place to themselves. It was time to finish with this mission and get missing. The authorities would be out for blood after the scene he’d just left behind.

Chapter 10

Joshue and Flip stood watching the sunset in the coastal town of Santa Marta, Colombia. The weather was beautiful, just like the hundreds of women laid out next to the Caribbean Sea trying to soak up the last rays of the disappearing sun. Since they didn't want the public to know they weren't trapped under the rubble of his father's estate, they were staring out at the scene from a third story balcony facing the beach. The chest-high glass surrounding them was tinted and bulletproof. Never knew when some maniac would run down the beach or sail his yacht onto the sand and try to execute a Cartel Boss.

The women and children had also survived the assault and had been flown to New York to stay with his mother. Juan was down on the first floor, high as a kite, being attended to by one of the Cartel's doctors. They had tried to get him to go to the hospital, but he wasn't going for it. The pain of his injury, and the realization that his left hand would be mangled forever without help, had led to this compromise. Now, the doctor had him in the medical suite where he swore he had everything he'd need to patch up his brother's hand.

Neither man watching the beach had said a word to each other since they had narrowly escaped being crushed by the collapsing structure. Joshue had hated to leave the bodies of his father and brother, but knew they had to abandon the area as fast as possible.

The assault on the house had been felt all the way in the security suite as it shook from the numerous impacts. Only minutes behind Mr. Burke's departure, they had boarded a small motor boat and got out of dodge before the authorities could descend on the scene. That being one of their prearranged escape routes in case of attack, 30 minutes after exiting the property, they were on a plane heading to the northwest part of the country.

Still looking out over the tranquil scene, Joshue said, "My father had told me parts of that story the first few months after you joined us. I didn't listen because I thought he was making things up to drive us apart. Of course, he hadn't had as many details as Mr. Burke, but who could ever have more information than the WRA?"

Flip stayed silent, just turned and walked his battered and beaten body back into the house. Making his way over to the bar, he poured an amber-colored liquid into a glass and tossed it back. Joshue sighed, and turned to join his friend inside.

They had all cleaned up and taken showers. New clothes made Joshue feel like a new man. Flip had gotten a few stitches in his shoulder to close his knife wound, and they were now both wearing jeans and t-shirts collected from their own rooms.

He stepped into the third-floor library, where Allorah loved to come and sit, looking at the ocean while devouring romantic fiction books for hours. Sandra Brown, Allison Brennan, Tami Hoag, Linda Howard. And then a new section of romantic fantasy by Laurell K. Hamilton, J. R. Ward, and Sherrilyn Kenyon. Just glancing over the titles made him yearn for his wife. He needed to call so he could hear her voice. Even when she was cursing him out, it made his day just to talk to her.

He took a seat at the bar next to the man who had just killed two members of his family. "You don't think I'm owed an explanation? You sat in the car a week ago, looked me in my eyes and flat out lied. Now, you don't have anything to say?"

Slinging his glass at the stone wall, Flip spun and yelled, "What the fuck do you want me to say? Huh? You want me to say that I lied? That I murdered my crew to save my life? That I chose to work for the devil so he wouldn't kill the only real family I had ever known? Okay, dammit! That's what I did. You fucking happy now?"

Joshue jumped up and slapped the shit out of Flip. "Don't try and turn this around on me! I've stuck by you through all of your bullshit! Even going against my own family. I don't give a fuck what you had to do to survive, I'm mad because you didn't tell me the truth!"

The men stood nose to nose, neither giving an inch. The breath huffing in and out of their chest the only movement. They were roughly the same size. Only one year separating their ages. Both raised to be ruthless and violent. But they both knew Flip was the true killer of the two. Joshue would kill to protect or if ordered to do so. The other man murdered wherever the proclivity hit him.

This time, though, it was Flip who lowered his gaze and took a step back. He paced, rubbing his hand across his stinging face before he turned to address his brother.

"When I was a kid, showing fear got you killed. You didn't run to Mommy, or call for Daddy to come help. You either handled your shit, or you died trying."

Joshue turned and made them each a drink, carried them over to his massive desk, and set them down in front of two overstuffed chairs. "Sit," he commanded his friend.

After sitting and sipping the alcohol, Flip leaned back and said, "My uncle, Pluto, was a fucking monster. He had no value of human life unless it was a life he owned. Training for his killers and whores started around the ages of five or six. The reason we were even living in that poor ass Favela was because of what he did to my older sister years before."

Flip explained how, when he was six, his 12-year-old sister had been kidnapped. They had been living in a condo in Rio and his uncle always made sure life was good for them. A week before his sister disappeared, his mother had found out a childhood friend of hers was whoring in their neighborhood. She took the woman in, cleaned her up, and gave her enough money to run away for good.

His sister had been gone a month before his uncle came to their home drunk one night. In his rage over Flip's mother interfering with his whore, he confessed that he'd sent someone to take his niece as payment for the lost wages.

The siblings had battled, and Flip's mom had demanded the return of her daughter. With a sick, sadistic sneer on his face, Pluto told his sister, "The girl was too much like you. I tried to break her of the offensive attitude but she wouldn't listen." Earlier that day, a man had slit her throat for not obeying his commands.

"That night," continued Flip, "my mother packed us up and we left with nothing but the clothes on our backs. My mother refused to live another day off my uncle's ill-gotten money. After that incident, our happy and protected family was never the same."

Silence ruled for a while because the situation seemed to call for it. Softly, Joshue asked, "What was her name?"

"Rosa Belle," he answered with a tear rolling down his cheek. "Rosa Belle Dos Santos." He sat looking into his glass for a bit, then leaned forward. "When those kids pulled us out of our homes and marched us to my uncle, for the first time in my life, I could taste true fear. I hadn't seen him since we left Rio, but he still looked the same. Smelled the same. I knew he would kill us all, so when he gave me a way to live, I took it.

"I live with that shame every day, and it shapes every decision I make. We can't pick our family, but we damn sure can pick our friends. I lied to you because I never wanted you to look at me the way I look at myself, when I can bring myself to do so. I needed to see someone look at me as if I wasn't a backstabbing piece of shit."

"It's nice to see you getting along with the man who just killed our father," said Juan, entering the room. His words were slightly slurred, his step a bit ungainly, but the fire in his eyes was fed by pure hate. "I should have stuck that knife in your chest instead of trusting you to pitch in and help!"

Juan was in no shape to head into war, his left hand being bandaged from finger tips to elbow. But that didn't stop him from dressing as the soldier he was. Black and grey fatigues, combat boots, and a black t-shirt. To complete the look, a nickel-plated pistol was in his good hand, hanging by his side. He had never been an official soldier for Colombia, but he'd fought in enough wars to have earned the distinction.

Joshue jumped up, placing his body between Juan and Flip, who still sat as if he wasn't being threatened by an out of his mind madman. Joshue said, "Hold up, Bro! It was a mistake. Mr. Burke had the lights turned off as soon as Flip started to fire. He didn't kill them on purpose."

Stumbling forward, Juan sneered at his younger brother. "You're not a killer, Little Bro. But, me and this scumbag right here, we are. I can read a scene just as clearly as any seasoned investigator. You didn't notice the concentration of shots? The chair where Reggie was sitting was shot to shit, then a trail of bullet holes led straight over to the couch. No Joshue, this wasn't a mistake. This was a cold-blooded execution."

From behind him, Flip asked, "Why are you acting angry?" Joshue turned to see that Flip had stood up, but had not unholstered his own gun. "Isn't this exactly what you wanted? Now that you're the oldest Noriega left, you have undisputed claim to the throne."

"Fuck you, you murdering bastard!" yelled Juan. "Don't act like this was done for me. If you could have explained how a few bullets made it into me, I would be dead right along with them. It's no secret that you want Joshue to head the Cartel so you can use him to go after your uncle."

The ring of truth in the statement, along with the story Flip had just told, made everything click into place. That was the true motive behind Flip's actions from the very beginning. All of the research into Joshue's assassination attempt from years ago turned up no motive for the would-be killer. Maybe his father had been dead on when he said Flip being where he was that day wasn't the coincidence it seemed to be.

Slowly, Joshue turned to Flip. "It was you," he said, with the scene of the attempted murder playing in his mind. "You paid the assassin to make the attempt on me."

The resignation on the man's face was all the confirmation he needed. Flip said, "I didn't pay the man anything. A few choice words here and there, I had the man believing that you were the cause of his every plight. But I was never going to let him succeed, I just needed a way to insinuate myself in your life."

Another thought crossed his mind. "The whorehouse in Rio. The guy you murdered…"

"Yes, I took the job to get close to my uncle's General. You see, this was the man who had raped and killed my sister. Instead of killing the man for his crime, Pluto added him to his organization. It took me over ten years to finally get close to him, and I murdered him the first chance I got."

"So, is Juan right? Did you kill my father and brother to further your plot for revenge?"

Flip thought on his answer before giving it. "Six years ago, when I settled on this plan, the Noriega Cartel was feared. Powerful. No one would dare to fuck with any of you. Under your father's rule, I watched this organization lose its bite. People are losing respect for the Cartel. His lust for money and women was causing him to not care about the state of affairs around him. I saw the system that I'd invested six years of my life in, crumbling to the ground."

"So?" asked Joshue slowly.

Rolling his eyes, Flip said, "Okay, I'll spell it out for you. I needed a powerful organization to combat my uncle's gang. I focused on the Noriega Cartel. I needed the weak part of the system out of the way, so I killed Carlos and Christian. I have no reason to kill you or Juan because, with the three of us at the top, we can restore the Noriega Cartel into the fearsome Big Bad Wolf it was meant to be."

Joshue looked around the room at all the fiction novels and wondered when he'd become part of one himself. Lies on top of lies on top of lies. He understood that the world was dog eat dog, but where had all the honor gone. He was sick of the games and deceptions. It was time he did something about it.

In one motion, he pulled his gun and pointed it at the traitor's head. Flip's eyes went wide, but he didn't attempt to bring his own gun out in defense. Instead, he smiled. Clearly not believing Joshue had it in him.

But the situation had triggered something inside of him. His mind flashed through the numerous times people had told him he was soft, not cut out for Cartel life. He acknowledged that he was always playing the small fish to the giant sharks swimming around him. Just waiting to be devoured at their leisure. Within a split second, he chose to rectify everyone's assessment of him.

He pulled the trigger.

Reggie and Meka sat down to a late dinner of Chinese food with laptops spread over most of the available space. As they ate, they worked. Both scrutinizing every word and motion coming from their subjects. It was laborious work, but important. One slip or loose comment could lead to the end of this horrid ordeal.

Now that Christian and Carlos were dead, it cut out two of the main suspects, but they still had to entertain the notion that one of the lesser Capos had ordered the hit. It seemed unlikely because of the talent level of the shooter, but no stone could be left unturned.

While Reggie was in Colombia on the front line, the WRA was anything but idle. His sister, Kashonda Wilson, their Head of Intelligence was using her vast network to make sure the CIA wasn't responsible for the hit on their mother. Although the two agencies have shared a long and prosperous relationship, acts by his mother before her death could have been the catalyst for the strike.

Phung Lei, the Head of the WRA's I.T. Department, was also using her considerable hacking skills to provide support for both operations. No firewall was safe. No encryption strong enough to keep her out of any system she wanted in. Any information they requested was delivered within minutes. Reggie knew the extremely intelligent woman would sleep with a computer in arms reach until they gave her the all-clear.

Dollis Truesdale, his younger cousin and Accountant for the WRA, was tracking down the money trail that was sure to exist. Her supremely analytical mind was pouring over data almost as fast as some computers. At a glance, she could dismiss a suspect because the odds were so low that the person was involved. She was the one combing through every possible database for the one small detail that would hang the guilty. And her integrity couldn't be compromised. Whoever was responsible, even if it was Reggie himself, that person would be held accountable.

The ex-SBI super-agent turned WRA Head of Internal Investigations, Walter Rogers, was looking for the shooter. Not many had the skills required to make that kind of shot, then disappear after not leaving a trace behind. He was attempting to locate everyone who could possibly have done it, and track their movements before, during, and after the relevant timeframe.

Meka waved her hand to grab his attention. He moved one side of the headphones off his ear and asked, "You got something?" after hitting the pause button on his screen. Everything would be recorded so he didn't miss something important.

"Not really," was her response. "Just curious as to if Felipe is being honest here." Since they weren't watching the same things, he grabbed her computer and rewound to the story. Speeding it up to catch back up to real time, he pushed the computer back to her, and focused back on his own.

He said, "Yeah, everything he said is truth. At least, as far as we know."

Shaking her head, she said, "Why didn't he just tell that story the first time? No one would hold what he did as a child against him."

He paused his screen again and told her to remove her headphones. He asked, "Have you studied the history of my family and the WRA?" She nodded, so he continued. "Our training started from the time we could walk and talk. Scientific studies show that a child starts to develop its personality before the age of 5-years-old. By 10-years-old, my mother and uncles could tell what role I and each of my siblings would play in our Agency.

"Unconsciously, we all have the ability to predict the trajectory of another person's life. Haven't you seen a child that was so evil you just knew he would be a criminal later in life? If Felipe had told Joshue the truth last week, it would have painted him as a coward and a deceiver, no matter the age he was when he committed the acts. And, it would have caused Joshue to second guess his friend's motives."

Her eyes flashed to her screen, and she said, "Oh, shit! Like he's doing right now!"

Reggie toggled his feed to bring up the video on his computer as they both covered one ear with the headphones to hear what was being said. They watched Juan and Joshue face off with Flip as he admitted to how deep the deception went and his true motivations. Reggie used one of the hidden cameras placed in the home over three years ago to get a better view of Joshue's face. He knew the second the young man decided he was done being a victim.

The scene played out with the gun being fired, but the drama didn't end there. They stayed glued to their screens for another ten minutes before coming up to look at each other.

Meka asked, "What the hell just happened?"

Reggie considered for a moment, then said, "The first step towards the truth." Focusing his attention back on the characters still in play, he said, "Maybe it's time to take a step back and let someone else take the lead. Someone who's motivated and ruthless and who'll get to the truth, no matter what."

Yanking his headphones off, he reached out and started shutting the lids to the numerous laptops. Standing up, he said, "Let's get all this stuff packed up. There's nothing else we can do here."

Meka, getting to her feet, asked, "Where are we going?"

He said, "Call the pilot and make sure the jet is ready to go. I'm going home, and I think it's time for you to rejoin your partner in the WRA."

Giving a huge smile and a small fist pump, Meka pulled out her phone to do his bidding. He chuckled, shaking his head at her enthusiasm, as the pair continued to pack for their return home.

Chapter 11

"So, what's your plan now? You just murdered a hundred cops. You know they won't stop coming until you're dead!"

Allorah was in a bathrobe in front of a fire that was really too hot to have going. Delmas acknowledged that her need for warmth had nothing to do with the outside temperature. Her small, bundled up body continued to shiver despite the heat. The hot bath hadn't thawed her, and neither had the food and hot chocolate. Only getting the information she sought would extinguish the persistent chill.

"You can act like you're Superman and not afraid of us mortals, but California cops don't play that shit," she continued. "The Cartel is the least of your worries now. You're pretty much a walking dead man."

Their new abode was on the scale of luxury they were both accustomed to. Large, airy rooms that flowed together to create an extravagant atmosphere. When they had first arrived, she'd been quiet and withdrawn. He'd been worried, but now he wished for the silent and calm of a few short hours ago.

"Where did you get a weapon like that, anyway?" she asked. "And is that what you planned to use on my family? You kidnap me, use me as bait, then murder my loved ones? What kind of man are you?"

"The kind that's getting tired of your shit!" he yelled. "You're so worried about those cops, let me show you what you should be focused on." He picked up the remote and switched the TV on. Turning it to an all-news station, of course it was showing the biggest story in the world right now.

"Oh my God!" she exclaimed. "That's the Cartel's compound in Colombia!" The reporter was giving a synopsis of the info they had thus far, and it didn't bode well for the Noriegas.

"It seems like no one made it out of the protective walls alive," the man was saying. "The local authorities are claiming that this was the work of, alleged, rival Cartel members. Based on how devastatingly one-sided this attack was, it's hard to attribute these results to gun-wielding drug dealers. It had the precision of a military operation.

"As we said, there hasn't been a single survivor found on the property. Police are not revealing any IDs at this time, but the body count is now over one hundred. The few people who witnesses the slaughter from outside the walls, speak of war-machines sweeping in and laying waste to everything and everyone trapped on the inside. A tragedy, as a number of women and small children have also been pulled from the rubble.

"If these are the kinds of weapons the Cartels now possess, we will surely see more scenes like this in the future." With a solemn look, he finished with, "May God have mercy on us all."

They went on, flashing picture after picture of the smoldering structure, as authorities worked tirelessly to find survivors. Photos of grieving families waiting outside the wall for word of their loved ones' fate, painted a vivid picture of the suffering delivered upon this community. Allorah stared at the screen, soaking it all in, before she fell to her knees in misery.

Something in his heart made him take a step towards the crying woman, then he regained control of his body. He stopped, turned the TV off, getting rid of the images, then he headed off to the kitchen to give her some privacy.

Sighing, he shook his head because he couldn't afford to soften towards his captive. It was explainable, in his own mind, why it was happening. He loved strong women. He'd been raised by, and around, them. Those silly, whiny things that shed tears because of a broken nail, held no appeal to him. But it always got to him when he saw a woman of obvious strength breakdown.

Heading back into the living room, he found her still in the same place. Walking over, he tossed another log on the fire, then took a seat in the chair opposite where she was kneeling. She was silently weeping, but he decided not to leave her alone with her destructive thoughts.

"When I was younger," he whispered across the fire-lit room, "as the middle son, I felt overshadowed. My older and younger brothers were exceptional at everything they did. I felt it made my inadequacies stand out all the more.

"Reggie, my older brother, was an athlete. Could have went pro in several different sports. By the time he was 15-years-old, he'd earned two college degrees, and two black belts to go with them. He didn't stop there. His only competition seemed to be an inner determination to be better than he was the day before. I tried to follow in his footsteps, but every time I came up short, I felt the disappointment of those around me."

Allorah, by now, was sitting on the floor with her back propped up against the chair, staring across at him with her tear-streaked face. She seemed to be enraptured by his tale, but he knew she just needed to part company with her own doubts and fears. He had no idea why he felt compelled to do so, but he wanted to do what no one had ever tried to do for him: Soothe and comfort.

"Then, fucking Daniel came along, and I knew I'd just pulled the shortest straw ever in life. IQ so high he made them rethink the whole test. They gave it to him three different times before he was 10, and he completed it each time with laughable ease. I tried to join in the family trivia games and puzzles, but they just made me feel stupid. Which is crazy because my own IQ is high in the genius range.

"They didn't do it on purpose," he conceded. "That was just how we were raised. Compete, compete, compete. Win, win, win. And the girls were expected to be just as tough as the boys. No tears. No complaints. Get it done or be a disgrace to the family."

She wiped her face on the sleeve of the robe and lumbered to her feet. The low fire was the only light in the house, a move he'd made so the police might not show too much interest. Allorah did her sensual stretch, something he was beginning to realize was just her way of moving, and then crumpled back into the plush chair. She asked, "Why are you telling me this?"

He considered the question, but decided to go on with his story. It wasn't that he ignored it, he just wanted to tell her in his own way.

"Through all the training, all the competing, all the failures and victories, there was one figure at the forefront. Driving us, teaching us, making sure we operated as a single unit. Loving and selfless, this person sacrificed everything she ever wanted in life to make sure that her family was well cared for and protected." He paused to make sure he had her undivided attention. She needed to understand that he wasn't playing a game.

"Yesterday, you asked me what the Cartel had done to me. Well, the Cartel took that person away from me. Someone in your husband's organization killed my mother. Now, my mission in life is to find them and make them suffer."

"I don't understand," she said with a frown. "Was she a bystander during a shooting or something?"

"No," he said, shaking his head. "They put a hit out on her and someone cashed in."

"But why would the Cartel wish to kill your mother?"

"Because my mother, Lucille Drake, was the leader of the American organization the Cartel was working with."

"Hold on a second." She paused as her eyes rolled up to gaze at the soaring ceiling. Focusing back on him, she said, "I don't remember ever hearing that name, or remember anything on the news about a high-ranking government official being killed."

Just in case she survived this ordeal, he had to be careful with how much he told her. "Nothing would have been on the news or social media because the world doesn't know anything about us. Let me explain it like this. Our country has to deal with people that would cause a public uproar if word got out. So, they cultivate contracts with private agencies, then give them huge amounts of leeway to perform their duties.

"My mother's Agency was formed in the 1960s by her father, a former spy for the US government. We're pretty much the spearhead of America's power. Just to give you an example, one agent did what you just saw in Colombia."

"But you just said you were still trying to figure out who did it! Why would you kill all those people and you don't know who's guilty?"

"That wasn't me. To be completely honest with you, I'm not officially part of the Agency anymore." She was still puzzled as she sat there shaking her head. "I'm not the only person searching for the truth. Everyone has their specialties, and they will individually employ them to find the guilty parties."

"So, your choice was to kidnap me and use me for bait to bring the Cartel to you?" He nodded. "And this other guy took the fight to them, then decided to just kill them all!"

"From the looks of it," he replied. "But, you and I both know the Noriegas have that security bunker under their compound. We just have to hope they made it inside."

"What do you mean, 'we'? Aren't you happy that they could be dead?" Angrily, she swiped the tear that leaked out of her eye.

"No Allorah, I'm not happy. I just told you that I'm trying to find out the truth. How the hell can I do that if they're all dead?"

"Well, it seems to me, these are the kind of scenes you guys specialize in. He killed a hundred Colombians, and you killed a hundred California cops."

Taking a deep breath, he said, "The fucking cops aren't dead, Allorah."

"Ha!" she barked. "I might have been in shock, but I'm not stupid. I saw the bodies."

"What you saw was the result of a device engineered by my little brother," he explained in exasperation. "I'm not 100% sure how it works, but it uses sound waves to send pulses. It can be set to kill or debilitate. I set it on a medium strength that would knock everyone out in a half mile radius. That was just to give us enough time to relocate. They were as good as new within minutes of us leaving."

"You're lying. I've never heard of anything like that. Just admit it! You killed them!"

He didn't answer, he jumped up and snatched the bag off of the couch. Quickly, he fiddled with something on the inside of the bag, then placed a set of headphones over his ears. She stood up and said something he couldn't hear. He flipped the switch.

She immediately bent at the waist with her hand plastered over her mouth. He could see her body heaving, so he switched everything off before he had another of her messes to clean up. Snatching the head gear off, he said, "Now, not only have you heard about it, you've felt it on a low setting."

Seeing how affected she was, he said, "Sit down," and went to the kitchen to get her some crackers and ginger ale to settle her stomach.

Reentering the living room, he found her bent over the bag, trying to figure out how to work the contraption. Gun out in a spilt second, he said, "Get the fuck back or you're in a wheelchair for the rest of your life."

She dropped the headphones and took a sidestep, her hate-filled eyes cutting him to shreds. "Why don't you just kill me? My family is dead! No one is coming to save me. Just get it over with! Stop fucking with me!" Like a lightbulb had lit in her brain, her eyes brightened. "Oh! That's what it is. You're keeping me alive because you want to fuck me!" Her hands went to the belt of the robe.

"Get over there and sit back down, Allorah. Just when I was starting to feel sorry for you, making my job so much harder, you go and make it easy again. I had already made up my mind to let you go."

"Oh, no! You can't let me go yet. You haven't had your taste." She snatched the robe from her naked body and let it float to the floor. She took a few tentative steps towards him and, unconsciously, he took the same number of steps back.

"Put the robe back on. I really don't want to hurt you." His gun was still pointed at her midsection.

"What? You don't like the view?" Her hands came up and toyed with her sleek breast. She licked her supple lips and moaned lewdly. "Come on, Middle Son. Isn't this why you told me your sad story? You wanted me to feel sorry for you, causing my thighs to fall open as a result? Isn't this what you've been dreaming of?" she asked, cupping herself between her long, sexy legs.

Rolling his eyes, he shot her in the shoulder. Well, he scraped her arm with a 9MM bullet. Graze or not, she responded as if she'd been hit in the stomach with a 50 caliber Desert Eagle.

She yelped in pain, grabbing at the wound, and dropped to the floor. Her yelp turning into a keening sound, like the pain was unbearable. She rolled back and forth on her back like she'd just received a mortal wound. He chuckled at her act, and said, "Get up, Allorah. Stop with all the drama. The bullet barely touched your arm." When she kept acting like she was dying, he laughed, went over and grabbed the robe, draping it over her body. After that, she curled up into the fetal position, and cried.

Taking a seat on the couch, he put his gun away and stared at the weeping woman. Eventually, the events of the day caught up with her, and she fell into an exhausted slumber. To her sleeping form, he said, "You're gonna be alright.

You'll make it through this, and be stronger for the experience."

Of course, she didn't respond, and he let his own body relax and fall into a light sleep. What seemed like minutes later, he became fully awake, but didn't move a muscle. Opening his eyes a fraction of an inch, he saw that Allorah was still stretched out on the floor. That wasn't good; a sound had issued from the back of the house. Not knowing what to expect, he quickly rolled to the floor. At that moment, automatic gunfire shattered the sliding door and shredding the spot he'd just vacated.

Chapter 12

Tano, Kamp, Fa'ness, and a tall, lanky, white guy named Jackson Smith, cruised pass the house, not being able to see a damn thing. The property was heavy with trees and vegetation, not to mention, dark as pitch. Shaking his head, Tano kept going around the curve and made his way back to the meeting spot.

He exited the borrowed, black Chrysler 300, and came face to face with 50 of his most battle-hardened soldiers. Everyone was expectant, everyone was ready. All they needed to be told was where to point their guns.

Tano looked over to his left and waved forward one of the foot soldiers. The kid couldn't be more than 15-years-old, but he put on a brave front standing before the grown men. He was the soldier of the hour. The one who had tracked down Allorah and the soon-to-be dead man who kidnapped her.

The young kid said, "What's hood, Gang?"

"Tell me again how you tracked them to that house," demanded Tano.

"Well, like I said OG, I was clocking the swag of the D-Boys and…"

"Little Nigga, speak fucking English! I don't have time to decipher what the fuck you saying! And take that flag off of your head. You want to announce to the world that the Bloods out here shooting shit up?"

"My bad, Big Homie," he said, removing the red bandana and picking back up the tale. "I was, um, watching a group of cops when they pulled up to the house by the beach. One of them went around back, then came running back to the front, signaling like he'd found something. I was up on a hill with the binoculars, so they wouldn't know I was following them. Within minutes, like a hundred cops flooded the area.

"Then, this old white man showed up, and he start barking orders and screaming at everybody. That's when all the cops got in their cars and left."

Punk ass, fuckboy cops, thought Tano. If it had been some old ass white bitch, they would have sealed the area and got her out of there. He bet, as soon as they saw Allorah by herself, they hatched the plan to use her as bait. If it wasn't someone close to him, he'd be happy with what happened to them next. But, what he was told happened, just left him disturbed.

"I started to leave, thinking it was a false alarm, but I saw a lot of the police were going into the woods and the neighboring houses. I was too far away to keep track of them all but, only the ones who moved the vehicles actually left."

He went on to tell them how this fly-ass Rolls-Royce SUV pulled up to the house and made a bunch of erratic movements. Finally, convinced everything was on the up and up, the driver entered the house carrying a bunch of bags.

"I watched three cops work their way to the back of the house, like one inch at a time. Then, all hell broke loose. The cops stormed the house. The cars returned, dropping off more police. It was like they were racing to see who could make it inside first. Then, like them old boxing videos of Mike Tyson, they all just fell on their faces, knocked the fuck out."

"And that's when you saw Allorah and the guy come out and enter the SUV?" asked Fa'ness.

"Yeah," said the little soldier. "The guy had to drag her to the car, but they both got in and pulled off. I watched for a minute to see which direction they headed, then I jumped in the whip and followed them.

"As careful as he was when he pulled up to the house, the driver seemed positive he wasn't being followed this time. He drove straight to the other house. I backed up into someone's driveway and waited to see if he would come back out. Unless there's another way out, which it could be, he's still in there with the chick."

Tano reached out and patted the boy on his shoulder. He asked, "What's your name, Blood?"

"They call me Lil 50," he answered with pride.

"I'm gonna ignore the fact that you disobeyed my order to only go out in groups. I know your Big Homie gave you those instructions." Lil 50 had enough sense to look contrite. "You know the white girl, Megan? Be hanging around the hood?" Lil 50's face lit up as he nodded. "She at the Spot waiting for you. We got it from here, head on back and collect your reward."

"That's what's up, Gang! That joint right there is fire!" He started to leave but then stopped and turned. "I don't normally disobey my Big Homie, but he sidelined me. Said I wasn't old enough to be trusted with this. I stayed out the way, but I knew I could do something to help."

Tano nodded, saluted him, and said, "Good job, Lil Homie. Now get out of here."

Tano and the other men laughed as the kid raced off. He said, "I hope he don't kill himself before she has a chance to." Everyone shared a hardy laugh. Most of them have had a taste of what the girl had to offer. But, quickly, it was back to business.

He turned to the white boy, Jackson Smith. "A place like that will have a top-notch security system. You sure you can by-pass it?"

He pushed the designer glasses higher on his nose. "Piece of cake," he said with confidence. "All of the homes in this area use the same company. It is top of the line stuff, but the owner of the company happens to be my father. I already downloaded the specs and programmed the code to disable the whole setup. As soon as you're ready to go in, you press a button, and everything shuts down."

Tano nodded. "You know if you fuck this up, I'm gonna have your whole family killed, right?" Jackson waved a long, thin arm, and said everything was under control. Then he turned his back, pulled out his phone, frantically going over everything again.

Turning back to his crew, Tano locked eyes with as many of them as possible. "Ya'll heard what the Little Homie had to say. This nigga got something that caused a hundred cops to pass out, then just walked away with the GF's daughter. But cops are sloppy. We will go in with Military precision, and get our girl back.

"Circumstances dictate that we have to be silent and fast. After the security is shutdown, Kamp and Fa'ness will use their training to go in and assess the situation. We'll meet ya'll back here and shore up the plan to eliminate any means of escape. Be ready, be safe, and understand that any mistakes could get us all killed." He let the silence drag on, then turned to his advance team and said, "Let's ride."

Within minutes, they were parked down the road from the target house, and Jackson was telling the three men what to expect. "Things like motion sensor-flood lights, and barking dogs, obviously I have no control over." Handing Kampaign a small device, he said, "Hold the button down until the light turns green. That's the signal to go. You'll have to watch out for any aftermarket additions. People in this area normally have secondary alarms that alert their phones to movement. If at any time the light turns red, stop all movement, hold the button down again, then go only if it turns green. If it stays red, come back as fast as you can."

The two black-clad men nodded at Tano, then each other, exited the car, and disappearing into the night. They had both been Special Forces, so Tano didn't worry about their aptitude for sneaking around. 15 minutes into the wait, of which Jackson was sweating the whole time, Tano's cellphone lit up.

It was Fa'ness. "OG, listen. I got this nigga in my sights right now, but it doesn't look like a kidnapping to me. They sitting in the living room, Allorah in a bathrobe, and they conversing in front of a fire. This looks like Allorah just stepping out on Ol Boy."

Tano frowned. "But, if that was the case, why would he kill all the guards at the beach house? If she wanted to leave Joshue, she could have just packed up and left."

"We don't know what kind of orders those guards had. Maybe the only way she felt safe was to have them all killed."

Shaking his head, Tano said, "Naw, Blood. She could have come to us and the Cartel wouldn't have done shit."

"Hold up," said Fa'ness. "The nigga doing something now. He digging in a bag and putting on some headphones. He…What the fuck…?" Then nothing but gagging sounds.

"Yo, Gang! You good?" It sounded as if the brother was about to throw up a lung. For a split second, Tano's own stomach felt a little funny. He yelled, "Pull back! Pull back, NOW!" He listened as the Homies retreated, then the phone went silent.

A torturous three minutes passed before the backdoor opened and the two men climbed inside. "Tano," said Kamp. "We have to get in there! He used that shit on her!"

"Used what? What did you see?"

"I was a little father back, giving Fa'ness cover, so the effects didn't hit me as hard. Whatever is in that bag, he used it on Allorah. It had her looking close to death before he turned it off. My guess, he set it on low to show her what it could do. Now we know how he took out the cops," Kamp added.

Tano didn't like that, not one bit. "Man, I don't know if I was responding to hearing Fa'ness, but my stomach felt funny, too."

"Oh no! It definitely reached us. I felt my guts liquify for a few seconds," said Jackson.

"That means, if he makes it to that bag, it's game over for us," concluded Tano.

"The good news is, we made it to the house with no problem," said Fa'ness, having fully recovered. "We didn't come across anything that would alert him to the presence of our guys surrounding the place."

"So, we can do our thing and bring everybody in. We just have to destroy whatever is in that bag first," said Kamp.

"Alright, so…" An all too familiar sound reached their ears. They looked around at each other in confusion before Tano said, "Get the fuck back up there and tell me what's going on." The two men opened their doors while Tano dialed Zero's number.

Jackson paused the two soldiers by saying, "Don't forget to activate the device again. Since you left the coverage area, everything reset." The men nodded and disappeared just as Zero answered the call.

He asked, "Ya'll got her?"

"Hell, we might have just lost her," he replied. After explaining the last few minutes, he finished with, "Get everyone over here. Tell them to come in quiet and park in the driveway where the 300 is. I'm going in, but tell everyone to call and warn me as they come in. I should…Hold on, Kamp's calling." He switched over and said, "What you got?"

"Yeah, Blood, this bitch ass nigga shot your girl. But it looks like it's not life-threatening. She rolled around on the floor for a while, but now appears to be sleeping."

"You sure she's not dead?"

"I can see she's still breathing. The dude is sitting on the couch right now. What do you want us to do?"

Tano thought on it for a minute. They damn sure weren't dealing with their regular adversary. And, one wrong move could result in Allorah's death. The plan had been to surround the home, flood the area with his troops, then slowly infiltrate to reduce the risk to Allorah. He didn't have any reason to deviate, so he told his Bro to stand down.

"Chill for a minute, I'm coming in. Tell me exactly where you are and how to get there." After Kamp told him, he clicked back over to Zero. "I'm heading in now, Blood. Get everybody mobilized, and I'll call you when we have her."

Zero said, "Good luck, OG. The crew is on their way."

The next hour was a flurry of activity. Tano joined up with Kamp and Fa'ness, and dispersed the crew as they arrived on-scene. It wasn't long before they had the house boxed in with every man holding an automatic weapon. Once he confirmed everyone was in their specified place, Tano gave the order to move in.

They moved with all the caution the situation required. Inside the dense wooded area, there was no illumination. The moon was obscured, the stars non-existent. It seemed as if the only light for miles was spilling out of the home's massive windows.

Closer and closer, every step tested and measured before weight was applied. Hand signals and body language telling others when to stop and when to advance. Everything going well, everyone stepping easy. They were 20 feet from the house when a tremendous *CRACK!* rent the warm night air.

Every person froze. Adrenaline spiked. Every gun in view started to sweep the area. The idiot who had stepped on the fallen branch took a step back. Too late, thought Tano, wanting to shoot the motherfucker himself. Kamp's frantic whisper brought him out of his anger and back to the mission.

"He heard it! We need to move!"

The man on the couch hadn't moved a muscle, but he wasn't gonna argue. He said, "Aim for the guy, but if you miss, take out the bag." No sooner had the words left his mouth, the man rolled to the floor, and Kamp's gun obliterated the couch.

A hand reached up, trying to snag the bag. Fa'ness said, "Not today, motherfucker!" as his own weapon released a prolonged volley. Soldiers from every direction joined in the torrent.

Tano heard Allorah screaming as her kidnapper scrambled towards the garage. Tano raised his gun, fixed the setting to three-round burst, and kept the man from exiting out that way. With nowhere else to run, and no cover inside the virtually all-glass room, he dove into a hallway leading farther into the house, disappearing from Tano's sight.

Five seconds later, he was in the living room, dragging Allorah to her feet. On instinct, she started to fight him. He yelled, "It's me, Lorah! It's T!" Recognizing his voice, she stopped and looked up at him with wide eyes. Then she crumpled against him, crying her eyes out in relief.

He glanced around and saw Charles, the NC Blood, standing at the backdoor. He signaled the big man over and said, "Take her out of here. We have to find this fucker before the cops come." Charles dashed over and gently unwrapped her from the OG. Holding her close to his body, he led the traumatized girl out of the house.

To his left, deeper in the structure, the gun fight was still raging on. It sounded as if the bastard had tried to exit some other way, only to find more of his crew waiting. Off in the distance, someone yelled, "He's still in the house!" In response, Tano nodded to the two Special Forces soldiers. They shouldered their weapons and disappeared after their prey.

He turned around and exited the way he'd entered, eyes scanning, trying to spot Allorah. He found her, trying in vain to pull away from Charles as she explained why she needed to go back inside.

"You don't understand! Let me go! I have to warn them!" It was clear that the robe was all she had on, and Charles was doing his best to hold her without injury to either of them, and allow her to keep her modesty intact.

"Warn us about what?" he asked, jogging up behind her.

She spun and said, "Oh my God! Tano!" She pulled away and this time Charles released her. "In one of those black bags is some kind of sound wave device. If he turns it on, he can kill us all. You have to get it!"

Hugging his little sister, he said, "Kamp and Fa'ness shot it to shit. One of my guys saw what it did to the cops, and we were out here when he tested it on you earlier. We got it covered, Lorah."

"Oh God, T," she said, squeezing him tight. "I tried to fight, I tried to escape. I was so scared. His people are the ones who hit the Cartel down in Colombia!"

"Whoa, whoa, whoa!" Tano said, moving her to arms-length. "What do you mean, his people?"

"He's with some Agency the Cartel was working with. They think somebody in the Cartel killed their leader. And the leader just happens to be this guy's mother."

"Oh shit!" Tano exclaimed, looking over at Charles. "It's what you were talking about!"

Charles immediately started looking up in the sky, backing away. "OG, we need to get everyone out of here, now! We got Allorah, we need to settle for that. If we kill this guy, we're all dead. We need to go!"

Only then did he notice that the gunfire had stopped, and sirens were getting closer by the second. He turned to give the order for everyone to fall back, and came face to face with Allorah's kidnapper. But, he wasn't free, he wasn't alone.

He was flanked by Fa'ness and Kamp, his hands were laced behind his head. Charles said, "This is bad, man. We need to get out of here." The trio exited the house and the two with the guns marched their captive over to Tano.

"Fucker killed six of our guys, and wounded some others. Only reason any of us survived is because he couldn't get to the rest of his guns. The guy is a fucking beast," said Fa'ness. "What do you want to do with him?"

Tano faced the man head on, smirked at his bravado, and launched a vicious punch at his stomach. His abs were rock solid and a quick inhale was all he was rewarded with. Tano drew back to deliver a hook to the captive's face, when a robotic sound echoed across the area. It was an ominous sequence that reminded him of a transformer changing out of its car form.

Charles said, "Don't move!" as he froze in place. One of the soldiers rounded the corner at a full sprint and was immediately vaporized by a spray of bullets. Louder this time, Charles screamed, "DON'T FUCKING MOVE! NOBODY!"

A few seconds of silence ensued before one of the war machines swooped down into the clearing and unleashed a barrage of bullets into the house. After whatever had caught its attention was dead, three rotating guns performed a 90 degree turn and faced off with the rest of them. Another drone joined the first. Then another. And another.

The captive chuckled and dropped his hands. The drones didn't respond to his movement, causing him to laugh out loud. Looking Tano in his eyes, he said, "It sucks to be you, right now. I remember being on the other end of those damn things, and it wasn't enjoyable in the least." Just to be a dick, he walked over and took a gun out of a soldier's hands. After thanking him for his service, he pushed him in front of the flying weapons.

Instantaneously, 50 holes appeared in the man. Tano knew the machines didn't have a soul, or thought process, but it was almost as if they dared him and his men to move. Wanted them to move. The kidnapper toyed with another man. Acting as if he was going to push him, but pulling his hands back at the last second. Then, with a laugh, pushed the man off his spot, forcing the drones to do his dirty work. A voice from the sky stopped his game.

"You done playing around?" the voice asked.

Laughing, the man said, "Sure, Little Brother. But, I need one favor."

Silence. Then, "I think I just gave you one. How you let these off-brand motherfuckers get the drop on you is baffling to me. You're becoming a disgrace to your name."

Losing all humor, he said, "We're a team. We work as a team, train as a team. All of us don't have your experience as a rogue asshole!"

Sighing, the voice asked, "What's your favor?"

"I still need the girl," the kidnapper said.

"Wait! No!" yelled Allorah.

Tano said, "Don't move, Sis. You're not going anywhere with this guy."

The man spun on him. "Who's going to stop me? You? One of your little toy soldiers?" He brought his gun up and shot another of his soldiers in his face. Allorah screamed as the body crumpled to the ground, the drones tearing him to shreds on the way down.

"You're not calling the shots here, little boy!" he yelled at Tano.

In a calm cadence, the voice asked, "Why do you need the girl?"

He said, "You know why. She's the key to getting the truth."

"You don't need her. I'll help you," said the voice.

That only seemed to piss the man off, as he twisted around and trained the gun on the drone. "You're fucking help is what put us in this predicament in the first place! If you would have trusted us instead of 'helping' us, our unit would still be whole. Now stop questioning me and let me do this my way!"

Almost a full minute of silence followed his outburst. Then the voice said, "Everyone, stay still." The drones dispersed. Some went into the woods, some entered the house. Tano watched as twenty of the machines swooped down and scanned every one of his brothers. Then, the four took back up their post while the rest faded into the night.

The voice said, "Remain where you are. My drones have taken biometric scans of every one of you. If you step within a hundred yards of the man facing you, you will die. Take the girl and get out of there. The cops are minutes away."

Tano said, "Allorah, it's gonna be alright. Just go with him and live to fight another day. We'll never stop coming for you."

The man grabbed Allorah's arm and propelled her towards the garage. Looking at Tano with a sneer, he said, "The next time I see you, you're a dead man." Then, they were gone.

Sirens seemed to be converging from every direction as the Rolls-Royce rolled down the path and disappeared from sight. Tano gritted his teeth as the drones held them immobile until the police cars started dumping officers from their interior.

Suddenly, the voice said, "I don't have an issue with you guys. Just go peacefully and I'll have you out in a few days."

Tano thought of all the bodies and didn't see how that was possible. He asked, "Who are you?"

"A good person to have as a friend. A very bad person to have as an enemy. See you around." The drones silently faded into the night, just as the police raised their weapons and told them to get on the ground.

He was fucked. His crew was fucked. Allorah was fucked. With so many dead bodies around, none of them would ever get out of prison. It didn't matter what the mystery man thought he could accomplish. All he could do was pray for his sister's safety as the officers started loading them into the back of their vehicles, one by one.

Chapter 13

"Get the fuck off of me! What are you doing?" Joshue asked his brother. His barrel had been lined up perfectly with the liar's face, the trigger about to depress, when Juan tackled him from behind, throwing off his aim. Now, his gun was halfway across the room, and Juan was holding him down with amazing strength.

"Calm down! Stop fighting me! I'll explain everything when you stop acting like a child," said Juan.

Taking a deep breath, Joshue forced his tense body to relax. He needed answers as to why his brother would help the murderer.

When he was sufficiently calm, Juan leaped off of his back and walked over to the gun. Joshue launched to his feet and eyed the other men as Juan tucked his gun in his waistband. Joshue said, "Talk, asshole."

"Well, you fucking idiot, it's two things." While he talked, he was typing something into his phone. "The first is that the WRA will be back looking for answers in less than two days. Flip here is a killer. We're in no position to take out the little bit of help we have, especially since no one survived the assault on the compound."

Juan swiped his screen and the video from the phone launched over to the huge television monitor hanging on the wall. A report on CNN was showing the devastation left behind after their run-in with the new WRA Head.

"Of course, we were there, but we got out pretty fast. With this amount of violence, does it look like the work of someone looking for answers? Hell no!" he answered his own question. "This is what you do for revenge. The WRA has already convicted us, and without a shred of proof!"

"And you think one extra gun, possessed by a man we can't even trust, is gonna make a difference?" asked Joshue, his menacing eyes locked on Flip.

"Think, dammit! Get out of your feelings and look at the bigger picture. Fucking Carlos ordered a lockdown, but not before all his top enforcers were inside with us. The WRA has killed the Noriega Cartel! We're finished! But the WRA isn't the only ones on the offensive right now."

He threw up story after story showing that, during the past 24 hours, their Capos in prisons all across Colombia and the US, had been murdered by rival Cartel members. "You get it now? We're all we got! Just us. I've contacted Mom and told her to take the women and children somewhere no one knows about, just in case either group strikes at them."

"SHIT!" exclaimed Joshue. "I need to contact Allorah." He walked over to his desk and picked up his cellphone. "Plus, we still have the 14 trained soldiers guarding her. They can meet us…"

"Joshue," Juan said in a tone that caused him to stop and look up. "They already got to her."

"What? Hell no!" he proclaimed. But the fact that she hadn't called him made him realize how likely the statement could be. He dialed her number anyway. Ring after ring, no answer. He dialed again and again, same result. When he looked up, Juan had the video already set to play.

Weakness laced his body and he fell back into his chair. The smoldering beach house in ruins; body bags lining the front yard. The reporter said that the 14 bodies were all male and all were dressed as security. Witnesses said the woman of the house had been home, but authorities had no idea where she was.

Joshue swiped everything off of his desk and roared his anguish to the heavens.

Juan gave him a minute, then said, "The WRA has her, so she should at least be alive."

"How do you know?" Joshue managed to spew out of his clenched jaw.

Juan cued up another video, this one with a young, white officer standing in the street in front of a home Joshue had drove pass a hundred times on his way home. The officer said, "The young woman was secured to a bed, but she didn't look injured or abused. We had over 50 officers out here, but we needed to get some experts to look for traps before we breached the home.

"While we waited for them to get here, everyone vacated the area because we didn't want to scare the perp off with our presence. Sure enough, he returned, performed some moves like he was checking if anyone was on to him, then he rushed inside.

"We deployed smoke inside the house, hoping to confuse and disorient the guy, then we moved to infiltrate. The culprit used some kind of weapon on us that knocked us out, allowing him to just drive off with his captive. We're searching the whole area for any clues, and we ask that if you know anything about this crime, call…" Juan stopped the video.

"Have you reached out to Tano?" Joshue asked his brother, gathering a speck of control.

He waved off the question. "Why? So the WRA can use the Bloods for target practice? They showed restraint in not killing the cops, I can promise you, gang members won't receive that same consideration."

Joshue brought up his phone and dialed half the number before he stopped. Juan was right. If he involved the Bloods, the WRA would target them. They didn't stand a chance against a foe of this caliber. He placed the phone down on his desk and turned to his brother.

"So, you're right, it's just us. My wife is missing. Dad and Christian are dead. The Cartel is finished. The rest of our family is on the run. We're now being hunted by the other Cartels. And we have less than two days to come up with an answer for Mr. Burke, or we all die. That sums everything up?"

Juan nodded. "Pretty much." He turned to Flip, who'd been standing quietly during all this. "So, as you can see, the

Noriega Cartel is gone. Your plan was actually a good one when you factor in the time and dedication you put into it. But, you're in this now. Just because your last name isn't Noriega doesn't mean the threat wasn't for you, as well. With that being said, what are you gonna do?"

Flip looked from brother to brother, then asked, "Do either of you have a plan?"

"Well, my plan was to blow your fucking head off," said Joshue. "You want to revisit that one?"

Before an argument could break out, Juan said, "Not much of a plan, but this place has a security bunker. I say we load up, lock in, and be prepared when the motherfuckers come."

"What if this is exactly what they want us to do? You see what happened in the last security suite."

"Nothing happened except what you did!" replied Joshue. "The deaths are on your head, not the WRA's." Turning to Juan, he asked, "How do we know this traitor isn't gonna shoot us the second we turn our backs?"

"This is about our survival!" roared Juan. "We separate, we die. We stay together, we still might die, but we have a chance. Flip, if you want to leave, leave. If you want to stay and fight these fuckers, then stay. Either way, you need to commit right now."

Without hesitation, Flip said, "I'm in. I'm not the scumbag you guys are making me out to be. I had an agenda, but that's out of the picture now. Let's show these WRA assholes who they're fucking with!"

The bunker was fully stocked and had a viewing room that displayed the video from the 30 cameras place around the property. Some were hard wired so they couldn't be manipulated from an outside source. All of them ran on electricity, but had double backups in the form of a generator and internal battery packs. They were certain that, when the WRA came, they would have some form of advance warning.

To make sure, they went around to all the entrances and placed mines connected to tripwires. These weren't necessarily for the WRA, their agents wouldn't be fooled by them anyway. But if the other Cartels came skulking around, their end would be painful and swift.

Since there was only one way into the bunker, they laid traps all along the entrance and directly inside, once they locked the massive, steel doors. Then, they settled in.

It wasn't as glamorous as the one at their father's compound, but it was spacious and livable. They turned on the TV and switched the channels, trying to find any updates on the multiple scenes involving their people. Nothing new was said, so they hit the small kitchen, ate a quick meal, cleaned up, then turned in for the night. They were relatively safe for the next day and a half; they needed to get as much sleep as possible before the deadline arrived.

Juan was already snoring lightly, the injury and subsequent surgery, draining most of his energy. But Joshue was wide awake. For one, he didn't trust Flip. But also, his eyes kept tracking over to the TV. Twenty minutes later, he launched up and grabbed the remote as his vigil paid off.

"Dammit!" he yelled. "Juan, look at this shit." Juan rolled over in the pullout, couch bed, and sat up to see the images on the screen.

The headline read, '13 DEAD AT PLUSH HILLS MANSION!' The camera swung through the scene just in time for them to see Tano being loaded into the back of a police car. Joshue looked over at Juan, who said, "I told you! Now the WRA has eliminated them, too."

"But that's not even his territory," said Joshue. "What the hell was he doing up there?"

"It doesn't even matter," said Juan. "13 dead? It's over for all of them. Get some sleep, Little Brother. What they have planned for us will be worse. They don't want to send us to jail, they want to send us to the morgue."

Juan turned back over and pulled the covers over his head, signaling an end to the short conversation. Joshue took one last look at Flip, then laid back in the recliner. He would love to go sleep in the king-sized bed he had in the back, but didn't think he should leave Flip alone with Juan. The man had confessed to being a coward pretty much since birth. All trust and loyalty were now remnants of the past.

Joshue said a silent prayer for the safety of his wife, then closed his eyes. Juan was right, the WRA would be coming for their heads. It was a shame, too. He was 99% sure that the Cartel hadn't killed Lucille Drake. But, even if the WRA felt the same way, that 1% of uncertainty was reason enough to find them guilty, and wipe them off the face of the earth.

"Will you please shut the hell up!" yelled Delmas.

"You're the one who wanted me to tag along," said Allorah. "If you didn't want to hear my complaints, you should have left me with my people."

They were cruising along the highway in a Range Rover Delmas had stolen from one of the dead, or locked up, gangbangers. It seemed that Allorah's new goal was to drive him crazy.

At first, she had pouted. Then, she tried to crash them by grabbing the steering wheel. After that little stunt, he had pulled over and secured her to the back seat. Since then, she screamed at irregular intervals, cursed him out constantly, begged for something to eat, promised him sexual favors, and now she was threatening to piss all over the interior if he didn't find her a bathroom to use.

"Listen, Allorah," he said, exasperated. "I'm not really well versed in keeping people alive. Normally, when I come out in the field, it's to kill someone. I need you to hear me and understand what I'm saying to you." He stared at her in the rearview mirror until she inclined her head. "I'm reaching the point where I don't give a fuck about you. I only brought you with me because all of your people back there are going to prison for a long time. They would have eventually figured out who you are, but in the meantime, you would have been living in a jail cell."

"So, you want me to believe that the reason you brought me with you was to help me? And I'm also to believe that it had nothing to do with using me as bait for the Cartel?"

"If your family is even alive, I really don't need you anymore," Delmas admitted. "I knew that they would run to their compound, but I didn't have the resources to go in after them. Now, thanks to my former colleagues, that's no longer an issue. As soon as we get to our destination, I'll be able to find out if they're buried in the rubble, or at one of their supposedly hidden retreats."

"And, what are you gonna do after you find out?" she asked.

"I'm gonna go in and move them to a site where no one will hear them scream. Then, I'm gonna torture them until I get the truth." He expected her to cry and plead for him not to go forward with his ruthless plan, but that's not what he got. Instead, she laughed.

"What are you gonna do? Pull out their teeth with some rusty pliers? Use a pipe-wrench to twist their legs? Oh no, I got it! You have one of those skin removers they used in that Russian spy movie!" She laughed until tears rolled down her face.

He let her have all the fun she could with the situation. Then, he said, "No, we've evolved way past that. Actually, what I'm gonna do is…" After he finished his description, all her humor evaporated.

"That's not funny," she stated.

Locking eyes with her in the mirror, he said, "I'm not laughing." She was silent for about ten seconds, then she exploded.

"You can't be serious!" she exclaimed. "What if they're innocent?"

He shrugged. "Cost of being a criminal in today's world. The line between innocence and guilt can sometimes become…Murky."

"You son of a bitch!" she screamed, pulling on her restraints. She wiggled and thrashed, but there was no escape from the leather cords holding her immobile. "I fucking hate you! My life was perfect until you came along. Now, you've taken everything from me!"

"Just like your husband and his Cartel buddies took everything from me!" he screamed back. "Fuck them, and fuck you, with your sob story. All my mother needed was Carlos to hold off while we dealt with a real emergency. But he couldn't show a little patience. Instead, he had her murdered! Now I'm supposed to feel sorry for you and your evil family? Fuck that!"

She raged for a while longer, inventing curse words to hurl in his direction. Then, like a switch had been thrown, the tears came. He had plenty of nieces and female cousins who used tears to get their way. His Uncle Kenny would tease him and call him soft because, whenever one of them cried, he undoubtably gave into their demands.

Over the years, that phase went away, just like his need to sleep with a Teddy Bear. If anything, a person's tears pissed him off now. Especially when he felt they were only being deployed for manipulation.

Eventually, she fell silent, and they continued on their way with the sky to the east getting lighter and lighter. He stopped for gas only once and expected Allorah to crank up and cause a scene. But, she surprised him by sitting quietly without voicing one complaint. When he asked if she needed to use the bathroom, she just shook her head and continued to stare out at the morning sky.

They reached their destination a couple hours later, and Delmas turned into the parking lot with the sun all but blinding him. He drove up to the desolate structure and stopped right in front of the door. The place had seen better days, but it wasn't there to look good. It was there to serve a purpose that he planned to take advantage of.

He opened the car door and pulled his weapon, placing it down by his leg. The WRA seldom used the decrepit airfield, but they still might have guards somewhere close by. Glancing in at Allorah, he said, "I'll be right back," and closed the door before walking off.

The building was two-story, with the top floor having a 360-degree view through its tinted glass panels. Realistically, if someone inside wanted to kill him, he'd already be dead. But, right now, they wouldn't be able to tell if he was just a meddlesome tourist or if he was a real threat. Only after he made his way to the other building, about a quarter mile farther along, would his intentions be made clear.

Boldly, he walked to the front door and turned the knob. Of course, the door was locked. He holstered his weapon, pulled out his pick-set, and had the lock disengaged in seconds. Taking a long, careful look around the area, he pulled his gun once more, then yanked the metal door open before stepping inside.

The interior of the cinderblock structure was clean, cool, and empty. Since the second story's floor was nothing more than a metal grate, he didn't need to go any farther to verify he was alone. He rushed over and made his way up the stairs so he could get a better view of the surrounding area. Everything looked deserted, like the land had been abandoned. For his purposes, he prayed it was only a façade, designed to look this way to discourage trespassers.

Returning to the first floor, he acknowledged that it didn't matter what he thought about their intentions with the property's look. He still had to be careful. The WRA always protected its assets.

Proceeding back out to the Range Rover, he climbed in, glanced back to find Allorah staring at him, but ignored her inquisitive look. Instead of engaging with her again and risk her cranking back up, he just drove the vehicle over to the other, much larger, building.

This time, when he exited the vehicle, he walked around and opened Allorah's door. He reached in and released her, directing her to step down onto the dusty concrete. Since she'd been dead set on playing her stupid game the night before, she was still barefoot, with only the robe to cover her body. The left sleeve, up near her shoulder, showed a light, red spot where her wound had leaked through. All of his senses tuned for the slightest hint of danger, he led the way to the side door, picked the lock, and stepped into the semi-dark interior.

He waited for Allorah to join him before he closed the door and reached up to his left to switch on the lights. Row by row, the florescent lights flicked on to reveal a wanted fugitive's dream come true. Planes of all sizes: Crop dusters, single engine puddle jumpers, global travelers. Every one of them, sleek, damn near brand new, and ready to take him wherever he wanted to go.

But, he needed to quicken his pace now that he'd breached the warehouse. He could almost picture the black SUVs hustling in his direction, full of gun-toting agents. With that image in mind, he grabbed Allorah's hand and took off for the front of the structure.

Once there, he slammed his palm against the green button to open the huge, roll-up door that comprised the whole front wall. Then, he reversed course, headed for a jet similar to the one which had brought him to the West Coast. But, as soon as he yanked the door open, Allorah pulled away in defiance.

"I'm not getting on that plane with you! Are you out of your fucking mind?" She folded her arms across her chest and cocked her hip to the side. She did everything except snap her fingers and roll her neck, something his sister's daughters were experts at.

Frantically, he said, "The people who own these planes are the kind that shoot first and never ask questions." Pointing to an overhead camera, he said, "They're definitely on their way, and they'll kill us both if they catch us. I still have to put fuel in this thing. We don't have time for you to throw a hissy-fit!"

When all she did was roll her eyes and lean farther to the side, he yanked his gun out and pointed it at her uninjured shoulder. "I'm done fucking around with you, little girl. I told you I don't need you anymore. Either get on the plane now, or get on in five seconds with an extra hole in your body!" She sucked her teeth and flipped him off, but she climbed inside the plane.

He boarded after her and secured the door before trotting to the cockpit. Allorah, still pouting, appeared at the door and asked, "Do you even know how to fly this thing?"

Hitting switches and preparing the plane to move, he said, "Been a while, but I hear it's just like riding a bike." With a playful glance, like he hadn't just threatened to shoot her, he said, "I hope they were right."

Shaking her head, she turned away and mumbled, "We're gonna die," before disappearing.

The engines roared to life and he taxied the craft out of the structure and over to the fueling pump. He cut the power off and exited the airplane with his head on a swivel. Allorah had apparently decided she didn't want to die while dirty, he heard the shower running in the back before he climbed down. He planned on taking advantage of the facilities also, but only after they were away from here. Right now, he was expecting bullets to start flying at any second.

His cellphone rang.

Considering the distance to their next stop, he figured about three more minutes of fuel was needed. That meant, whoever was calling him from the unknown number had two and a half minutes to deliver their message. “Hello?” he said, answering the call.

“Really?” Daniel asked in disbelief. “You couldn’t go to a charter service like everyone else?”

“Are you calling to reprimand me, or is there another reason?” His little brother mumbled something under his breath that sounded suspiciously like ‘stupid motherfucker.’

Louder, he said, “They’ll be there in about four minutes. If you’re not in the sky by then, they’ve been ordered to use deadly force.”

Just out of curiosity, he asked, “Reggie?”

Daniel said, “No, but that doesn’t matter! You need to hurry because I can’t get involved this time.”

“What? You afraid your mentor will disapprove?”

He was silent for a few seconds, then, “Fuck you!”

Before his brother could hang up, Delmas said, “Hey! Hold on!”

After a pause, Daniel said, “What?”

Taking a deep breath, Delmas said, “I’m sorry for voting to leave you in prison. And I’m sorry for going after Alisha and Gabby. For what it’s worth, I’m happy your life turned out so good.”

Delmas could hear the shock in Daniel’s silence. Finally, with emotion in his voice, he said, “Take all the time you need. I’ll take care of the agents.” Then, he hung up.

He took his little brother at his word and, two minutes later, heard the assault happening a couple miles away. Plane fueled and ready to go, he climbed back aboard and found Allorah in the copilot’s seat. He looked over everything to make sure she hadn’t sabotaged them, then directed the plane to the end of the runway.

Revving up to full power, they launched. Seconds later, they were lifting into the bright, blue sky. Below them and to the left, Allorah pointed and asked, “What’s that?” He had already spotted the three smoking vehicles in the middle of the road.

Feeling his own emotions well up, he said, "The true definition of family." She paused, waiting for him to continue. When he stayed silent, she shrugged, as if to say 'whatever' as they climbed higher and higher.

They hit their cruising altitude, and he engaged the autopilot before pulling out his phone to do a little research. Finding the needed information, he stored the phone and stood up to go take his shower. Allorah grabbed his arm and asked, "Where are you going? You can't just leave me by myself?"

He looked down at the hand clutching his arm before he glanced back at the controls. "It's on autopilot. Don't touch anything and it'll be okay."

Settling a bit, she asked, "Where are we going, anyway?"

He disengaged his arm from her grasp, then said, "Turns out, your husband and his brother, Juan, survived the attack on the compound. So, we're gonna pay them a little visit." Walking towards the bedroom, he called over his shoulder, "If it looks like we're gonna hit something, yell so I can come change our course."

Almost laughing out loud, he looked back to find Allorah studying the horizon intently. Smiling for the first time in what seemed like ages, he felt like his life was on the mend. Now, all he had to do was torture the truth out of two Cartel Bosses, murder whoever was responsible for his mother's death, and then hide from the law for the rest of his life.

Whistling a jaunty tune, he stripped off his clothes, thinking, oh what a joy it was to be a Burke.

Chapter 14

This time, Zero could hear the moans, groans, and pounding flesh much clearer than the last. That was because he was now the man stroking in and out of Megan from behind. Her juicy ass vibrated and rippled every time he lunged forward. Which, in turn, forced her face firmly into the notch between Ciera's thighs.

Watching Megan bring Tano's girl so much pleasure was a sight to behold. Ciera's body, bent and twisted in the throes of ecstasy, was perfect. Glistening with sweat, back arched, head thrown back, the only time she was more alluring was after she came down from a climax and she stared into his eyes until Megan's tongue sent her back up once again.

They'd been at it all day. Zero had taken a major risk this morning when he woke up to their shouts of release. Deciding it was worth whatever price he'd have to pay, he walked into the bedroom, not wearing a stitch, and boldly asked where they wanted him. Megan had reached back and lifted her plump cheeks, that's where he'd been ever since.

The up-close view of Ciera was what really got him going. He'd been dreaming of being with her for years now, but he could never be the one to make the first move. If she took offense to his overture, and she told Tano, the OG would blow his fucking head off. But wait! Tano was in jail, charged with multiple bodies! What the hell was he hesitating for?

Softly, he whispered in Megan's ear, "I think Ciera looks hungry." The beautiful white girl looked back and nodded before disengaging from him and climbing up her lover's torso, planting herself right on her face.

Now that the view was unobstructed, he could clearly see the moisture gathered all around Ciera's opening. With her legs splayed wide, and her hand clutching handfuls of Megan's ass, he knew a better opportunity would never present itself. Even though he longed to find out if she tasted as good as she looked, another part of his body was demanding attention.

He eased forward, almost afraid that any perceived movement on his part would bring her out of the sexual daze she'd been enjoying for hours. Lining himself up, he pushed forward and realized that the ringing in his ears was actually his phone down the hall.

Fuck that! he thought. He wasn't even all the way in yet. Intent on rectifying that, he rocked his body into her tight, wetness, until he felt himself tapping her cervix.

SHIT! he screamed in his head when Ciera's phone started ringing on the dresser. There was no way he could stop now. Leaning forward, he pushed Megan down, hoping that her thick thighs clamping on the side of Ciera's head would drown out the noise. When it looked as if Ciera was trying to move Megan off of her, he decided he needed another plan.

He'd been so excited to be inside the goddess, he'd only been gently rocking, trying to prolong his pleasure. Now, he turned his body into a piston. He reached up and worked her nipples, causing a fresh flood of heat to engulf his manhood. Up, down, round and round, the sound of hammering flesh doing what Megan's legs couldn't. Zero wasn't gonna pass this up. It might be the one and only chance he had to make a lasting impression.

All of a sudden, Ciera's legs lifted straight up into the air. She let out a raspy scream, forcing him to hook his arm under Megan's leg and toss her to the side. Seeing Ciera's drenched cheeks, her straining neck, and wide-open mouth, he yelled, "Look at me!" As soon as her passion-filled, hazel eyes focused on him, he exploded.

Still hammering, he roared his victory to the heavens. Ciera went into a series of whole-body jerks that caused pride to swell his chest. A giggle to his right drew his attention to Megan. She said, "Been holding that one in for a while, huh?"

They all laughed as Zero continued to grind his pelvic area into Ciera's. Her gasps, and her gripping heat, were firming him back up for round two. Then, her phone rang again.

Ciera sighed and rolled her hips as she patted him on the ass. She said, "Let me up. Playtime is over." Reluctantly, he pulled out and fell beside her onto his back, his flesh still hard and sticky with her juices. Laughing at his satisfied expression, she swung her sexy body out of the bed and swayed over to the dresser.

A hand wrapped around him. Megan whispered, "I'll take care of that," and dove down to continue his pleasure.

She was a pro. She knew exactly what to do to drive a person wild. But his attention was tuned into Ciera as she leaned on the dresser with her ass poking out, watching them in the mirror. She winked at him, which proved to be more than he could handle. Spasm after spasm wracked through him, Megan didn't stop until he was truly drained. Then Ciera's eyes went wide.

She screamed, "Dammit, Tano! Why didn't you start with that!" She listened for a few more seconds, then said, "I'll call you back in half an hour. By then, we'll either both be dead, or I'll have answers for you." She hung up and spun around. "The GF is on his way! Megan, you need to go and…" She didn't get to finish before the door was opened, and the man himself stepped into the room. Two of his henchmen stepped in with him, took in the scene, paid a little too much attention to Ciera's body, then left them alone.

Ciera and Megan stayed exactly as they were, but Zero jumped to his feet, wrapping the sheet around his waist. He was exposed, vulnerable, a position he hated to be in when in the presence of an Alpha male. And you couldn't get anymore Alpha than Antwan 'Poppy' Parks.

The 6’4” mountain closed the door gently behind his men, then pulled out his gun. His platinum and diamond grill sparkled as a sneer spread across his face. He stepped to the side, swung his waist-length dreads behind his head, and pointed the gun at Megan. “Get out,” he said softly, causing Megan to leave all her shit, and dash to the door, butt naked. He opened it for her like a gentleman, and she skittered through before he closed it back.

His gaze bounced between them a few times, then he chuckled and shook his head. “So, let me get this straight,” he stated with false amusement. “My daughter, your so-called friend, is out there, still being held by some madman, and ya’ll up in here getting your freak on with the white girl!” Looking at Zero, he added, “Not to mention, your OG only been in jail for three days, and you already fucking his bitch!”

Zero kept his mouth shut, Poppy would kill him in a heartbeat. The only reason he hadn’t killed him already was because, 50% of their line was already locked up or dead. Since everyone with a higher or similar rank than Zero fell into one of those categories, he was now the decision maker for his line. That might grant him a small reprieve, but his life was still very much in jeopardy.

The GF turned his attention to Ciera. “Put some fucking clothes on, silly ass bitch!” Rage flashed across her face before she moved, and Poppy caught it. “You got something you want to say, BITCH?” With downcast eyes, she shook her head and started to get dressed. He added, “I told that boy not to add no slutty ass whore to his line. Matter of fact, get your shit and get out. Let the real gangstas handle their business.”

Zero could damn near see the steam coming out of the top of her head. It was well known that Poppy had little respect for female gang members. If one so much as rolled her eyes at him, the discipline was harsh and left lasting imprints.

Zero knew that Ciera was real with her shit, but it would be suicide to show it at this moment.

After she was gone, Poppy pulled out his phone and sent a text. He waited for a reply before focusing back on him. "Tell me what's going on with Tano. I'm getting too much secondhand info that sounds like some Syfy shit. For some reason, Tano won't call me himself. I know he got a phone."

Zero wished he had some clothes to put on, but he'd left them in his room. Making sure the sheet wouldn't fall down in the middle of his report, he explained it exactly like Tano had told him. "Some Scrap clocked the pair when the police found them, then followed them to a mansion up in the hills. Tano told me and Ciera to come here so, if anything happened, we could continue his line." That wasn't relevant to the report, but it might help keep a bullet out of his ass.

He continued. "They went to check it out and found that the guy had some sort of device that he demonstrated on Allorah. It made her, and everyone around them, sick. Then the fucker shot her in the shoulder. Just a nick," he added when the GF's eyes flashed. "Since she seemed to be okay, they waited and rushed the house when the man appeared to be sleep. He wasn't. They ended up getting into a shootout."

"With Allorah in the house? They shot it out with this guy?"

He shrugged. "He didn't go into detail, except to say they got the guy and Allorah. But before they could get away, fucking flying war machines, his words not mine, came down and started murdering our crew. The only people who could move without being killed were the man and Allorah." To end the report, he said, "The machines held them until the police got there, now all of them are charged with multiple bodies."

Poppy stood there, waiting for the punchline of the joke. "You're serious?" he finally asked.

"That's what Tano said. He was on a cellphone, so he could speak freely. But that's what he claims happened."

"And you up in here getting some pussy!" Shaking his head, Poppy asked, "Why you aint out there looking for this guy and my daughter?"

"Tano said that we stumbled onto some Cartel business, and not to do anything until he gets out."

Softly, Poppy said, "That nigga is a known, high-ranking gang member. It doesn't matter how he makes ya'll dress and act, they still know ya'll Blood! He got 13 bodies hanging over his head. What? Ya'll gonna search for her in the next life?" He visibly collected himself, then raised his gun and shot Zero in his shoulder.

He yelped and sat down hard on the bed. Thundering footsteps could be heard coming their way. Calmly, the GF opened the door and said, "I'm good," then closed it back.

He turned to Zero and said, "Everything is on you now, Blood. My daughter gets shot, you get shot. If she dies, you die. Tano and them niggas are finished. I better hear of some kind of progress every fucking day, or I'll come back. And, Zero," he said, ominously. "If I have to come back, I'm putting holes in places you won't be able to walk away from." Then, he turned and walked out of the door.

Zero ripped the covering off one of the pillows, using it to apply pressure to his bleeding shoulder. A few seconds later, he heard a brutal smack, followed by a feminine cry of pain. Then silence.

Carefully, he made his way to the door and opened it a crack. No one was in sight, so he walked out into the hallway and rushed over to the room containing his stuff. "Son of a bitch!" he cried, noticing his bunny-eared pockets. Since his gun, phone, and wallet were still there on the floor, he knew it had to have been Poppy's boys looking for an easy payday. They hated the fact that everyone in Tano's line was rich. Not willing to get worked up over a few hundred dollars, Zero dashed into the bathroom to better bandage his wound, he got dressed, and then went to find Ciera.

When he found her on the couch in the living room, he pulled up short and yelled, "What the fuck!" He rushed over to her, but didn't know where to place his hands. "What the FUCK!" he yelled again, lightly touching her swollen face. "Oh my God! Why would they do this?"

She was naked, curled up in the fetal position, but with a calm expression on her face. She was bleeding from several cuts on her lips and around her eyes, but the blood that worried him the most was coming from between her legs. He asked, "Can you get up, Homie?" He added the last part to try and make her show the strength he knew her to possess. She nodded and slowly got to her feet.

A tear leaked out of his eye as the condition of her body was revealed. The fuckers had bit, punched, and brutalized her, all while he'd been only feet away. He was amazed at her control because, only at the end had she made a sound. He said, "We have to get you to a hospital." She nodded as he gently helped her put her clothes back on. He noticed they weren't torn up, so she must have been forced to undress herself.

She wouldn't meet his eyes, but she must have read the curiosity in his posture. "They said if I made a sound, they would wipe out the rest of our line." Only then did she look at him, and it broke something inside his heart. He had to find Allorah because she was his family. But after that was done, retaliation was on the horizon.

She said, "I'll drive myself. If you go with me, they'll see your gunshot wound and hold you for questioning." He knew she was right, but it hurt his soul to watch her turn around and slow-step over to the door. Blood was already starting to seep through the seat of her jeans.

When she reached the door, she opened it and stopped. Without turning, she said, "Please don't tell Tano." She waited a few beats, then exited, closing the door behind her.

He sat on the chair, sickened as he stared across at the couch, stained with her blood and other body fluids. Forcing his mind away from things he couldn't change, he switched to what he perhaps could. Pulling out his phone, he called the rest of their crew. Then, even though he didn't really know him that well, he called Joshue Noriega.

When the man picked up, he was shocked to learn that the Cartel Boss knew less than he did about what was going on with Allorah. They talked candidly for almost an hour before Zero hung up feeling more confused than before the call.

Secret government Agencies. Flying war machines. Super Soldiers on the hunt for an assassin. What the fuck had they stumbled into? He flashed back to the Homie, Charles, telling them about the Crip Set being slaughtered in North Carolina. If they were dealing with the same people, they would be lucky to escape this ordeal with their lives.

Figuring it was time to talk to his OG, he dialed the number to Tano's bulletproof cellphone. When he answered, Zero immediately got to the point. Well, actually, two points. "Allorah is gone and we're gonna have to kill the GF." Then he went on to tell him the events that brought on these conclusions. Not holding anything back, even the part he was now ashamed of, he told him everything.

The man reentered the massive house after stowing the last bag in the back of the maroon Porsche GT4, and headed for the kitchen. He smiled and slowed down when he heard the feminine voices raised with excitement. He was kind of in a hurry, but the topic being discussed made him pause.

"Ewww! I don't need anything from some smelly boy! I got my dad and that's all I need!" Gabby exclaimed. His chest swelled with pride at the words from his newly-minted 12-year-old daughter, Gabriella Burke. He peeked in to see her beautiful face scrunched up in disgust. The next voice made his eyes roll.

"Gabby, you say that now. In a few years, you'll have your pick of all the boys on the planet. With that flawless skin, and long, flowing hair, they'll be on you like flies on…"

"Tyiesha!" yelled Alisha. "What did I tell you about putting that stuff in her head? If Daniel hears that crap, he's gonna have your ass."

"Too late," Daniel said, stepping into the kitchen. "And just to set the record straight, my baby girl doesn't need some snot-nosed, stank-breath, perverted boy up in her face. She's gonna stay here and live with her dad until he grows old and gray and dies in his sleep at the age of 120."

"Dad, I love you," said his daughter. "But you gonna have to hire some nurses if you live to be 120. I'm not changing your diapers!" Everyone laughed as he hugged her from behind and planted a kiss on her head, her smile making his heart warm.

He made his way over to Alisha, still clad in her black, spandex, work-out clothes, and leaned in for a kiss. She dodged him and said, "I'm sweaty. Let me go freshen…" Before she could finish, he had her off her bare feet, wrapped in his embrace.

The kiss started out G rated, but quickly turned rated R when Alisha locked her legs around his waist. Gabby yelled, "Come on guys! Kids in the room!" He chuckled and lowered his fiancé back to the floor, but continued to steal little pecks. When he finally pulled back, he couldn't help but stare at the amazing woman who owned his heart.

Skin a deep, dark chocolate that always made him want to lean in for a taste. At 5' 8", she possessed the perfect balance between long and slim, mixed with a curvaceous thickness that could bring a man to his knees. Her brown eyes were mesmerizing and alluring, her love for him never failing to shine through. A gagging sound issued from his left making him glance at his fiancé's best friend.

The young Rhianna look-alike was shaking her head like the sight in front of her was unbearable. “Will you two give it a rest? He was only gone for like two minutes,” she told Alisha. “You don’t have to inhale each other every time your eyes touch.”

“Aww!” said Alisha while Daniel nibble her neck. “I think Tyiesha is jealous.” The singsong, baby voice was funny, but it sent an image to his brain of Alisha bent over talking to their own baby in the same tone. It definitely wasn’t an unpleasant dream. In fact, he wished he had time to start on it right now.

Tyiesha jerked back as if slapped. “Jealous of what? Don’t nobody want no man hanging all over them every second of the day!” Scratching her arm, she said, “Just seeing it is giving me a rash.”

“Well,” said Daniel, hugging his future bride from behind. “You don’t have to see it. You can always leave.”

At different points in his former life as the Prison Guard Killer, these three young ladies had crossed his path. He had actually met Gabby first, but it wasn’t until the end of their second encounter that she’d asked to come with him. With open arms, he’d taken her in and made her his official, adopted daughter.

Alisha and Tyiesha had been affiliated with a gang that Daniel decided had to go. While very attractive, Tyiesha didn’t stir a thing in him. Alisha, on the other hand, had stolen his soul the first night they met. They’d gone through a rough patch of revelations on his part, but love won out. Now, they were set to be married in a little over a month.

Two years after their official meeting in a club, Daniel had spared Tyiesha at Alisha’s request, and she’d been with them ever since. Technically, he’d kidnapped her. But it was either that or death. He didn’t think she would complain about his choice.

Now, the reminder that she didn’t have to stay with them anymore only seemed to piss her off royally. Jumping to her feet, she drew up to her full 5’ 9” and said, “Fuck you, Daniel! You want me to leave? Fine! I’ll pack my shit and be gone before you come back!” Then she stomped off towards her room.

Gabby rose and yelled, “Auntie T, come back! He was just playing!” When Tyiesha kept walking, Gabby spun on him with a fierce expression. “Stop treating her like that! She’s our family, too.” She turned and raced after her aunt, but not before he caught the glint of tears in her eyes.

Immediately, he made to follow. “Gabby, I’m…”

“Let her go,” Alisha said, cutting him off and wrapping him in her arms. With a sad smile, she said, “I’ll handle it, I know you have to go.”

Running both hands over his face, he said, “I was just joking with her. Why does she always take what I say so seriously?”

Leaning back so she could look into his eyes, she said, “Tyiesha has a lot of the same issues that Gabby has. They have both been through so much that they fear abandonment is always around the next corner. Gabby is still in the fear phase, while Tyiesha is fully invested in lashing out in anger. Go do what you have to do and let me handle this.”

Kissing her succulent, pink lips, he whispered, “How did I get so lucky to find you?” After one more lingering kiss, he said, “I love you, Alisha Saffiyah Harden.”

She gave him the megawatt smile. “I love you too, Daniel Manuel Burke.”

They both laughed as Daniel said, “Oh! You got jokes?” Manuel ‘Manny’ Adams was the alias he’d been using when they first met. That name had almost become an obstacle to their relationship. He thanked God that they could now laugh about it.

Backing up, he kept ahold of her hand until the last possible second, then he let go. He yelled, “Love you, Gabby!” Then whispered, “Make sure our little girl knows how much she’s loved and wanted.”

Alisha wrapped her arms around her midsection and said, "I will. Be safe." He nodded and turned away, every fiber of his being screaming for him to stay at home with his family.

But duty called. There were still things he had to do to make sure his family was safe. Leaving the house and returning to the Porsche, he set his mind for the task at hand. One trip to California, a couple of days on the ground, and he could return to his girls. Pulling off, he felt his phone vibrate on his hip.

Edging down the driveway, he read the message and slowed to a stop as tears blurred his vision. All was right in his world. The text was from his daughter. It simply said, 'I love you too.'

Weight lifted off his chest, he exited the gate, ready to leave his protected castle and take on the world.

Chapter 15

"I'm telling you, they're not coming!" shouted Joshue. "It's been three days! Maybe they found the people responsible and don't need us anymore."

"Sit down and shut the fuck up!" Juan yelled, jumping to his feet. "We're not leaving until they make their attempt. If they say they're coming, they're coming."

"Fuck you!" Joshue said, getting in his brother's face. "My wife has been taken, and I'm not even sure she's still alive. I don't have time to sit around while she could need my help."

Pushing Joshue away from him, Juan said, "Have you heard me talking to my wife? Have I gotten to talk to my son and daughter? No! I want to make sure my family is alright, too. But me going out there and getting killed, possibly making them targets in the process, isn't gonna do them a bit of good."

Joshue grabbed two handfuls of his hair and continued to pace back and forth. He knew his brother was right, but the wait was fucking with his mind. Maybe if he was sure one of the Burkes had her, he wouldn't be so worried. But some of the other WRA agents, he wouldn't trust them to care for a pet goldfish.

Fucking mercenaries, psychos, and savages. Most of them would murder their own mothers if paid enough or ordered by one of the Burkes to do so. He'd only met a handful of them a few times when they were picking up and dropping off merchandise, but those few times were too many. Killers with no conscience, they made Felipe look like a choirboy. Speak of the devil, he glanced at the piece of shit who used to be his best friend.

"Why the fuck are you so quiet?" he asked him. "Don't have anymore lies to tell? I bet your sister never even fucking existed."

Flip was out of his seat and in his face in seconds. "Say something else about my sister and I'll kill you!" he growled. The men stood chest to chest, eye to eye, until Joshue turned away with hate in his eyes.

"You hear back from that guy, Double O?" Juan asked, attempting to disperse the tension.

"It's Zero," said Joshue. "And no, nothing since he told me her father is going crazy, Tano is locked up, and he really doesn't know what to do. He does know that some kind of secret organization is involved, but that's based on some shaky intel from one of his guys from North Carolina. And since he wasn't personally in on the raid when they found the guy and Allorah, all his info on that is second hand."

"Hey, the fact that she was alive three days ago, and the man said he needed her, is a good thing. Obviously, they're gonna try and use her to pull us out." In a show of love uncustomary between the brothers, Juan gave him a quick embrace. "We'll get her back, bro. No matter what, we'll make sure she gets through this."

For the next couple hours, they were all quiet, deep in their own thoughts. Joshue's mind raced with fear for his wife. Why hadn't he insisted his dad allow her into the compound? She would have gone through the terrible ordeal the other women experienced in the Security Suite, but she would be by his side now.

Allorah wouldn't have run away with the rest of the women and children, that wasn't how she operated. She would have been sitting right here with a gun within reach, waiting for the WRA to show up. His warrior. His equal. His best friend. She could be a huge pain in the ass, but his life would be bland without her in it.

For the hundredth time over the last 48 hours, his phone lit up and he shook his head. Poppy, Allorah's father, was reaching out, no doubt to curse his soul and threaten his life. The tone of his text messages was getting worse and Joshue decided to stop putting off the inevitable and answered the call. "Hello," he said with trepidation in his heart.

"Where the fuck are you, you piece of shit!" were the first words he heard.

"I'm doing fine, thanks for asking," he replied smartly.

"I don't give a shit how you're doing. And say something else out of the way and you'll be rejoining your father and brother in hell." The authorities had indeed finally reached their bodies late last night and it was all over the news. There was still speculation about the rest of the family's whereabouts.

"Look man," Joshue said standing up. "If all you've been calling me for was to issue your threats, I have more important things to worry about."

"Have you found my daughter?" asked the high-ranking Blood member.

"The people who have her won't hurt her. They're just holding her until they get what they want." He tried to sound confident in his assumption, more to convince himself than her dad. "The second I have her back, I'm sending her straight to you. Just stay calm and…"

"You remember what I promised you if you got my baby tied up in your Cartel bullshit?" the man rudely cut him off. Not waiting for an answer, he said, "You ever show your face in California again, you're a dead man. And when you have my daughter, you better give her a long farewell kiss. It will be the last time you ever get to see her." Then the bastard hung up on him.

Joshue laughed as the personnel against him continued to stack up. Juan asked, "Poppy?" Joshue nodded, feeling sick to his stomach. He wondered if he could now convince Allorah to stay in Colombia for good. The last time he'd broached the subject, she'd laughed in his face. But Poppy didn't issue empty threats. If he went back to Cali, he would have a million Bloods trying to earn their stripes by killing him.

His phone rang again as he sank back down onto the couch.

He almost didn't want to look at the screen, thinking it was Poppy calling to add more predictions concerning his impending death. But he looked down, and his heart leaped to his throat. Allorah's beautiful face filled the screen. He fumbled and dropped the phone in his haste to answer it. Snatching it up, he brought it to his face. "Oh my God! Baby! Please tell me you're okay!"

A pause. Then a deep, masculine voice said, "I'm doing pretty good, but I don't think you know me well enough to be calling me baby."

Juan and Felipe, thinking it was Allorah from his reaction, flanked him and started demanding information. He shouted, "Shut the fuck up!" before he focused back on the call.

The man said, "Okay, but you'll wish you had listened to what I had to say."

"No, wait…I wasn't talking to you! Hello? Hello?" But the caller was gone. He screamed in rage, squeezing the phone while staring at the ceiling. Then he focused his attention on the men.

"Get the fuck away from me," he growled, pulling his gun out. Both men heeded his warning, raised their hands and slowly backed away. He was just about to light into their hides when the phone lit up again. Anger vanishing at once, he shushed the two men, laid the phone down on the table, then answered it on speaker.

"You ready to listen, or should I keep shutting up?" the voice asked.

"I'm sorry, I wasn't talking to you. I'm ready to listen," he said calmly.

"I know you wasn't talking to me, Little Capo, that was the problem. I need your undivided attention. Do I have it now?"

"Yes, Sir! Yes, you do!"

"Good," the man said. "Well, first, let me tell you who you're dealing with. This is Delmas Burke." He paused to let the information sink in. "Of course, we've met before, but we were friends then. Now, since we're enemies, you get to meet the real me!" The last statement was said in such a tone, it sent a shiver down his spine.

Delmas continued. "Normally, when I deal with my enemies, I communicate with bullets. I've decided to try and use words this time. You following me?"

"Yes, Sir! I'm following loud and clear." Just hours ago, he had hoped Allorah was being held by a Burke. His prayer had been answered, but now he felt like a fool. Delmas Burke was ruthless, an animal. He was the one the WRA used to control the monsters they had in their employ. For him to have that kind of power, how much worse did he have to be compared to the minions.

"So, I'm gonna make this message plan and simple, because I don't want to lose you," he went on. "You have three options. Options that I am graciously offering you to solve our mutual problem. One, you can tell me who killed my mother, I kill whoever's responsible, and everyone else goes on their merry way."

"Ok, but Mr. Burke, we don't know…"

"Two," interrupted the WRA man. "You don't tell me, and I kill your wife, Joshue. Your family, Juan. And your mother and grandmother, Felipe." The three men looked at each other in silence. "Just to interject a little more information into the situation, I have Allorah, and I know exactly where to find the others."

Joshue clinched his jaw as the need to rage, but also cooperate, warred inside of him. He noticed that his brother and Felipe, two guys who didn't take shit from anyone, wore expressions similar to his own. All three remained still and silent as they waited for the man to finish his list.

"Or three," he said after a minute. "I give you an address, all three of you come down for a nice chat, I release Allorah, and leave the rest of your families alone. I'll give you guys 30 minutes to talk it over, and I'll call back." The call disconnected.

Juan and Felipe immediately got on their phones and tried to contact their families. The calls wouldn't go through. They were able to dial the numbers, but the process would stop as soon as they pressed send. Juan looked up and asked, "How far away can he be and still block our calls?"

Joshue shrugged. "This is the WRA we're talking about. He could probably be in Germany and do it."

Felipe finally gave up with his own phone, then joined into their conversation. "Listen, everyone understands Cartel business is kept secret from non-members, so no one would expect me to know anything. But if either of you knows who killed that bitch, now would be the time to tell it. I've been through hell trying to protect my family. I don't want them to die because of something one of you are deciding to keep secret."

"You selfish ass coward!" yelled Joshue. "This bastard has my wife! He could be bluffing about knowing where your family is, but it's no bluff with mine. Add on the fact that we've already lost two family members because of you, I think it's time for you to shut up and let the honest men figure this out."

Felipe shrugged. "Not much to figure out. I'm not turning myself in to save your wife. So, the only option is to tell the man the truth. If push comes to shove, blame it on Carlos and it's over after that. He's already dead." At that point Joshue came to a decision in his head. He didn't show any outward sign, but he'd made up his mind what to do.

He turned to Juan. "What do you think?"

Without a word, Joshue could tell that Juan was thinking along the same lines as him. Running his uninjured right hand through his full beard, he said, "I'm with whatever you want to do." Pausing, he strolled off before turning back with his arms wide. "We can't stay in this bunker forever. The other Cartels will keep coming for us. The WRA will get to us, eventually. Plus, I told you we're gonna bring your girl home. We can't let her suffer over Cartel business."

Joshue almost shed a tear over his brother's words. They'd never been super close, but Noriegas are loyal to their own. The fact that he was willing to sacrifice his life for a woman he barely knew, spoke of something deeper than loyalty. It spoke of love.

Shaking his head, though, he said, "We need to come up with a plan. There's no way we can just blindly turn ourselves over to him without safeguards in place to protect our families."

"Why are you still talking about that option?" asked Felipe. "The man said all three, and I've told you I'm not turning myself in to him."

"Look!" said Joshue, spinning to confront the man. "Delmas knows you're not Cartel. Since that's common knowledge, he should also be aware that you wouldn't be privy to our secrets. I'm gonna talk to him when he calls and see if I can remove you from his stipulation. Just calm down and let us try to work this out." Flip nodded and walked off to let the brothers talk.

They started by thinking over the problem as a whole. Turning themselves in would hopefully save their families, but what could they use to save themselves. No matter what the WRA thought, the Cartel had nothing to do with Lucille Drake's death. How were they supposed to convince the lunatic they were innocent?

The brothers were brainstorming arguments they could make when Flip burst out laughing from across the room. Joshue looked up and asked, "Something funny?"

"You guys just don't get it," he said in way of an answer. Shaking his head, he added, "They've already found you guilty. The WRA might can't determine which one of the Noriegas did it, but they know it was one of you. This guy isn't going to question you, he's gonna execute every Noriega to make sure he gets the right one."

Joshue was forming a retort in his mind when his phone rang, making any response irrelevant.

"Hello," Joshue said after Juan and Flip had joined him back at the table.

"So, what's it going to be? Option one, two, or three?" Delmas asked without preamble.

"I want to speak to Allorah to make sure she's still alive," demanded Joshue.

After a brief moment of silence, Delmas asked, "You don't trust me, Joshue?"

"Ah, no, not really," he answered.

Delmas barked out a laugh. "Smart man, but your request is denied. I give you my word on my mother's soul that she's safe, I'm just not near her to grant your request. Now, give me your answer so we can move forward."

"I have one more question." Delmas sighed and told him to proceed. "From the start, this has been between the Cartel and the WRA. I think we can both agree that anyone not in the Cartel wouldn't be in the loop on something of this magnitude. Do you agree?"

"Get to the point, Joshue."

"My point is, Flip is not part of the Cartel. He was my security, but he was never a member of the organization. Me and Juan want to turn ourselves over to you, but we want to leave Flip out of the transaction." Juan eased away from the table as the conversation progressed.

"Okay, let me make this simple," said Delmas. "The compromise was the choices I offered you. That's as far as I'm willing to go. Either all three of you agree to turn yourselves in, or pick another option. I know your dad made sure you were fluent in English. Use your skills to comprehend what I'm saying."

Joshue looked at Flip who stood up straight and started shaking his head. The Brazilian, making sure he was loud enough to be heard over the phone, said, "I'm not Cartel, I'm not a Noriega, and I have no knowledge of your mother's death. And I'm not turning myself in to be executed for something I didn't do!"

Delmas said, "I'm getting bored with this. Since all three of you won't come in, that takes option three off the board. You have ten seconds to choose another option, or I pick one for you."

Joshue stood up straight and looked Flip in his eyes. "You won't change your mind?" he asked his former friend. As soon as he shook his head no, Joshue nodded and said, "Do it." Juan, standing behind Flip, brought the wooden bat down on the top of his head.

Flip fell to his knees and Juan delivered one more solid blow before he fell face first to the floor, unconscious.

Into the phone, Joshue said, "Option three is back in play. Flip is coming. Give me the address and we're on our way." He gave them the address to a place in the city of Villavicencio, and told them they had two hours to get there. Joshue promised they would make it, then disconnected the call.

Juan was already over by the entrance disabling the mines and, after checking to make sure Flip was still alive, Joshue joined his brother. He said, "We can't keep hitting the man in the head every time he comes to. We need to tie him up."

Juan said, "You keep working with the mines, I'll secure the sack of shit." Ten minutes later, they exited the underground bunker carrying a mummified, still unconscious, Flip.

They laid him down and dismantled enough of the traps for them to enter and exit the garage. That done, they came back and carried the wrapped body over to the back door of a Dodge Ram 1500, and the brothers maneuvered him across the backseat. They both climbed in, Juan in the driver's seat, and he turned the key to start the truck.

The engine wouldn't turn over.

Glancing at each other in alarm, the brothers grabbed their door handles just as the locks engaged to prevent their escape. Then they heard a slight hissing sound coming from the back compartment.

Turning, they found a thick fog seeping into the vehicle through a hole in the floor. "Son of a bitch!" shouted Juan, Joshue tearing his shirt off to use as a plug for the hole. It slowed down the flow, but enough of the gas was coming through to make the shirt pointless. Juan pulled out his gun and pointed it at the driver's side window.

"Whoa! Whoa! Whoa!" yelled Joshue, grabbing his brother's arm. "You trying to kill us, motherfucker." Knocking on his own window, he said, "Bulletproof glass."

"Fuck!" roared Juan, turning the gun around and uselessly hammering on the glass. After a while, he gave up and sat back with a dejected look on his face.

Joshue assumed his own face mirrored his brother's expression as he sat there waiting for the effects of the gas to take place. All he could think was how good the WRA was at these types of games. The options, the threats, none of that stuff had been real. There were four vehicles in the garage. He would bet his life that all of them had been set up in this same way. Since all the games had been geared towards getting them inside one of them, ultimately.

"Look at this arrogant fucker," Juan said, bringing him back to their present situation. The gas was pulling him down fast. He could barely keep his eyes open. But he used the last of his strength to focus forward, and almost laughed at what he saw.

Fucking Delmas Burke was sitting across from them on a work bench, jerking his phone this way and that as if he was playing a game. Then, almost like he felt their eyes focused on him, he looked up and waved. That's when the spell of the gas overcame his will to stay awake and covered him in a shroud of darkness.

Chapter 16

When Joshue finally pulled himself out of the abyss, his body felt like it'd been put through a cement mixer. Everything hurt. For a minute, the pain was the only thing that confirmed his status among the living. Because he was still in darkness, a darkness that could be felt more than it could be seen.

Wherever he was, he wasn't going anywhere soon. The material securing him to his seat was almost soft, but it was a holding embrace that couldn't be broken. He strained and pulled, got nothing except frustration for his efforts. Since the binds seemed to be unescapable, he turned his attention to the chair he was secured to.

His legs were free, so he tried to use his lower body strength to tilt the chair in each direction. Nothing doing. Then he tried lunging his weight from side to side. Ultimately, that proved to be a fruitless endeavor. Deep in his mind, he knew the WRA man wouldn't leave any avenue of escape. Dammit, he still had to try. He was a Noriega! He couldn't just lay down and die.

A skittering sound to his left made him freeze so he could better hear. He slumped when he realized it was the same sound he'd made a minute ago when testing his own binds. He whispered, "Juan?" and the noise abruptly stopped.

"Joshue?" his brother whispered back. "What the fuck is going on?"

"Don't know. I just woke up a minute ago. Can you even take a guess at where we are?"

"Tunja!" said a voice booming out of the darkness. The echo sent fear streaking down Joshue's spine as he realized how massive the area had to be. For some reason, it made him feel very vulnerable and small.

The next sound was an electrical buzz that proceeded a line of hanging, florescent lights blazing to life. Joshue squinted to save his eyes, but he could clearly see his surroundings now. What the light revealed was Delmas Burke walking towards the two men from across what appeared to be an evil villain's hideout.

Delmas said, "We're in a cave outside the city limits of Tunja. You know, just north of Bogota?" Joshue nodded because he did indeed know where the city was. "The WRA had this area fixed up just in case we ever had problems out of the Cartels. It's pretty much half prison, half torture chamber." Rubbing his hands together in glee, he asked, "Guess which one it's gonna be used for today?"

The room was maybe half the size of a football field, with the roof about six feet near the walls, and closer to thirty feet at its center. A glass enclosure was sitting in the middle with the inside darkened to hide its content. Here and there, other enclosures hid things that Joshue hoped to never find out about. His heartrate spiked when he thought of Allorah tied up inside the glass room, ready to be tortured to get some truth out of the Cartel brothers.

Delmas stopped about ten feet from them and said, "All I wanted was the truth and we wouldn't be here now. Well, it doesn't matter anymore, this is the end. I'll take my pound of flesh, get my revenge, then move on to the next phase."

Pleadingly, Joshue said, "We've done nothing but tell you the truth! Our organization didn't kill your mother!" Juan wasn't even trying to talk, he just renewed his efforts to break free from the chair.

Delmas laughed and said, "I know you didn't, Little Capo. I wasn't talking about you two," which caused Juan to cease his struggle. Turning and pulling out his phone, Delmas swiped the screen and said, "I was talking about this piece of shit!" The light in the enclosure turned on to reveal Flip secured to a vertical board facing them.

Both Joshue and Juan jerked back in confusion. Joshue said the only thing that came to his mind. "Where's my wife?"

Delmas waved the question off like it wasn't important. "She's fine, don't worry about her." He turned back towards them with a speculative look. "Why were you asking me questions about if I needed Flip to come along?"

Juan shrugged. "He didn't want to turn himself in. We pretty much decided to kill him if you only wanted us two."

Nodding, Delmas said, "That's what I thought." Focusing on a spot over their heads, he said, "I told you what I would do to the ones responsible. These guys were just a means to an end. You can cut them loose now."

"What!" exclaimed Joshue as a feminine squeal came from behind his back. He turned just in time for Allorah to wrap her arms around his neck and kiss him like it would be the last time she got to do so.

Juan yelled, "Hey! Hey! Hey! You can do all that after you cut us loose."

Pulling back with a huge smile on her face, Allorah said, "Oh, sorry. Just happy to see my man." She used the knife in her hand to cut through their ties before they all fell into a group hug. It wasn't long before Joshue was holding a crying Allorah as the fears of the last few days finally overwhelmed her.

Joshue was whispering endearments in her ear as his hands roamed all over her back and head. He needed the contact to convince his unbelieving mind that this wasn't some kind of trick. It wasn't.

Her smell, her sound, her feel. This was home, this was safety. Juan stood by his brother's side, silent tears rolling down his face as he took in the happy scene.

Delmas finally walked over and said, "Excuse me, I just need to grab this," as he took the knife out of Allorah's hand. Then he retreated over to the enclosure, entered, leaving them alone.

Juan said, "Okay guys, I don't know how long he's gonna be in there. Allorah, fill us in on what's going on."

She kissed Joshue one more time, running her hands down his chest, before saying, "I don't know much, but he told me his latest research had cleared the Cartel of any responsibility."

"So, why take us through all of this?" asked Joshue. "Why kidnap you in the first place?"

"Like I said, I don't know much. It's not like we were buddies, sitting around telling all our secrets. I know he confirmed something on the plane ride over here that cleared you two and implicated Felipe. And I also know that he's not working with the organization he was once with. They're running two different investigations."

"Alright," said Juan. "So, we're cleared. We're free. Let's get the fuck out of here!"

"Oh, no!" said Allorah. "He's not letting us go yet. He said something about a big reveal that you guys need to hear." On cue, Delmas emerged from the enclosure and made his way back over to them.

Looking contrite, an expression that looked almost painful on his face, Delmas said, "Because of the actions of me and my family, we have cost yours a great deal of anguish. As an Intelligence Agent, I should have been able to see the facts for what they were and reach the right conclusion from the start. I have no excuse for my sloppy work and I hope one day you'll be able to forgive me."

Juan looked back and forth between his family and Delmas. With a humorless laugh, he said, "You can't be serious! Forgive you? My father and brother are dead because of your people. Look at my fucking hand!" he demanded, holding it up. "And you come over here with a sad expression, say you're sorry, and all is supposed to be forgiven? Fuck you!"

Looking as if he was digging deep for patience, Delmas said, "I understand where you're coming from, but all the stuff you just named wasn't on me. I had nothing to do with the WRA's assault on your home. Plus, after my demonstration, you'll know the truth behind your father and brother dying. And let's not forget that my mother was murdered. If I hadn't been diligent in my hunt for the truth, all three of you would be dead right now."

Ready to get the show started and over with so he could spend time with his wife, Joshue said, "So, what's this big reveal? How is Flip involved in all this?"

"Well, let's hear it straight from the horse's mouth. Come on," Delmas said, leading them over to the enclosure. Once they were standing in front of the glass wall, he said, "You'll be able to hear everything said inside, but he can't see or hear you guys. I'm gonna make him believe that all of you are dead and the only way he can survive is if he tells the whole truth. I actually already figured out most of it, but I want him to tell you out loud."

He turned to enter the room, then stopped once more. "There's only one way in or out, and the code to the door is 15 digits long and changes according to the day and time. Don't try to escape, and don't try any bullshit when I come out. If you do, you'll all just be stuck in here. I'll let you guys free after this is over." Then he went in, securing the door behind him.

They stood and watched as Delmas fiddled with a few machines, then lined up three spray bottles the size of fire extinguishers. It was only then that Joshue noticed what Delmas was wearing.

It was yellow and shiny and conformed to the contours of his body. It was some kind of fire-retardant suit that hinted at how he would get Felipe to confess his sins. The show hadn't even started and his stomach was already rolling in rebellion.

Allorah was glued to his side, constantly touching and stroking, reassuring herself he was still there. She hadn't said a word, just stood watching the preparations being made in the room.

Juan was excited. He was smiling and kept saying how happy he was the fucker was gonna get what he deserved. When Delmas picked up the first bottle, which happened to be yellow like his suit, Juan clapped loudly and, bright eyed, turned to Joshue. "Damn! I wonder if there's a kitchen down here? There's nothing like a little buttered popcorn to go along with a good show."

Then the spectacle commenced.

"Well, my man, you're the last one left," Delmas told the semi-nude man strapped to the board. "Your two friends tried to feed me some bullshit about Carlos being the guilty party. What they didn't know was that we already know part of what happened. So, just a warning: When you talk, and trust me, you will talk, if your story doesn't line up with what we already know, you'll be joining them in death."

Speaking through the oxygen mask strapped to his face, Felipe said, "I'm not Cartel. I don't have a clue about what they do in secret. Joshue hired me to be his bodyguard and that was the extent of my job description."

Delmas tapped his chin in thought, then clasped his hands behind his back and began to pace. "Eight years ago, I had to go to Turkey to pick up a shipment of guns that was destined for the Cartel. I was sitting in their warehouse while they packaged everything up, and they had this fascinating way of doing it. After the pallet was piled high with the equipment, they would drape a plastic sheet over it, spray it down with these chemicals, and then light it on fire.

"The first time I saw it, I jumped up in surprise and the whole warehouse burst out laughing at my alarm. I didn't think it was funny because, anyone with intelligence knows not to set a bunch of guns on fire, right? But, to my surprise, the fire burned hot for a few seconds, then died out on its own, revealing an airtight, plastic seal encasing the product.

"The process intrigued me, to say the least, so I asked how it was done. After the chemist explained the procedure on how to make the mixture and apply it, I asked if he could make some for the WRA." He stopped talking for a bit and walked over to the three multicolored containers. He caressed each of them before turning back to Flip.

"Over the years, our own chemist has taken the formula and perfected it for different uses. The first one," he said, picking up the yellow container, "is the original produced by the Turks. It's effective, gets the job done of sealing plastic, but it's weak, burns too fast. Not really suited for many applications other than that. Let me show you what I mean."

Delmas pulled the hood of his suit over his head, then sprayed Flip's legs with the fine mist from the yellow bottle. Flip had no protection as all he had on was a speedo made from the same material as the suit Delmas was wearing. Only after Delmas walked over and picked up a metal pole, igniting one end with a striker, did Flip start to talk.

"Hold on, man! What the fuck are you doing? I told you I don't know anything!" He tossed his body this way and that as Delmas got within range with the pole. "Don't do it, man! Wait! Nooo!" he screamed when the fire touched the mist, causing flames to crawl up and down his legs.

It only lasted about three seconds, but the pain seemed to be intense. Flip threw his head back and screamed into the mask as his body convulsed. When the flames died away, he slumped. The metal clamps securing him to the board, the only thing keeping him from puddling onto the floor. His breathing was fast, steam billowed off of his skin, but the only evidence of trauma was a series of red splotches on his legs.

"You see what I mean?" Delmas asked after lowering his hood. "This formula is pretty much water with an alcohol base and a fire suppressor, all mixed to produce a fast, but hot, burning fire. Now, this next one," he said, picking up the red bottle. "This one here was the first generation attempt to make it stronger. It's about ten times stronger and burns twice as long as the Turkish mixture. It burns so hot that it melts the muscles off of your bones. Do you need a demonstration?"

All defiance was gone. The Brazilian had no tough talk or threats for his tormentor. "Please! I swear I don't know anything! I'm just a bodyguard. Come on man, let me go!"

Delmas crossed his arms over his chest. "You don't get it, do you? If you don't know anything, then you're a dead man. The only thing that can save you is knowing something. So, do you know anything, or do we move on to the next canister?" Flip went silent. Delmas shrugged, put his hood back in place, and picked up the red can.

"Oh, God! Please! Please don't do this!" Flip begged as Delmas sprayed his legs with the thick mist. He lit the end of the pole once more and, without hesitation, placed the tip in the mist.

This time, blue, orange, and purple flames rippled and danced all over the affected area. Flip screamed and thrashed as the skin, tissue, and muscles melted down his legs like hot wax. Then, just as fast as it started, the fire disappeared, leaving behind a scene straight from a horror movie.

Felipe continued to cry and squirm as Delmas went and picked up a body-length sized mirror from over by the door. Since Flip's head was bracketed in place, this was the only way for him to see the extent of the damage. When Delmas stopped in front of him, revealing to him the condition of his legs, the kid lost his shit. Literally and figuratively.

He soiled himself as his eyes went wide. Bellow after bellow issued from his mouth, gaze steady on his wounds. Even Delmas felt a little sick as he removed his hood and the smell reached his nose. It took all of his training not to gag and reveal that this was the first time he'd actually used any of this stuff on a human being. But the show had to go on. So, he waited until the shouts turned to whimpers, then went on with his plan.

"I want to show you something." Delmas picked up a remote and directed Flip's attention to a screen hanging to his left, near the door. Turning it on, the screen revealed four different rooms, one of which they were standing in. The other three contained blackened, burning bodies, shackled to tables just like the one Flip was now secured to.

Walking over, Delmas pointed to each one as he explained. "Allorah. Juan. Joshue. None of them knew a thing, so they all made it to the black canister. The contents of the last can are drastically different from the other two. While the goal of the Turks was to make something that burned hot and fast, I gave our Chemist a different objective for that one. I told her to make something that would burn slow and at a temperature that would keep the subject alive as long as possible. Of the three, Joshue lasted the longest at 22 minutes and 18 seconds."

Making his way over to the last bottle, he picked it up and moved closer to Flip. "The oxygen mask is the secret. When I used this the first couple of times, as soon as the subject started to scream, the flames burned their lungs. It was pretty much game over after that. The mask and its tubes are treated with a fire retardant that the low temperature flames can't penetrate. So, you can scream and cry and beg, but you'll stay alive, suffering, until the fire dries you out and you die from dehydration."

This time, a light mist didn't issue from the can. A heavy foam-covered Flip's head and torso until Flip screamed, "Alright! Alright! It was me! I'll tell you everything." Delmas stopped spraying the foam and sat the canister on the floor. He pulled over a chair, sat down, and gestured for the man to talk.

"A little over six years ago, the WRA cut off my uncle's gang and started sponsoring another group out of Western Brazil. On that day, Pluto made up his mind to have Ms. Drake killed. I didn't have anything to do with the planning or her execution. My job was to come to Colombia, get in with the Cartel, then figure out a way to blame her death on them when the time was right.

Flip paused, moaning in pain, but Delmas showed him no mercy. “Keep going. Tell me everything.”

After a minute, the kid was able to go on. “I told Pluto that my price for doing this was the life of the man who had killed my sister. After I was allowed to murder my uncle’s General at the whorehouse, I came over here to start my infiltration.”

Flip described how he convinced a mentally unstable Cartel flunky to kill Joshue when he came to their prison. Then, he sat back and watched, stepping up at the right time to save the young Capo. He’d done his research and knew Joshue had nobody to protect him while he did his rounds at the hardcore prisons. So, he put on the exhibition as his interview for the job.

Once he was in, it was just a waiting game. He was to keep his uncle abreast of what was going on with the Cartel, and Pluto would decide when to make his move. When the WRA seemingly turned its back on the Noriega Cartel, Pluto thought the time was right to get his revenge.

“Just out of curiosity,” Delmas interrupted. “Did you ever reveal any of this to the Noriegas?”

“Hell no!” he said emphatically. “The whole plan would fall apart if any of them found out. I had to integrate and really become a part of their circle.”

Delmas nodded. “The plan was perfect, and it actually worked, as far as the WRA was concerned. They were fully invested in blaming the Cartel. There was just one weak point that led to you being strapped to this board. You want to guess what it was?”

Flip thought about it, then slumped when the answer became clear. “The emails,” he said.

Delmas nodded again. “The emails,” he repeated. “It was small, so small the WRA didn’t pick up on it. Two years ago, you moved your mother and grandmother to Medellín,

Colombia to get them away from the warring gangs over in Brazil. Now, when the WRA heard you telling Joshue about your family being dead, it made sense that any correspondence you had with them would have to be secret. But, they missed the fact that, after they moved, your messages were still going straight to Rio."

"I told my uncle years ago that we needed a better way to communicate. I even asked if he could send someone who I could give a verbal message to. That would eliminate any trace. But, with Pluto, any idea that's not his own, is a bad one. So, we kept doing it his way."

"Well, Felipe, I only have a couple more questions and I can get out of here."

"If I answer them, you won't kill me?"

Delmas crossed his heart. "Cross my heart, hope to die, stick a needle in my eye."

Flip exhaled in relief and said, "Ask away," now feeling a little better about his chances to survive.

"How did Pluto know when my mother would be exposed?"

"I know he has someone either on the inside or very close to the core group at the top of the WRA. I never got to see or talk to him, but several times before I left for Colombia, Pluto took meetings with someone he referred to as 'The Mastermind.' I wasn't involved in that part of the scheme, so that's all I know."

"Okay," said Delmas, getting to his feet. "Last question. Why did you kill Carlos and Christian Noriega?"

"Carlos just wouldn't stop digging. I don't know if he sensed something or if he actually had facts, but he kept insisting I was a plant. I saw an opportunity when your brother attacked, and I used it to finally rid myself of the threat."

"And Christian?" asked Delmas.

"The fat bastard saw me in Medellín with my mother, and my hasty explanation about her being the mother of a friend of mine from Brazil, didn't seem to convince him. Before that, he'd always been civil towards me. After, I would see this suspicion deep in his eyes that needed to be dealt with. So, I killed him."

Delmas nodded and started to peel out of the fire suit. "Well, as promised, you answered my questions. The info you gave lined up with what I already knew. So, I'm not going to kill you."

Flip sagged with relief. "For what it's worth," he added, looking confident now, "I'm sorry about your mother. If mine had been murdered in the same fashion, I'd be doing the same thing as you."

"It's not worth a lot since I can't bring her back, but I do appreciate the sentiment." Delmas was now in a pair of black tactical pants, a black t-shirt, and black boots. He gave Flip one last nod, then walked off towards the door.

"Wait!" cried Flip. "Where are you going? I answered your questions!"

Delmas pushed the door open and looked back at Flip. "Yeah, and I told you I wouldn't kill you. But these guys might not show the same restraint." Juan and Joshue appeared at the door, smoldering expressions on their faces.

Walking inside, Juan turned to Delmas. "Will this foam shit actually do what you said it would?" He nodded. "Show me how to light the pole thing." Delmas showed him with a smile on his handsome face.

Flip started to wail. "No! I helped you. I answered your questions. You said I could go free! Joshue, come on man. Don't do this! I'm begging you. Think of my family!"

"Like you thought of mine?" asked Joshue. Delmas walked out of the enclosure to the sound of Joshue saying, "Fuck you! Light his ass up, Juan!" Then the sound of the pole igniting.

Chapter 17

"Tano Jackson?" yelled the guard after knocking on his cell door.

Tano hopped up from the bed and said, "Yeah, what's up?"

"Your lawyer is here to see you."

"Alright," said Tano, reaching for his rag. "Give me five minutes to get myself together."

"10-4," the guard said before walking off.

Normally, the LA County Jail was loud and boisterous, a very dangerous place to be. But, because of his charges, and his known leadership role in the Bloods, Tano was being kept in Administrative Segregation where it was quiet. They say it is for his own protection, like he needed protecting. The real reason was because the officers had a tenuous stranglehold on the jail at the moment. Someone of his fame and stature added to the mix could turn the tide back towards the inmates. That was something the Administration couldn't allow.

Tano yelled down the hall, "Yo! CO! I'm ready." The guard that came this time wasn't the skinny white guy that had first approached his door. This guy was massive, black as midnight, and had a killer's stare. Tano had never seen him before, and he wasn't wearing a name tag.

In a voice filled with bass and menace, he said, "Step back!" Tano eyed the man up and down, then backpedaled to the wall. The man eyed him back and then nodded to the right for the door to be opened. When it did, the behemoth stepped inside and said, "Give me any weapons you have and you might live through this."

Tano said, "I'm in AD-Seg for the duration of my stay. I don't have or need a weapon." The man nodded but still spun him around and, very thoroughly, patted him down. After that, he tossed his bed and his meager belongings, standing up with his hidden cellphone clutched in his hand.

Smiling, which made him look scarier than the earlier scowl, he tucked it in his pocket and said, "One way or the other, you won't need this anymore," before exiting the cell. Looking at someone off to the side, he said, "Take all the time you need, Mr. Burke. Kill him if you have to. We've gotten very good at making anything look like a suicide." Then, another man stepped into view, paused, and entered the cell.

He said, "Hello, Mr. Jackson. You ready to go home?"

Tano squinted. The look was slightly different, but the voice was directly out of his nightmares. He said, "You're the brother! The voice coming from the drone!"

The man nodded and leaned on the wall. "Very good. You already passed the first test. Being detail oriented and a deductive reasoner are skills you must have to survive in my world."

Shaking his head, Tano said, "I have no idea what you're talking about. There's only one world."

Cocking his head, the man asked, "The gang world is different from the civilian world, is it not?" Tano nodded in concession. "Well, my world is the one that actually dictates what the other ones are allowed to do. A world that the movies and books hint at, but they can't fathom how much we actually control."

"Like what?" Tano asked, curious.

"Human rights, laws, elections, gas prices, taxes. Basically, anything that effects the population of the planet, we have a hand in it."

"And who are 'we'?" asked Tano.

"First, let me give you a warning." The man came off the wall with the grace of a born predator. That one simple movement alerted Tano to how dangerous this man actually was. The expensive, dark blue suit couldn't hide the fact that the man was a certified killer.

He continued. "If I fill you in on who 'we' are, then today will be your last day being out of the loop. You accept my proposal, you'll be in the know and you'll join an organization that makes global decisions on a daily basis. If you don't accept it, then you will die, and all your people will stay in prison until they die. I can't have people walking around with knowledge of us who are not under some type of contract."

"What if I don't want to know anything and I tell you to leave?"

The man chuckled. "Then, you get to explain to the DA, judge, and jury how you just happened to be found holding a gun, standing over 13 dead bodies, and some secret Agency is really the one responsible." Shrugging, he said, "In other words, I leave, and you're on your own."

"Doesn't sound like I have much of a choice, Mr. Burke was it?" asked Tano. The man just smiled.

"You can call me Daniel," he finally said. "And you definitely have a choice. Ballistics and science being what it is today, you'll spend years fighting the case from cells just like this one, but eventually you'll go free. The thing is, I like the way you do things. I like how you lead your people, and I want you to use your leadership skills on a much grander scale. That's if you choose to accept my proposal."

Tano considered the man for a bit, then turned his thoughts internal. This was an opportunity of a lifetime. He could feel it in his bones. Just from the small amount of exposure he'd already gotten, he knew that this wasn't a joke. Most gang leaders had visions of conquering and running the world. He didn't think that he would be given that kind of power right off, but this was definitely a step in the right direction.

He tuned back into the man, said, "I accept. Tell me everything." And the man, Daniel Burke, told him an earful.

Thirty minutes later, he concluded with, "I have a compound in San Diego where you and 25 of your top people will go and train to survive and flourish in the world of true power. Your training will last about two years and you will be sequestered during that time. After you complete your training, you'll be sent on missions all over the world. Your life will be good, you'll always have everything you want and need, but your actions will follow a path set forth by others." After a pause, he added, "At least until you reach a management position. Then, you'll be granted free will to do whatever you think is necessary."

"How do I get my people to commit to this? I mean, we'll be signing the rest of our lives over to your Agency!"

Daniel said, "Not really. After the first two years, you'll be on call, and all of you will be tested regularly to make sure you're keeping up with what you learned. When the probationary status goes away, no agent will ever go on more than two missions a year. Plus, after you prove yourself as a sufficient supervisor, you'll get the power to choose who goes on which missions."

Tano nodded, liking the sound of that. "Okay, what kind of pay are we talking about. I'm expecting something in the six-figure range, with all expenses paid on your end."

"Did you just say six-figures?" Daniel asked with a laugh.

"Listen, Mr. Burke. Most of the people I'd want to bring along are millionaires already. These people aren't gonna be motivated to join for bologna sandwiches."

"No! You misunderstand my amusement. I have a twelve-year-old daughter whose allowance adds up to six-figures a year." Shaking his head, he said, "Every agent will be issued a special Black Card that draws from a pool of money set aside for your crew. During training, because none of you will have expenses, you'll get $1 Million a year. After training, it jumps to $10 Million, with bonuses for completed missions. And, of course, supervisors are paid more."

Tano's mouth gaped in astonishment. "And this is each agent, per year?" Daniel nodded and the Blood leader said, "Oh! We can definitely work with that!" His eyes went bright with the possibilities. Then he paused. "What about the guys with families?"

Sighing, Daniel said, “Sadly, that’s one of the sacrifices. The first two years, there can be no outside contact, period. Afterwards, everyone can return to normal life, they’ll just be obligated to respond to any summons. And all illegal activities will have to come to an end.”

Waving that off, Tano said, “The illegal activities are nothing. Most of what we do is just to get guns. After what I saw the other night, I don’t think that will be a concern. Now, the family thing might be a problem. I encouraged all my top guys to go out and start families because it helps to put things into perspective. When you don’t have something to come home to, you might do something stupid, because coming home isn’t important. Getting 25 guys is easy, but getting 25 guys who will excel at this kind of stuff, and are willing to give up their families for two years, might be a little harder.”

Shrugging, Daniel said, “Ultimately, who you choose will be your responsibility. You pick a guy who’s not up for the job, he’ll never leave the compound. Not alive, anyway. Oh! And speaking of who you choose, you’ll have to make them understand that this gangbanging shit will have to take a backseat. I can’t lose agents in the streets, getting shot over what colors they wear.”

“Understood,” was all Tano said on the subject. Then, “So, when do I get out to start recruitment?”

Daniel reached in his inside pocket and pulled out an IPhone. “You get out after recruitment is done.” Handing over the phone, he said, “None of your people’s phone calls will be monitored or recorded. And no one will search you or take your phone. There’s a number saved in the contacts. As soon as someone agrees, you tell them to call that number, say their name, then hang up. When you have 25 names, you and all your people will be freed within the hour. But, be careful who you choose. After the commitment, if they change their mind, they will be disposed of.”

Tano smiled and said, “Be ready to get us out by tomorrow!” But a shadow crossed over his face, snuffing some of his excitement. “There is one problem though, and none of this can happen until it’s taken care of. It would be a favor and an imposition, but it’s a necessity.”

Daniel said, “Shoot.” So Tano told him what had to be done.

He ended with, “If you can give that person a role in the operation, that would be the icing on the cake.”

Daniel considered him and then extended his hand. They shook and he said, “Give me 24 hours to get it done. Get to work on your people. The faster we can get you guys in, the faster we can get you out.” With a small wave, he turned and left the cell without another word.

In seconds, the huge officer was back at his door, holding up the cellphone he’d taken earlier. He smiled and said, “I see you got a thing for Brittanya and Lexi. I heard that they were mother and daughter. On one level, it’s kind of hot to think about being with both of them together. But, then it’s kind of sick.

“On the real, though, you need to get up on that chick, Mia Khalifa. Or even Dani Banks. Both of them girls bad as hell! And you can never go wrong with a big-booty white chick. Am I right?”

He stood there with a smile plastered on his face like he was waiting for Tano to say something. Finally, after an uncomfortable silence, Tano said, “Uh…Okay…Thanks.” The officer nodded, signaled for the door to be closed, then walked off with his eyes glued to a porno playing loudly on the confiscated phone.

Shaking his head at the stupidity of some people, Tano sat on the bed and got to work. He’d told his visitor to be ready by tomorrow, but his goal was to be out by the end of the day. The first call was to his number two, he had to let someone know the whole picture of what was going on. When the call was picked up, he said, “Zero, it’s me. Let me tell you what the fuck just happened. We about to take this shit to a whole nother level, Blood!”

"So," said Delmas. "Do you think somewhere deep down in that wonderful heart of yours, you can find some form of forgiveness for me?" His most charming smile was on display, but Allorah's mean-mug didn't even twitch. "I guess not," he said, frowning.

After exiting the torture chamber, he'd posted up next to Allorah and watched the festivities while working his phone. Juan and Joshue were having a ball listening to Felipe scream as the fire slowly ate away at his body. Allorah wasn't exactly doing her happy dance, but her eyes hadn't left the spectacle since he'd joined her.

Glancing over at him now, she said, "You burned my house down, killed my guards, kidnapped me, beat me up, shackled me to a bed, and that was after you made me strip butt-naked in front of you!"

"Okay, but…" he started.

"And," she said, talking over him. "Let's not forget the threats and insults. Then, you fucking shot me! Now, I'm supposed to forget all of that and use my big, wonderful heart to forgive you?"

She was an absolute vision with her beautiful, brown eyes sparking with anger. Her jean-clad hip, tossed to the side with attitude. Blue pullover stretched taunt from her arms being crossed over her chest. Delmas almost smiled as she focused her heated gaze on the side of his face, but even he knew that any sign of amusement would surely get him smacked.

Turning to face her, Delmas said, "I am truly sorry for the stress and pain I've caused you and your family. I promise to reimburse you for everything you've lost. It was never my intention to hurt you, and I apologize from the bottom of my heart."

With hate-filled eyes, she spun back around, ignoring him as she focused back on her husband and brother-in-law. He really did feel like shit, but there was no other sequence of events he could have set in motion to reach his goal. What saddened him the most was that, he liked the young woman. Strong, brave, gorgeous, and smart was just the tip of the iceberg in naming her attributes. Turning himself, he noticed that Flip had finally succumbed to the damage, and the brothers were on their way out.

Out of the corner of his eye, he saw Allorah's arm fold outward, fist extended in his direction. Dumbly, he stared at it, not sure what she was doing. Sucking her teeth, she asked, "You want to be cool, or not?"

Nodding, he cautiously bumped his fist against hers. She immediately tucked her arm back under the other, then grudgingly said, "I know your people would have been content with killing my husband if it wasn't for you exposing the truth. For that, I thank you, and we'll call it even, except for the money you owe us to replace what you destroyed."

Delmas fought it with everything he had, the smile still slipped through. "So, you forgive me? We're friends now?"

Smugly, she looked down her nose at him. "I wouldn't go that far, but I don't hate you."

Extending his arms, he said, "I think we should hug it out!" The look she gave him had his arms folding back to his sides. "Too soon?" he asked. The hip cock was all the answer he got. Nodding, he said, "Too soon," and turned when the brothers exited the enclosure.

Both of the Colombians sported smiles as they rehashed what they'd just witnessed. "The best part was the swelling of the veins, then watching them explode," said Juan. "I wish we could have kept him alive for days, melting his ass like ice cream!"

Stepping up to Delmas, Joshue extended his hand. "Thank you for exposing that son of a bitch. Your brother was going to kill us, and Flip would have gotten away scot-free."

He shook his hand and said, "I'm sorry I didn't figure it out before he killed your brother and father. But the trail doesn't end here. It might take a few days, but I'm taking a trip over to Brazil." Pausing to appraise the two men, he said, "You're both welcome to join me if you need to."

The brothers glanced at each other and shook their heads. Juan said, "I think we can trust you to handle it. Plus, we still need to pick up the scattered pieces of our lives. And, the other Cartels are still gunning for us."

Delmas said, "I sent Reggie the confession video and he messaged and said he would take care of everything. The fact that the WRA never publicly severed its relationship with you guys, and the other Cartels still felt safe enough to attack? Let's just say, he's going to make them see the error of their ways."

Joshue, hugging Allorah to his side, said, "The Noriega Cartel is dead. As long as our family, and whatever Cartel members are left alive, can live in peace, that's all I ask for."

Chuckling, Delmas said, "I have a feeling he'll make a bigger statement than that. Anyway," he said, clapping once, "I say we get the hell out of here so I can go finish this thing."

Allorah sighed while hugging her husband. "Sounds good to me." Turning to look at him, she said, "Good luck on your mission. Be safe."

"I will," he said with a brief nod. "Who knows, after it's done, we might can all go out for drinks to celebrate!" His grin was met with uneasy glances among the trio. "Too soon?" he asked them.

"Too soon," they said in unison.

Delmas led them across the wide-open area to the exit, where Juan asked, "Don't you have to clean up the, um, mess we left behind?"

Shrugging, he said, "I'm not WRA anymore. It's their problem." He entered the code, opened the way out, and they made their way through the moonlit night, down the side of the mountain.

Looking puzzled, Juan asked, “How the hell did you get us up here?”

Allorah laughed and said, “If I hadn’t seen it myself, I wouldn’t have believed it. He actually carried both of you on his shoulders. He must be half Billy-Goat; never missed a step the whole way up. But I still think he only carried you guys so I wouldn’t try and push him over the edge.” Both men eyed him with a mixture of awe and disbelief. The path was barely wide enough for two people to walk side by side.

Turning a bend, the foursome entered a parking area where the champagne-colored Dodge Ram sat waiting for their return. Delmas immediately launched into detailed directions on how his companions could make it back to civilization. The brothers listened intently, nodded their understanding, bade him farewell, then hustled over to the vehicle. Allorah hung back.

For a minute, no words were spoken. The pair just stood, staring into the other’s eyes. It wasn’t romantic in the least, but it was intimate. An acknowledgement of a shared experience that had created a fragile bond. Then, still without a word, they found themselves in a deep embrace.

She sniffled and Delmas smiled. With her face buried deep in his chest, she said, “This better be an ‘I’ll see you later’ hug. You owe us too much to just disappear.”

He set her back at arm’s length, then nodded over to her husband, who stood waiting at the truck. Turning, she glanced at Joshue, briefly brushed Delmas’ hand, then walked off to join her family.

Right before she entered the vehicle, he yelled, “See you later!” She glanced back with a smile, then climbed in, disappearing from his sight.

Delmas watched the red glow of their taillights until they made the first turn into the woods, feeling an uncommon loss as he pulled out his phone. Entering the number, it only rang once before the call connected. Into the silence, he asked, "Did you review the video?"

Reggie said, "Yeah. Now we can finish this." After a pause, he asked, "Or, do you want to finish it yourself?"

Delmas hesitated with his answer. Lucille Drake was Reggie's mother, also. But none of her children had been as close to her as him. He was thinking of an answer that wouldn't sound too selfish, when Reggie saved him.

"I understand," he said. "Just tell me what you need."

"Not a thing," was his response. "At least not on this mission. As far as the other thing we talked about…"

"Already in the works. By sunrise, there will be no doubt as to where we stand."

Gratitude for his big brother filled his heart. "Thank you," he said, hanging up before he embarrassed himself.

Walking over to what appeared to be a sheer cliff face, he touched a sequence on a hidden panel. A door, 20ft by 15ft, separated from the rock wall and began to roll up. Accessing a website on his phone, he sent a command that made the lights flicker to life inside the WRA warehouse. He stepped inside to do a little shopping for the next leg of his mission. Reggie thought it would end at the next stop; Delmas knew there would be at least one more after that.

Twenty minutes later, Delmas exited the concealed structure in a bulletproof, Military Edition, Rezvani Tank. The satin-black finish, and custom, almost silent, engine would make sneaking up on the enemy a piece of cake. The arsenal he'd stacked on the inside was just in case stealth wasn't possible.

Closing the door with another command, he set off to find the truth. Confirmation to a feeling he had deep in his gut. Flip said the codeword for Pluto's contact had been 'The Mastermind.' Delmas just wondered if the object of everyone's suspicion was the culprit, or if the real puppet master was still lurking in the shadows. One way or another, he would find out within minutes of meeting with his next target.

Chapter 18

Tiago Dos Santos, known the world over as Pluto, was convinced that American men were idiots. Pluto had twelve children, eleven of which were girls. His youngest, only five-years-old, was his only boy. He thanked God every day for his girls, but didn't want to risk bringing any more of them into this cold, brutal world. So, he got snipped. And now, he could enjoy the pleasures of life without the fear of an unwanted pregnancy.

But, back to the topic, American men were imbeciles. They traveled all over the world searching for beauty, when they had the most stunning smorgasbord of women he'd ever seen. Where else could you find a thick, chocolate, doe-eyed, queen, in the same room as a willowy, blond-haired, blue-eyed princess? Nowhere he'd ever been, except in the good old U.S. of A.

Turning the water off after his latest shower, he smiled as he heard the two young women giggling. They were in Rio on vacation, but it had been clear to him from the beginning they'd been searching for an adventure they could talk about once they got back home. American, 20-something, college students, and their dads had paid for them to experience a week in the exotic locale of Brazil. You see, stupid, thought Tiago. Only American men would pay to send their hot and horny little girls hundreds of miles away, just to get fucked.

His own daughters, ages ranging from 7 to 28, were kept in the neighboring mansion to where he lived now. None of them went anywhere without one of his men playing bodyguard\babysitter. His babies would never turn into the cum guzzling, porn star wannabes that men searched for in today's world. He would find nice, rich, handsome men that he had total control of to marry into his family.

Stepping out of the marble enclosure, he dried off and then padded naked into the huge, master bedroom. His

American conquests were still laying naked on the bed, waiting for his return. The Ebony and Ivory pair giggled again at his awestruck gaze when he posted up and stared at their perfection. His appreciation was becoming clearer by the second.

"Aww! He misses us," the chocolate bunny said, eyes flashing with mischief as he continued to rise. At this rate, it might be cheaper to just bring the duo into the shower with him. They had been with him for about five hours now, and he'd just finished his third wash and rinse cycle.

"He looks ready for round four," the ice princess surmised as her fingers slipped, slid, and spread her lower region. Pointing at the massive screen across form the bed, she said, "I think we should try that!"

He shook himself out of his stupor, stepped farther into the room, and almost choked at the spectacle on the screen. The two, heavy-bodied women had the man contorted in such a way, it looked more like torture than sex. He watched as the man threw his head back and screamed as the women showed him no mercy. At 48-years-old, what he was seeing definitely wasn't on tonight's menu. He wasn't sure that, had he still been in his prime, he could perform at that level.

Amber, at least that's what he thought the white girls name was, started to moan as the actresses set their bodies to a faster pace. Vanity, her African-American friend, reached up and twisted Amber's cherry-colored nipples savagely. She yelped, shuddered violently, and shot a clear liquid about two feet across the bed. That was all the visual stimulation Tiago could take. Within seconds, he was on the bed, slamming away at the still coming Amber.

Vanity rubbed his back for a while, then whispered that she was going to get something to drink. He nodded, but his full attention was on the moaning sexpot absorbing every one of his deep, punishing thrusts. Her clutching heat had him ready to explode in minutes, so he used powerful strokes to bring her off just as he himself launched into orbit.

Both breathing heavily and dripping with sweat, he rolled over and closed his eyes. She still wanted more, so she licked all over his neck and chest as her hand playfully pistoned up and down. Eventually, reality set in and she understood that he was done for the night. Then she said, "OK, girl! That's what I'm talking about! I need a few more poundings before calling it a night."

He opened his eyes to see what the freaky girls had come up with, and damn near shit himself. Vanity, snaking her body all over the newcomer, said, "He was sitting in the living room, in the dark, playing a game on his phone. I figured Amber and I could show him a better time. So, I brought him to ask if he could join us."

Pluto had only met the man once before; six years ago, when he and his brother had told him the WRA was moving on. There was only one reason why he would be standing in his bedroom, so he asked the one question he needed to know. "Where's my nephew?"

The girls were starting to pick up on the tension and used their arms to cover themselves. Delmas finally released Pluto's eyes, glanced at the women, and said, "Both of you, get dressed, and take whatever you want on the way out." After a pause where he focused back on Pluto, he said, "He won't be around to use any of it."

The young women didn't know what the hell was going on, but they'd seen enough movies to know when to get out of dodge. They didn't even stay long enough to dress. They just grabbed their belongings, jogged from the room and, seconds later, slammed the front door behind them.

Then…Silence.

Eventually, Delmas Burke walked over to the TV and turned it off. He said, "Cover yourself," before pulling his phone out and sitting it on the dresser, to record the scene, thought Tiago. Then, he sat down in the roll-chair at his desk and placed a gun on his lap.

Tiago, now covered with a sheet, asked, "What about Felipe? What did you do to him?"

Nodding towards the bedside table, he said, "I sent you a video about 15 minutes ago while you were bouncing on the blond. Check it out."

Snatching up the phone, he saw that, indeed, there was a video waiting. Because the WRA Agent was sitting in his home, he knew his nephew had talked. But, whether that had been enough to save his own life was the question. Glancing once more at the man wearing the indifferent mask across his face, Tiago pushed the play button, hoping there was enough of Felipe left to save.

The video started with Delmas Burke explaining that the Noriegas were dead and Flip could save himself by telling the truth. Right then, Tiago knew Felipe was dead. While his nephew was still a babe in the woods in the world of deceit, he could read the lie plainly on the agent's face. Then the torture started, and it broke something inside of him. He knew that what his nephew was going through was all his fault.

Since Felipe had been a little boy, Pluto had been grooming him to take a leadership role in his organization. The forced poverty, the indifferent attitude, the murders of his friends. All that had been fostered on the boy so he could survive later in life. The training had been brutal, and Tiago showed the boy no mercy. But, that was the only way Pluto knew how to achieve his goal.

He looked over at Delmas with tears coursing down his face. "He's just a kid!" he yelled. "How could you do this to a boy?" The man didn't acknowledge his outburst at all. Just sat, unblinking, uncaring about the devastation he'd delivered upon Tiago's world.

When Flip gave his confession, Pluto could see the hope dawning in his eyes. Even with his legs utterly destroyed and useless, the chance to survive fueled his tongue to move. It only caused Pluto to cry harder, being a witness to the childish dream of hope and redemption.

When the Noriega brothers stepped into view, Tiago leaned his head back and let the torturous screams of his ward consume his heart. The two men laughed and prodded Flip, delighting in his anguished existence. He couldn't look, but he listened until the hellacious bellows melted away, the crackling fire the only sound left. With his vision blurred beyond sight, Tiago threw the phone at the agent, sure that someone would be watching his video soon.

They sat in the soft lighting, the atmosphere far from the romantic one of an hour ago. It felt more like a wake as Felipe's soul hung heavy in the air between them. Tiago wasn't naïve in the least; this would be his last day on earth.

"You know," he finally said into the oppressive gloom. "I really did love that boy. But, for men like us, there's a knowledge that we possess that makes it necessary to treat the coming generation a certain way. It would almost be neglectful to fill them with hope and love and kindness. Those things make you a target in this day and age.

"The sad truth is, it's only going to get worse. I hate to see how cold and callous the future world will turn into."

"Well, you don't have to worry about that," said Delmas. "You won't be around for it, anyway."

Getting angry, Tiago said, "I'm still a father! My children will now have to live in a merciless world, with no one to protect them from people like you!"

The agent sat up and tapped his head like he'd just remembered something important. He pulled another phone from one of the hides in his black tactical gear, and started pressing buttons. In less than a minute, his TV switched back on. Tiago's world crumbled beneath his feet.

All twelve of his kids were laid face down on the living room floor of their mansion. Eyes terrified, they dared not move as each body was stretched across some kind of plate with explosives attached to it. His older girls were begging the younger ones not to move, but his young son kept insisting he needed the bathroom.

Tiago looked at the agent with hands clasped in total surrender. “I beg you! Not my kids. Please! I will tell you everything, but spare my children.”

The man shrugged. “The explosives are localized. As long as they stay in place, they will deactivate when I send the code. If one moves before the time, only that child will die. All of your guards are dead, but the deaths can end with you, if you tell me what I want to know.”

Speaking fast, almost in a panic, Tiago asked, “How do I know you won’t just kill them all after I tell you? What assurances can you give me?”

A wolfish grin split the agent’s face. “You don’t trust my word?”

Pluto closed his eyes and sighed in defeat. All he could do was trust the man, trust that this lifestyle hadn’t taken every shred of integrity he possessed. “You want to know the identity of The Mastermind.” He made it a statement because it was the only logical conclusion.

“I want to know his name,” Delmas said. “You give me that, and I promise your children will live. Give me the name of the man inside the WRA who helped you murder my mother.”

Pluto shook his head in confusion. What the hell was the man talking about? Then, a revelation. This man had no clue who The Mastermind really was. He’d thought the premier Intelligence Agency on the planet would have a list of names and would only need his confirmation on the guilty party. But the reality was, they were completely in the dark.

He leaned back and laughed. And laughed. Oh, this was rich! The Mastermind was truly the supreme puppeteer. He wasn’t sure now, when he said the name, he would even be believed.

"I'm glad you are amused," said Delmas. "But remember, it's your son who has to go pee pee." Those words took the laughter right out of Pluto's soul.

He leaned forward and said, "It just caught me off guard to realize how little you know." Having a thought, Pluto said, "This information is a lot more valuable than I figured. I'm not telling you shit until you release my children!"

Delmas smiled. "I remember the first time my mother hugged me and said she loved me. It wasn't because I aced a test or won some sports trophy. No! It was because a kid was picking on my little brother on the school yard, and I put an operation together to kill him. I didn't ask for help or permission to carry it out. I just set the plan in motion, got the kid where I needed him to be, then I slit his fucking throat.

"I burned the clothes, got rid of the weapon, and to this day, the case is unsolved." After a meaningful pause, he said, "I was 8-years-old. So, if you have some scheme floating around in your head that you think will save you and your children, dead it. Because, I'm warning you, I don't negotiate. I don't compromise. You're a dead man, and your kids will join you if you don't tell me what I want in the next ten seconds."

Cold water dashed his fiery hope when the man pulled the gun and started a countdown. "Alright! Alright! Alright! I'll tell you the name. But, I'm warning you; it will be hard to believe."

"Let me be the judge of that," said Delmas. "Give me the man's name!"

"You see, that's the thing," Pluto said, animatedly. "You keep saying 'man'. The Mastermind isn't a man at all. It's a woman. And her name is…"

The gun might have been silenced, but the impact between the bullet and Pluto's head sounded like a watermelon being squashed by a sledge hammer. The glass in the sliding door shattered as Delmas launched himself to the floor. The computer behind the chair he'd been sitting in exploded into a million pieces.

Delmas Army-crawled out of the room as bullets knocked chunks out of the walls around him. The sniper had to be using some type of heat imagery because, no matter which direction he went, the shots got closer and closer. Then, off in the distance, a huge explosion. The shooting stopped.

The first thing Delmas did was pull out his phone and deactivate the explosive under the children. He didn't alert them as he'd told them he would, because being inside, surrounded by the thick walls, might be the only thing keeping them safe.

Gaining his feet, he dashed back into the bedroom and grabbed his other phone from the dresser. There was no need to check on Pluto, his soul had vacated the premises. His phone rang in his hand, and he answered, stopping directly outside the bedroom. He asked, "Was the explosion you or them?"

Daniel said, "It was me. The shooter had a blind up in the woods about a mile away. It was too dense for gunfire to guarantee a kill, but the shooter is dead now. I need you to head in that direction so you can confirm identity."

"On it," said Delmas as he ran from the house and backtracked to the Tank.

Brazil being what it was, only one siren could be heard off in the distance. The cops seemed to want all the bad guys to have ample time to get away before they arrived. Once they found the bodies he'd left scattered all over the estate, the narrative would change. The full investigation would launch, and officers would flood the area.

Daniel was giving him directions for the fastest route to the wooded area. You couldn't take a direct path because roads dead ended and curved without rhyme or reason. But, after three minutes of navigating the maze-like streets, Delmas slammed on the brakes, the whole area heavy with smoke-filled darkness.

Exiting the vehicle, Delmas immediately reached back inside and unhooked a gas mask. The heavy-duty flashlight was clutched in his hand, and his face was covered before he ventured into the destruction left by one of his brother's drones.

All of the trees were leaning towards him as he made his way to the epicenter of the blast. Branches and leaves were burnt, blackened by the immense heat. He trudged through the result of a Burke making sure his kill was true.

Phone tucked in his gear, but on speaker, he said, "The body could be anywhere. How am I supposed to find it in this shit?"

"Hold a sec," answered Daniel. A soft metallic ping issued overhead, then the darkness receded as a sun-like orb brilliantly lit the area. Delmas became transfixed with the apparatus. He'd never seen anything like it. The sphere floated just below the canopy of leaves and illuminated everything. No more shadows. Delmas stored his flashlight and spotted the body in seconds. At least what was left of it.

He rushed over to the corpse and focused the lens of his phone on the blackened buddle. "Little brother, I think we have a problem." After recording it from every angle, Delmas forwarded the video. "ID isn't gonna happen today."

"No worries," said Daniel. "We can always use DNA. Just scrape off the burnt flesh, and get a sample from the fresh meat underneath."

His stomach rolled. "You want me to skin the corpse, dig around for some medium rare meat, then cut some of it off?"

Daniel sighed. "Cops are already descending on Pluto's estate. They'll be making their way to your location soon. Stop acting like a baby and try to get us some good samples."

This is some real-life bullshit, thought Delmas. He knew Daniel could scan the body and get all the info he needed. His brother was still punishing him for voting to keep him in prison. Issuing a sigh of his own, he pulled out his knife and got to work.

Five minutes later, he was back in the Rezvani, motoring away with several meat samples stored in the back. Delmas asked, "Where do I need to take these samples?"

Daniel chuckled. "If I fill you in on a secret, you promise you won't be mad?"

Shaking his head, Delmas said, "You motherfucker! You already know who it is!"

Full on laughing now, Daniel couldn't control himself enough to keep up the charade. "Oh my God!" his brother proclaimed. "The video of you hacking into the corpse is going to everyone except Gabby. I just knew you were going to throw-up!" He fell out laughing once again.

Delmas tried to hold onto his anger, but it felt too much like old times for him to be mad. Letting his own amusement show, he said, "Make sure I get a copy, too. Who knows when I'll need something to give me a good laugh?" Then the brothers disconnected.

Navigating the Tank back across Brazil, Delmas was troubled. He sent the video of Pluto's investigation to both Daniel and Reggie, inquiring what they thought of it. Two hours into his drive, all three of them were on the phone, along with his sister, Kashonda.

Daniel said, "I ran the video through every lie detector software I have, and he seems to be telling the truth. Whoever this Mastermind is, at least Pluto was convinced it was a woman."

"Flip said that his uncle met with the person numerous times," said Delmas. "I think he would know if he was meeting with a man or a woman."

Kashonda added, “But, if the person he was meeting was just a stand-in, then without her identity, we’re back at square one. The Mastermind could be anyone.”

Kashonda Wilson, at 48-years-old, was the oldest of the siblings. At 5’ 1”, with her flawless, brown complexion, and hazel-colored eyes, she could ensnare any target with her beauty. But when that wasn’t an option, the WRA’s Head of Intelligence could conquer any foe with her mind. Her network was legendary in the spy world. With one call, she could get the rundown on anyone.

Reggie finally spoke up after a minute of silence. “Since everyone on this call is up to date on the Uncle Situation, I think that is the most logical solution to this mystery.”

Daniel said, “I don’t think it’s wise to jump to conclusions on this. I’m sending each of you a file on the shooter down in Brazil. Since Delmas is driving, I’ll give the abridged version out loud.” He paused as if to gather his thoughts, then went on.

“White male, age 51, goes by the name of John Hester. Marine sniper, dishonorably discharged after pleading guilty to assault with intent for shooting a fellow soldier. Picked up by the CIA in the early 2000s, but was let go after his third unsanctioned hit.

“A lot of training dealing with land survival and staying off the grid. Last time he surfaced was eight years ago when a Sheriff’s deputy in the mountains of North Carolina tried to bring him in for hunting out of season. Neither Mr. Hester nor the deputy was seen again.

“I cross-referenced his name with the personnel files of everyone in the WRA and came up empty. I also went ahead and studied each person’s travel to and from South America, but 85% of all agents have been to the area in the last five years. And, because the targets are normally men the WRA was trying to get closer to, of the 85%, three quarters of them were women.”

"So," said Delmas, "the shooter is a dead-end, but not every female agent who has been to the area would have had the information on our mother's departure place and time."

"On top of that," added Kashonda, "a female agent who fits into those parameters, but would also have a reason to want her dead, cuts the list down even more." They stayed silent as each of them thought about that.

Reggie asked, "Are we assuming that this was the same shooter who took out Mom?"

"I have a theory on that, but I can't prove it at this time," said Daniel.

"Come on, Little Brother, share," said Delmas. "We're getting along too well to hold back now."

Daniel mumbled something derogatory about his intelligence before he continued. "Well, I've studied the videos of the scene and the surroundings at the time of the murder. I wouldn't expect any of you to have noticed it because I'm the one who set up the security for the HQ. But, one of the surveillance drones was off course."

Reggie said, "Right after the hit, I ordered the drones to the area I thought the shot came from. That might be what you saw."

"No," said Daniel. "About a mile away from headquarters, a drone that was supposed to be facing out, all of a sudden, blinked off. Phung might have attributed it to the weather or the fact that diagnostics were being run around the clock to make sure all the updates I sent were installing properly. But, seconds after the shot, it blinked back on, and it was facing the other way, and was only ten feet off the ground. From that position, the drone could have been used to fire the shot. That would explain why no human presence was detected immediately following the hit."

Delmas said, "All this is news to me. I haven't seen the video. But, if what you are suggesting can be taken as fact, Mom's murderer was in HQ when all this went down."

"Exactly," said Daniel. "Any computer in the control room, or in the family wing, could have been used. Insert a small virus to take the drone off the main server, then control it from the same station. After it's done, destroy the virus, log it back into the system, and the culprit sits tight knowing to run would be a red flag."

"There are cameras all over the control room," said Kashonda. "And, to use a computer, you have to use a personal log-in that would link you to any action taken."

"That's why no one would do it in the control room," said Reggie. "They would use the family wing where there are no cameras or log-ins needed."

After a short pause, Delmas said, "Well, that means the woman Pluto was meeting with was a stand-in, after all."

"Or," said Daniel, "it was with a woman who has access to the family wing."

Another silence.

Reggie asked, "Would this person have to be present to carry it out, or could it have been programmed beforehand?"

"No, the person would have had to upload the virus, direct the drone to lock onto a target, then delete the evidence of the conspiracy," said Daniel.

"Kashonda?" asked Delmas. "Why are you so quiet? You have something to confess?"

"Fuck you, Delmas! I had no reason to kill her," she stated.

"We'd all just found out she killed our father after setting him up. And you were a pawn in that scheme as you were one of the ones who found the 'evidence.'" he reminded them. "Maybe Uncle Ronald started whispering in your ear and you decided to take action."

Daniel said, "Delmas has a point. Kashonda wasn't in the control room when this went down."

"You know what?" asked Kashonda. "Fuck both of you! If anyone could have pulled off a drone hit, it's Daniel. We're taking his word on all this speculation, anyway. For all we know, he stood right out in the open and shot her down. Then, he messed with the drones so we couldn't see him. It was his updates that supposedly provided the cover for the drones to be moved around."

"Alright guys," said Reggie. "The bottom line is, we have to find this woman. We can sit here and speculate until we're blue in the face. Until we have solid evidence, we all need to focus our energy on uncovering this woman's identity. And Delmas, you need to stay as far away from the US as possible. Every cop in North America is looking for you."

"Yeah, I know." He merged onto the highway and said, "Thanks a lot, family." The dig didn't illicit a response from any of them. "Hey Reg, did you handle that for the Noriegas?"

"Been handling it for over a day now. When we hang up, I'll make the calls to set everything right."

"Well," said Delmas. "I have to admit it's good to be working as a team again. Maybe I can hide out down here for a while, and the WRA can use its influence to clear my name."

"There's one obstacle in the way before we can handle that," said Reggie. "But, I have it on good authority that the obstacle won't be there much longer."

"I hope this authority is reliable and fast," said Delmas. "I want to come home."

Kashonda, hearing the melancholy in his voice, said, "Soon, little brother. We'll all be together soon. Stay safe and call if you need anything. Even though you all just accused me of killing our mother, I love you guys, and I'll talk to you later." She hung up after they returned her endearment.

Delmas said, "I'm going back to Tunja. I'll use the facilities there to continue my research and stay off the radar."

"Be safe," said Reggie.

"You know I got your back," said Daniel.

Feeling himself getting emotional, he said, "Later," and hung up.

He had hours to go before he could rest in safety, but even that rest would be short lived. He would keep at his task, tracking down whoever was responsible for his mother's death. No matter where the trail led him, he'd follow. Delivering death until he was convinced that his mother was resting in peace.

Chapter 19

As soon as Delmas hung up the phone, Daniel said, "Okay, tell me what you have."

Reggie, sitting on the couch in his living quarters, frowned. "What makes you think I have something?"

"Let's not play games, Big Brother. It's late, you still have to make your calls for the Noriegas, and I'm getting less and less sleep the closer this wedding date gets."

"Why less sleep?" asked Reggie. "You getting cold feet?" Once upon a time, Reggie had been married. In his ignorant youth, he thought love could overcome all. Too many late nights and not answered phone calls ended the marriage before it even got underway. He wasn't gonna dish to his little brother about the pitfalls of their way of life, but forever doesn't last always.

"Stay on topic, Reggie," Daniel said with attitude. "Just tell me."

Heaving out a breath, Reggie said, "Until you filled us in on your theory, I didn't think it was important. Now that I know how it could have been done, I think I know who's behind all this."

"Alright," said Daniel. "Tell me."

"Uh, I think it will be better just to show you." Reggie pulled up the video file on his phone, then sent it to Daniel's email account. "It's about 30 minutes long, but only about five of them are relevant. The other 25 just establishes a time frame. Anyway, this is a compilation of ten cameras following the progress of the subject."

"Okay, let me watch it, and I'll call you back. Go ahead and make your other phone calls." Daniel hung up.

Reggie picked up his remote control and flipped through numerous news channels until he found one reporting on the fires spreading all over Central and South America. Dialing the first number, he sat the phone down, put it on speaker, then turned the volume up loud enough for the other person to hear.

When the call was answered with an annoyed, "What!" Reggie stayed silent and let the young lady do the talking for him.

She was saying, "…Cartels seem to still be at war as explosions and fires spread across the lower Americas. Compounds, businesses, vehicles, pretty much anything of value that is a suspected Cartel holding, is being targeted. We recently reported on the virtual extermination of the Noriega Cartel, and we can only assume that the survivors are launching a massive retaliation effort for the insult."

Wildfire-like scenes played in the backdrop; landscapes that looked as apocalyptic as a warzone between heaven and hell. Chard scenery and smoldering buildings were shown by the dozens. "Thousands of people had to be evacuated as fields and structures linked to the manufacturing of cocaine burned and created toxic clouds over villages."

The reporter paused as villagers could be seen running through the dense fog with shirts wrapped around their faces. She ended with, "If this continues, the death toll could reach into the thousands; property damage could reach into the billions. Let's just hope that as many innocent bystanders as possible can escape before this battle escalates even further."

Reggie muted the TV and picked up the phone. "I don't know who thought that it was okay to defy a WRA directive, but the Noriegas are still under our protection. Any further aggression shown towards them, will result in swift retaliation against your organization. Are we clear?"

Grudgingly, the man said, "Clear."

"Are you sure you got it?" asked Reggie. "You don't sound convinced."

"I got it," said the man. "I understand. We thought…"

"Don't think," Reggie said, cutting him off. "From now on, I'll let you know what to think." Reggie didn't give him time to respond, he just hung up and moved on to the next number.

He'd just finished up with his fifth call when Daniel's number popped up. He answered with, "So, what do you think?"

"It was definitely her," said Daniel. "I did a deep dive into the system and the terminal in that room was where the virus originated. What do you want to do about it?"

Reggie thought long and hard before he answered. "If we had found out that Uncle Ronald was the culprit, what would we do?"

Without hesitation, Daniel said, "Killed him."

"I don't think it should be different for her," he said. "But, I don't think it was a coincidence that she did this right when our uncle returned. I think they're working together."

"Anything is possible," said Daniel, sounding tired of the whole situation. "You want me to handle it, or do you want to?"

Reggie sighed. "No, I'll handle it. You're already taking care of the other problem." Switching gears, he asked, "What's happening with Tano and his crew?"

"He has twenty of his people committed so far. I have something going down first thing in the morning that I feel will convince the other five he wants to sign on. Everyone has been vetted and, barring any delays or unfortunate deaths, we should have them in San Diego in a day or two."

Reggie had decided that Terrell 'Big Zoe' Rilley and his crew were doing so good with the businesses on the East Coast, it was time to expand to the West Coast. They would start buying up the businesses while the new crew was in training, then use the fresh batch of agents to develop another revenue stream. Not to mention, the WRA would have 26 more soldiers to call upon.

"Okay," said Reggie. "Let me know if you need anything to supplement your plan for Uncle Ronald, and I'll do the same."

"10-4," said Daniel before he ended the call. Almost immediately, Reggie got an encrypted message from his brother on email. He read it and sent a reply back in acknowledgement, leaned back, thankful for his brother's planning.

This fucking family, he thought. He shouldn't be surprised, but the depths these people would sink to was getting ridiculous. Sitting on the couch, he thought for hours of an alternative to killing The Mastermind. Nothing surfaced. So, he did what the Burkes have been doing for longer than he's been alive; he sat and planned the murder of a member of his family.

The first thing Ronald said when he stepped inside her apartment was, "They know about you and they're planning to kill you!" He said it as if she was supposed to jump up and run for the hills. Instead, she looked at him and shrugged.

"It doesn't matter anymore," she said, flippantly. "As long as the bitch preceded me in death, I'll die with a smile on my face."

The Valduero wine, one of her favorites, flowed down her throat with the grace of an Olympic ice skater. She was perched on her couch, still dressed in her lambskin skirt, and Max Mara turtleneck. Her only concession to the time of night being her suede pumps removal; her bare, painted toes peeking from underneath her legs.

"I don't think you understand," said Ronald, impatiently. "They won't just shoot you in the head and send you painlessly off into the fade. They think you're working with me, so they'll torture you to find out the truth."

"Listen to me, Ronald," she said, finally setting her glass down and focusing on him. "The bitch needed to die! I did this family, and this Agency, a favor. I'll explain everything that she did, and everything will be fine. Just because you foolishly let them find out about your true identity doesn't mean we're all fuckups like you."

Throwing his hands up, he said, "How the hell was I supposed to know that the new Internal Investigator would find a hidden file that Lucille kept? Or that the file even existed? Daniel scoured the WRA servers hundreds of times and never uncovered it!"

"That's because you had his mind mastered. But, look at history. There's always something small and stupid that brings down an empire. In this case, it just happens to have a name: Ronald Burke!"

"Hey!" he exploded. "You better watch your tone, little girl!" He took several advancing steps before he stopped, right by her side. Looking down on her, he said, "If you think for one second you'll be able to talk your way out of this, you will die a slow and horrible death. I've fine-tuned Daniel into the instrument he is today. You can undermine his training by playing on his emotions, but Reggie is a different animal."

Standing up, she faced off with the idiot. "Don't worry about me, I'm a real Burke. Unlike you, I wasn't thrown away to be raised among the other family castoffs. My intelligence is far superior to yours and I don't need advice on how to survive a Burke man!"

He had the audacity to laugh in her face. "And yet, with all of your advance intellect, you didn't think someone would break the rule about cameras in the family wing? You are as arrogant as you are naïve, and those traits will be the death of you. True Burkes survive. Look at what I've been through! You've never been tested. A protected Burke Princess that's about to get a rude introduction into the real world."

Amused, she said, "You really think you're a survivor?" At his nod, she tossed her head back and roared with laughter. When she could talk, she said, "You're a coward! A scared ass little boy who ran from one of those Burke

Princesses you refer to with such disdain. Now, you're face to face with another one. One who has been on the frontlines, steering this family like a real leader. I don't think I need to point out that you decided to take a less dangerous route.

"Instead of proving and claiming your heritage, you ran off and hid, accepting your fate as the runt of the litter. Even today, when you could flex your inheritance and take over with a word, you still tuck your little wee wee and piss down your leg like the pussy you are!"

The slap came out of nowhere and tumbled her over the coffee table to land, splayed across the floor. She screamed in outrage as she clamored to her feet. Only to freeze when she saw the gun pointed at her head.

Barring her teeth, hair wild and in her face, she said, "You better shoot me! I'm gonna kill you if you don't!"

Clinching his jaw, he said, "I should, but I'd never be able to explain it away." Backing up a few steps, he added, "I think I'll just leave you to die by Reggie's hand. He might be on his way to get you right now." Continuing his backpedaled escape, he tucked his gun and gave a little wave before stepping into the sally port. He smiled as the door closed between them.

Rushing over to the couch, she grabbed the gun that was stuck between the cushions. "Stupid fucker!" she mumbled as she watched him exit out of the door to her rooms. Hitting the button to be used only in emergencies, both doors locked open as she dashed into the hallway behind him.

"HEY!" she yelled to his retreating back. Just as she knew he would, due to his inferior training, he ducked and spun while reaching for his gun. He never made it around to face her.

Two shots took out the arm reaching for the gun. Two more destroyed both his knees. On his way to the ground, she put one in his throat before rushing over to look down into his startled eyes. As he began to choke, she had one last message for him.

"Fuck all that Princess shit! I'm a Burke Queen, motherfucker! And this Queen will be the one to send you to hell! Remember this face, because one day, I'll join you. And I'll be the one responsible for extinguishing your worthless soul." She spit in his face, then put one more bullet between his eyes.

Contrary to her boast, she didn't want to die anytime soon. So, in true Burke fashion, she was prepared to disappear at a moment's notice. Dashing back into her suite, she pressed the button to seal the doors behind her. She ran full out to her bedroom and changed into clothing conducive to running. Grabbing a bag filled with nothing except money and documents, she shouldered it, then returned to the living room.

The true training of the Burkes meant that, she knew she would be found out eventually. And, knowing how ruthless her family could be, she had invested in an escape route that no one else knew about. Pressing a button on the side of her couch, it swung 90 degrees to reveal a trap door. She entered the code and yanked the door as soon as the lock popped.

Descending the ladder into darkness might have been unnerving to some, but it was a comfort to her. Reaching the bottom, she pressed the button to return the living room back to its normal state. They would run an x-ray of the room at some point and find the hatch, but she would be long gone by then. Hopefully.

Flicking the switch on the wall, a soft glow filled the tunnel. She took one deep inhale and exhale to force herself to calm down. After living in almost debilitating fear for so long, discovery was its own kind of relief. She was far from being safe and secure, it was almost impossible to hide from the WRA. But, if anyone could do it, The Mastermind, as she'd been known for the past six years, could. She just had to stay diligent and always be prepared and she'd be just fine. Anyway, it wouldn't be long before she would be in a position where she wouldn't have to run from anyone.

Making it to the exit, she was almost afraid to open the door. Paranoia paralyzed her as she envisioned Reggie or Daniel waiting on the other side. Pulling her gun, she entered the code and stepped back as the door lifted from its setting.

Nothing or no one made a sound.

She crept to the edge and peered out into the pitch blackness of the night. Nobody jumped out to grab her. Taking a glance at her watch, she realized that she still had four minutes until the blind spot in the rotation would appear. Facing back into the tunnel, she kept her gun trained forward until the time indicated it was safe for her to carry on.

Stepping fully into the cold air, she led with her gun, but couldn't find a target. A tear actually trickled down her face as she started running across the wooded landscape. If she had miscalculated by a second, one of the drones could pick her up and lead the WRA patrols directly to her, but she couldn't think about that. Making it to the next tunnel door, she quickly entered the access code, dropped and rolled into the foot-wide opening, then surveyed her backtrail for pursuit.

Now, she started to relax.

Closing everything up, another switch filled the tight tunnel with light. This one, a man would have to turn sideways to chase her, and the construction pattern would be confusing and deadly to anyone not familiar with the layout. She jogged for an hour. The stale air and the pack strapped to her back made sweat pour down her body. But she made it to the end.

The same anxiety hit her before she opened the door and entered another wooded area several miles from the WRA headquarters. She trotted to the tree line and scanned the gas station parking lot for anything that didn't fit. After a 15 minutes study, she walked out of the trees and jumped into the driver's seat of a 20-year-old Honda Accord after tossing her bag on the backseat.

Labeled as one of the most reliable cars on the road, the designation proved to be true as its engine turned over and she took off into the night. Hour after hour, mile after mile, she was on high alert for any sign of being followed or surveilled.

Nothing. Nobody was on her tail.

Finally, the relief of escape filled her heart and soul as she blended into the early morning traffic on the Georgia highway. A smile lit her face, accomplishment causing happiness to course through her veins. She was free. Finally from under the thumb of her secret life of fear.

Faces floated into her mind, but she pushed them away. There was no room for regrets. She could never return. Always had to move forward. Could never afford to look back.

Pulling into another gas station, this one remote and almost empty, she left behind the only connection she had to North Carolina. The car had to stay. She abandoned it and took off walking, a smile on her face, and a pep in her step.

The Mastermind was dead. Now, she was just a woman. A normal woman, looking for a life where she never had to be afraid again.

Chapter 20

Reggie was still deep in thought, plans manifesting, analyzed, and rejected, one after another. He knew what needed to be done, and he would do his duty. But this single act might be the catalyst that brought the WRA to its knees.

Then the alarm sounded.

The piercing *Beep! Beep!* was quickly followed by his cellphone ringing, the normal response made by security to alert him to the cause of the alarm. "Yeah," he answered, somewhat annoyed with the interruption. Then the security guard told him what was going on, and he was on his feet, running as he demanded, "Get the whole family over there, now! If you have to drag everyone out of bed, I want to see each and every one of them. And keep everyone away from the body. I'm on my way!"

He didn't have far to go as he bolted out of his suite and rocketed down the hallway. He passed guards awakening his family members, the lights still flashing, the alarm blaring. Slamming on the brakes, he turned the corner and came face to face with Mike, the head of WRA security.

The old man had obviously been aroused from sleep himself, he was still in his pajamas. Silver hair unruly, and face ashen, he said, "The facility is locked down. Guard found the body four minutes ago on his 15-minute round. Silencer had to have been used because no gunshots were heard. Nothing has been touched, as per your instructions."

Reggie nodded, patted the man on his shoulder, then walked around him to view the body of his uncle, Ronald Burke.

The man was laid flat on his back in a pool of blood, staring into nothingness. There would be no resurrection this time around, the bullets doing the job that the airplane crash had failed to do. Reggie skirted the body, seeing at least five, possibly six, gunshot wounds. The killer hadn't taken any chances as either the neck or head wound would have been enough to take his life. A scream behind him signified the arrival of the family. Reggie turned and pointed, said, "Hold them back! Don't let anyone through!"

The family crowd continued to grow as Reggie stepped off to the side to watch the video of what occurred on his phone. A hidden camera, just feet away, revealed the murderer executing Ronald with a horrifying deliberateness. Six shots in total, the final one delivered at point blank range. Then she scurried off, no doubt with plans of escape floating in her mind.

He watched as two guards approached Mike and they had a heated discussion. Mike turned toward him, dropped his head, and trudged over with uncertainty blanketing his every motion.

Before the man could speak, Reggie said, "Let me guess. You have no record of her leaving HQ, but her suite is empty. Nothing looks disturbed. Nothing packed?" Mike nodded with confusion lacing his face. "I'll have to fill you in later on. For now, go ahead and secure her rooms. And get forensics working on this scene. They might turn up something important that we can't see." Mike nodded and started issuing orders to the men around them.

Ignoring the shouts of his family for the time being, Reggie made his way over to the suite belonging to The Mastermind. He entered through the two wide-open doors, head on a swivel, eyes scanning for any sign as to where she'd gone. Twenty minutes to a normal criminal wasn't enough time for them to do much. To a Burke on the run, it was akin to an eternity.

He walked through, the two security guards still poking around looking for any hiding places. He spent about 15 minutes opening every drawer, every closet, hoping something would catch his eye. He thought about Daniel's tunnel system and how The Author had been able to gain access. It was almost two in the morning, but he called his brother anyway, praying that it wasn't too late to pick up a trail.

Daniel answered with, "You see what I mean? Less and less sleep."

Reggie didn't beat around the bush, he explained everything that had happened since he'd talked to him hours ago. He ended with, "I was hoping you had some kind of way to tell if she'd used your tunnels to escape."

"Hold on a sec," he said. Reggie waited patiently as his brother did whatever he had to do before hearing, "Well, she didn't use my tunnels. I suggest having someone come in and x-ray the room. My tunnels might not be the only ones available."

"Alright. The bonus in all this is that she made it so you can stop planning how to kill Ronald. I'm sending you the video. She annihilated him. They had a meeting before it happened, so your email was spot on. Our call was definitely ease dropped on."

Daniel scoffed. "Did you doubt what I said? I could have killed it, but I wanted to see what would happen. My guess, he heard us confirm her identity and went to warn her and make sure she kept her mouth closed about him. They disagreed on something and it cost him his life."

A ruckus occurred that had the phone rattling around for a few seconds. Daniel cursed and said, "I have to go before Alisha kills me for keeping her up. Get with Phung, I sent her some security upgrades that covered all of the outside blind spots. If she finished them, you should see her leaving. Talk to you later," he said before hanging up.

He called Phung.

The dark-haired, beautiful, IT Head was already inside the compound because she was personally handling the upgrades to their system. She answered the call with, "Is it okay if I turn off the alarm?" At his permission, the alarm and flashing lights quit, leaving behind blessed silence. "OK, Boss. What can I do for you?"

"I just talked to Daniel and he mentioned some perimeter blind spots that the new security would cover. By any chance, have you taken care of those yet?"

"The second thing I did after strengthening our firewalls," she answered. "Why? Do I need to try and locate someone?"

"Check all the footage and tell me if anyone was seen leaving the area in the last hour."

"That won't take long. Part of the package Daniel sent included a priority movement recording. It's a simple system, something we should have had long ago. But basically, it picks up all movement and puts those videos in a priority file for easy viewing. You get a lot of animal and bird videos, but after I configure it a bit, we will…Hold on, I got someone…What the hell is she doing?"

Reggie perked up. "How long ago was the movement?"

"Hold on, I'm tracking."

Reggie jogged over to the door and yelled for Mike to come. When the Head of Security arrived, he said, "Phung has found the subject's escape. I need you to get a squad over there to see what they can find. I also need you to order an x-ray of this whole suite so we can find how she disappeared."

"Ok," he said. "Where do I send the men?"

"Uh, Reg?" said Phung. "This is not good. I'm sending you the clip now, but she's gone. Um, why is she running, anyway?"

"Let JT take over in the control room and get yourself down to the family wing. I'll tell everyone at the same time."

"Oookkaayyy," she said, slowly. "I'm on my way."

Reggie watched The Mastermind as she emerged from a hidden door on the side of a hill. Mike, watching over his shoulder, began using the radio to direct men to the shown area. She ran full out as the drone captured her every movement through the woods. With just his vision, he could barely make her out, but the drone was using technology that highlighted her body for easy following. All of a sudden, he saw her go down, almost like she tripped. But then, she disappeared altogether.

Mike said, "We're on it. I sent some agents to tag along with my security guys. We'll access the tunnels and find out where she went." The man might look ridiculous in his orange and blue, striped pajamas, but he was utterly confident in the performance of his duties. Reggie nodded and exited the suite, the x-ray tech entering as he left.

As he made his way towards his family, he skirted the WRA forensics team, still processing the body and the scene. When his family caught sight of him, the questions were launched in rapid-fire succession.

"What the hell is going on?" "Who killed Glendo?" "Do we have them in custody?" "Why are you keeping us in the dark?" "Why won't you talk to us?" "You need to tell us something, now!"

He had just raised his hand for silence when Phung turned the corner, took in the scene with razor-sharp understanding. She yelped, hands coming up to cover her mouth in disbelief. Her eyes bounced from Reggie to the body and back again, revelation dawning in her eyes.

She dropped her hands and said, "It's not possible! Please tell me she didn't do this!"

The family swarmed her.

"Who is 'she'?" "What do you know?" "Tell us what you know!"

The shouted questions peppered them both as Phung backpedaled, eyes searching his own. It was clear that she was wondering why he hadn't told the crowd what was going on. He ignored her gaze as he wadded in to gain control of the chaos.

"HEY! HEY!" he screamed, pushing and pulling until his body was between his family and Phung. "Calm the fuck down!" After the noise died down, he pointedly looked at the security standing around watching them before saying, "Follow me," and headed off down the hall.

The group followed him in silence. This close to answers, none wanted to fuck up and be excluded. He opened his own suite's door and everyone piled into the narrow sally port, waiting for the outer door to close and the inner one to open. Once it did, he turned right and ushered everyone into his personal library. He said, "Have a seat."

The oak-paneled room was lined with shelves of books and knick-knacks. Some of the volumes were worth buckets of money, as they were rare finds or first editions. This was the first time some of the attendees were seeing his space, but none took more than a cursory glance as the mad dash for a seat commenced.

Because the room was so big, 50ft by 75ft, the rush was unnecessary, but he could feel the anticipation filling the space. When everyone was seated and eagerly looking in his direction, he pulled out his phone and made a call. He said, "Come to my suite, security will let you in," before hanging up and telling his family, "Give me a couple minutes, then I'll fill you in."

The training level of everyone in the room was off the charts. Assassination missions, personnel recovery, infiltrations of enemy countries. All of that was done with barely a twitch in their stoic outer shells. But now, legs twitched, feet tapped, knees bounced, hands were wrung. A powder keg of energy about to explode if he didn't tell them something soon.

Every head turned when they heard the inner door to the suite open and close. Heavy footfalls announced the advance of the man he had called to join them. When Walter Rogers appeared at the door, he looked just as confused as they were. Figuring answers wouldn't be coming from him, all eyes focused back in Reggie's direction.

He told Walt, "Join me so we can explain what's going on to the family." When Walt stood next to him, he said, "Explain to everyone who the body is out there, and how you reached that conclusion." Walt eyed him for a bit, then turned his attention to the family. Finally, he shrugged and launched into what he knew.

"Well, it started when I found a note in one of Lucille's personal files. It led me to…" He talked for a solid ten minutes, and his message left mouths hanging open and postures rigid in shock.

Before the inevitable avalanche of questions rolled over them, Reggie picked up the tale. "So, my mother was innocent after all. But the plot thickened when the real Mastermind exposed herself."

He went into detail about how Delmas had inadvertently stumbled into an assassin that was used by The Mastermind while trying to lockdown evidence on Ronald. This led them to the discussion where Daniel explained how the sniper might not have been the trigger man on Lucille.

"Now, I have to inform you all of something that might piss you off, but you'll see why I thought it was necessary." Huffing out a breath, he said, "A while back, I installed tiny cameras in the family wing so I could keep track of a certain individual's movements." This statement was met with silence, so he continued before they could launch an attack.

"When Daniel explained how this murder could have been perpetrated without a human shooter, we used the videos to identify The Mastermind. I'll show you the proof now." He powered up his 80 -inch monitor and pulled up the video that showed The Mastermind killing Ronald. Then he showed them the video of her using underground tunnels to escape the compound. Once again, everyone sat in stunned silence.

Finishing up, he said, "We have agents and security out combing the woods and infiltrating the tunnels to try and find where she went." Just then, his cellphone rang, and a picture of Mike's pasty face filled the screen. Reggie picked it up and said, "Yeah?"

"Mr. Burke, I was calling to give you an update on what we've found."

"Hold on, Mike," said Reggie. "I'm gonna put you on the big screen so the family can hear it firsthand." After connecting the phone to the monitor using Wi-Fi, he said, "Go ahead with the report."

"So, we used the video to locate the two tunnels she used to escape. The first, we backtracked and found a hatch leading up into her suite. With the help of the x-ray tech, we found the access door under the couch and JT hacked the code."

JT was Joseph Tarlton, a young computer whiz that Daniel had tracked down and made him a job offer he couldn't refuse, at least not if he wanted to live. Once he was transported to their HQ, he was put through rigorous testing to see if he could make it in their world. After proving he could, Phung made him her personal assistant, and soon after, because of his outstanding work, her second in command.

"Now," continued Mike. "The other tunnel was a different ballgame. It was designed so close pursuit by a man would be damn near impossible. It is long and narrow with zigzags that kill any line of sight. It contains several false tunnels that are littered with traps and snares, but we made it to the end. The exit came out at another wooded area a few miles away at a gas station.

"A hack of the store's cameras showed her getting into an old, blue, Honda Accord. We are using the IT Department to track her from there, but I'm sending you what we have so far."

"Thank you, Mike." Reggie hung up the phone and focused on the room. For a few seconds, everyone was stunned by the information dump. Then it happened. Complete and utter mayhem.

"There is no fucking way!" "How can you even think…" "This is bullshit!" All shouted at once as a surge of angry people jumped up and surrounded him. Voices raised, fingers pointed, teeth bared. Faces, mask of fury, the family not believing for a second the identity of the so-called Mastermind.

Reggie sighed and sunk down into his chair as the family continued to question his sanity and intelligence. It didn't take them long to figure out that he wasn't gonna answer their questions until they calmed and sat back down.

Walt, having no previous knowledge of The Mastermind, or her role in Lucille's death, was taking the news remarkably well. Certainly better than his own family. But Walt wasn't emotionally involved with the situation. That made it easier for him to see the facts for what they are.

Finally, the mob quieted. Their expressions still belayed their feelings, but they were giving him a chance to explain. Instead, he said, "The evidence is there for everyone to see. And, if she isn't guilty, why did she run?"

On

e feminine voice spoke up from the crowd. "If this guy is really some guy named Ronald and not Glendo, which I am certainly not ready to accept, maybe she found out and that's why she killed him!"

Someone else yelled, "Cameras and videos can be tampered with! Files can be forged! How do we know she isn't being set up?"

"And none of this means Lucille was innocent!" shouted another voice. "That hidden file could have been fake. A hole card for if she ever got found out. She was just killed before she got to use it."

"Okay," Reggie said, leaning forward. "All of your concerns are valid. Most of this information hasn't been cross referenced or confirmed through secondary sources. So," he said, looking around, "I think we have a lot of work to do. We need to dig into these videos and make sure they haven't been altered. Personnel files need to be studied and cross checked with other agencies. Travel itineraries need to be verified.

"As far as the story about Glendo and Ronald, we need to get with family in New York and either verify or debunk what we think we know. With the amount of talent we have in this room, and the resources at our disposal, I expect to know everything involving this situation in the next 24 hours."

Standing up and studying the familiar faces around him, he said, "And while all that is being done, we have an issue that is just as pressing. We are the most advanced Agency on the face of the earth. We are the best of the best. With that being said, I want to know the whereabouts of The Mastermind within the hour. Hack every network. Use every resource. I don't care what you have to do, or how you feel about what's been presented to you: Find The Mastermind, now."

When everyone just stood staring at him, he roared, "NOW DAMMIT!" which lit a fire under their feet and they scrambled to comply with his command.

Once everyone vacated his suite, he slumped back down into the chair, feeling more tired that he'd ever felt in his life. For once, just once, he wished his family could be like a normal family. No killers. No masterminds. No puppeteers. Just normal, everyday people who loved each other and lived together in harmony. He was really getting sick and tired of his devious, manipulative, secretive family.

His regained isolation didn't grant him the peace he expected. Thoughts of Ronald's murder, and the tunnels, spoke of a plan of escape years in the making. Eventually, they would find her and get the answers to the questions destroying his family. The one-hour time limit was impossible. They wouldn't even know what state she was in by then. But they would get her, and she would stand trial. Then he would put a bullet in her skull.

Reggie was now the leader of the family, officially the Head of the WRA. The oldest male Burke alive. Then a thought: Actually, he wasn't the oldest male Burke alive. But that issue would have to take a backseat. His problems with The Author just didn't seem that important at the time.

Pulling out his phone, he got to work. A King couldn't ask his people to fight in a battle that he was unwilling to be on the frontline of.

Chapter 21

The early morning drive up the Pacific Coast Highway was majestic in its beauty. Out of the driver's side window, emerald green waves showed the true power lurking just below the ocean's surface. The sky overhead, a clear, flat blue that turned normal men into thinkers and dreamers. And off to the right, the Santa Monica Mountains contrasted nicely to provide some toughness to an otherwise soft landscape.

The platinum colored, Mercedes-Benz GT zoomed along with the driver not caring one bit about the picturesque surroundings. She was too busy listening to her friend spread doom and gloom all over her mission. "Ciera, don't do this! Tano said the guy could handle it without you getting involved. Don't give them a chance to hurt you!"

Shaking her head, she regretted ever getting intimate with him. Sure, it had been in the heat of the moment, and it had felt damn good, but now Zero was treating her like a doll he needed to protect, instead of the gang soldier she was.

"Stop talking to me like you're my dad or my man!" Her patience was gone and he needed to remember who he was talking to. "Just because you went up inside me doesn't mean you get to dictate what I do! I'm doing this, and if I get hurt, or killed, use one of the substitutes for the new team. Bottom line, I'm getting my face back!"

"But, Ciera…" She hung up before he could say anything else.

Looking around at all the luxurious, black leather and woodgrain, Ciera admitted to herself the real reason why she didn't want to hear Zero's doubts: All of his mirrored her own. Tano was already taking them into a whole new world, an escape from the everyday gangbanging lifestyle. She shouldn't care about seeing the look on her enemy's face when he died. Knowing that Poppy was dead should be enough to satisfy her revenge.

It wasn't.

She wanted to look him in his eyes and make sure he knew why he was gonna die. As long as the guy, Daniel, kept his word, she should be able to do just that, then drive away unharmed.

He'd already followed through on the first part: The armored Benz and the automatic AK-47 had been delivered to the gang house late last night. Daniel told Tano that she would be safe as long as she stayed inside. Since she had no real way to test that statement, she had to trust the fact that Tano trusted the man.

In the sense of distance, the drive wasn't that far. But, when comparing prestige, it was like traveling to another galaxy. Their LA properties were by no means poor, but Poppy's Malibu mansion surpassed every American dream she'd ever heard of.

Then again, growing up, Ciera had only one dream: To make it out of her abusive home in one piece.

Tano and Allorah had played a major role in her making it out alive. Her mother had skipped out on her and her father when she was only 5-years-old. When she turned 12, about the time she started to fill out her previously skinny body, her dad's two brothers had moved in with them.

The abuse started out as jokes and insignificant touches. When she told her father, he'd whipped her ass and told her to stop lying. Then berated her for not dressing properly like a young lady should when around grown men.

After her uncles saw that her dad took their side, the men became bolder and more demanding. The rapes started on the night of her 13th birthday.

She, Tano, and Allorah had been inseparable until that point. But, the things the men made her do caused a deep shame to fill her being. She stopped hanging with all her friends, and pretty much stopped going home. In her time of need, the most vulnerable episode in her life, Tano came and became her savior.

Living on the streets of South Central hadn't been a picnic, but the gangs knew that Tano was her protector. Even at 15 years old, his reputation in the Bloods was becoming legendary. To his people, he was a bonified knight in shining armor. But to his enemies, he was the devil personified. Knowing that she was somewhere roaming the streets alone, he sent every soldier he had to track her down.

She still remembered their reunion like it was yesterday. Three o'clock in the morning, he arrived at a party she was attending and shut the whole celebration down. Once they were the only two left in the house, he demanded she tell him why she ran away. When she did, he paused and stared at her for a few long minutes. He asked, "Why didn't you tell your father?"

"I did!" she exclaimed. "But he didn't believe me," she added sadly.

This look had crossed his face. She'd taken a step back because she had never been exposed to this level of anger. He'd grabbed her hand, said, "Come on," and dragged her to his car.

When the car stopped in front of her house, he opened the car door and said, "Let's go." She didn't want to ever step foot in that house again, but being with Tano made her feel courageous. Safe. She pushed her door open and followed him up the walkway to her front door.

Everything happened quickly after that. Tano rang the bell and Ciera's father had wrenched the door open. He'd rushed out and swept her up in his arms, tears of relief flowing down his face. She'd been gone for over three months.

Not even acknowledging Tano, her dad had turned and walked into the house with her wrapped in his arms. But her eyes had never left Tano's. He followed them in, shut the door, then pulled out the biggest gun she'd ever seen.

Her uncles, hearing a commotion, had made their way into the living room. Smiles lit their faces, until the gun came out. Then both men raised their hands, thinking they were being set up for a robbery. Two blasts, she'd flinched on each one, rid the world of her rapist. Her father had dropped her to her feet and spun, using his body to protect his daughter. But she wasn't the one who needed protecting.

Tano laughed. "Now you want to protect her? You want to be a real father, now? You scumbag motherfucker! One day, I'll see you in hell!"

"Wait!" her father had yelled, hand extending with his plea. One more blast removed the top of her father's head, blood and brains splattering her face and clothes. After that, she'd moved in with Tano and joined his gang a year later.

One of the main reasons she had to see this through now, Poppy knew about her past. Knew about the abuse she'd suffered as a child. For him to order his crew to do that to her, it was unforgivable. The man had to die.

Pulling the Benz over at the entrance to Malibu Park, the exclusive neighborhood where the leader of their gang lived, butterflies filled her stomach. This could very well be her last day on earth. If Poppy and his boys didn't kill her, she still had to worry about the police.

Daniel said he had everything covered. Listening to the story Tano had told her about how connected the guy was, it eased the tension a bit. But she wasn't the kind of woman to jump out the window on blind faith that someone would catch her. Daniel might be 100% accurate and truthful about how this would go down, but she was still preparing herself to die.

Taking a deep, fortifying breath, she turned into the park filled with multimillion-dollar homes, with resolve and revenge prominent in her heart. It was time for some retaliation.

Gazing at the tucked away, mammoth structures, she marveled at the stone and glass designs that told all interlopers that they were on hollowed grounds. Everything gleamed in a uniformed tidiness. Hedges just so, grass manicured to the blade, not one iota of litter floated on the cool, ocean breeze.

Turn after turn, as she got closer to the water, the abodes became more exuberant. Each home vying for the title of being the most appealing. Once again, she was very aware that she didn't fit in with this level of wealth. The funny thing is, neither did Poppy. If it wasn't for the dues paid by Tano and his line of millionaires, their leader would still be in South Central robbing dope men to eat.

Heart pounding, she knew she was close because, even at 8:30 in the morning, she could smell the exotic weed smoke floating on the air. And there it was. Rounding the last turn, the white, concrete and glass, two-story mansion came into view. Exhaling loudly, she lightly pushed the gas pedal and clutched the AK to her side.

The house was tucked in on the side of a hill. Because of the decline leading down to the ocean, the occupants of the home would have the high ground. The element of surprise would gain her a few seconds, but that was it. She would have the opportunity to gun down a few of the sentries, then she would be under heavy fire until she killed everyone, died, or escaped.

Poppy's home wasn't inside of a fence. In fact, he assumed his status was all the protection he needed. Under normal circumstances, he was right. Today would be anything but normal for the gang lord and his minions. If everything went as planned, Poppy and all his boys would take their last breaths in the next couple of minutes.

Stopping in front of the structure, three pairs of eyes zeroed in on her vehicle, and those were just the eyes she could see. Putting the car in park, she kept the engine running as she opened the driver's side door. The windows were blacked out, so she kept the weapon low as she stood up and faced the men with a smile on her face. She waved and, recognizing her as one of their own, they waved back and went on smoking and talking shit.

She yelled, “Is Poppy up yet?” She had to repeat the question again before one of the guys deemed her worthy of a response.

“Take your ass in there and see. I don’t keep up wit dat nigga.” Seeing as the man was literally there for security, it seemed to be a pretty ignorant response.

“I don’t need to see him, I just need you to deliver a message!” She bent low, making herself as small a target as possible. Setting the barrel across the roof of the Benz, she yelled, “Death before dishonor, motherfuckers!”

Too late, one of them screamed, “Oh shit!” and they went for their weapons. The automatic rounds tore them to shreds. They never even got off a shot.

Activity picked up tremendously as the weapon of mass destruction sprayed death over the front lawn. The gun was powerful, but modified to have little kick. As shouts filtered out from inside the house, she ejected the first clip and reached for another. The front door opened just as she slammed it home. The menacing face of one of her rapists stared out at her from the threshold. A grin split her face as she pulled the trigger, shock registering as the bullets launched him backwards off his feet.

Within seconds, bullets were peppering the car and street. She was forced to duck down and pray that the armor on the vehicle held up. Where the hell was her help? Dammit Tano, she thought. Trusting this guy was gonna get her killed before she reached her target.

A quick peek through the tinted, bulletproof glass sent her spirits plummeting. Probably twenty soldiers were lined up waiting for her to give them a target. Shaking her head, she accepted defeat and went to climb in the car to escape the warzone. That was until she heard a voice taunting her from behind the protective line of men.

Antwan 'Poppy' Parks had been sleeping the sleep of the rich when the automatic gunfire had him rolling out of bed onto the floor. He reached under the bed and grabbed the Mossberg, pistol-grip shotgun, hearing his home descend into chaos. Boldly, he jumped to his feet, slammed out of his second-floor, master suite, and began barking orders.

Dreads flying, his head turned this way and that as his men poured out of the other rooms with guns at the ready. "Don't look at me, stupid motherfuckers!" he roared. "Go kill whoever had the audacity to attack my home!"

The entertainment from the night before, shrieking and screaming, the women hid behind whatever they thought could keep a bullet out of their asses. Still barefoot, holding the shotgun, he ran towards the steps to get in on the action.

One of his personal guards, Mario, snatched open the front door, and was rewarded with a chest full of heat. Someone with more sense yelled, "Go out the side doors! We need to flank her!"

Her? thought Poppy. There was no way some bitch was out there shooting his shit up. He flipped through his mental rolodex of women he'd done dirty recently, couldn't think of one who would pull some shit like this. Stopping one of his guys as he ran for the side door, Poppy asked, "Who the fuck is out there?"

Screaming over the gunshots, he said, "That bitch that be with Tano! Ciera, or some shit like that."

Poppy gave a wolfish smiled. "Pass the word. I want that bitch alive!"

Laughing out loud, he made his way over to the living room window just in time to see Ciera duck down as his men sprayed the vehicle with bullets. Interesting, he thought as he watched the bullets ricochet harmlessly off the car. How the fuck could she afford to buy a bulletproof Benz. It had probably been a gift from that fool, Tano. No matter. After his guys grabbed the little, wanna-be gangster, slut, he'd add the car to his personal fleet.

Shaking his head, he felt a fresh surge of disappointment towards Tano. Sure, everyone had been upset about the little girl being molested by her uncles. Poppy had even given Tano $100,000 to help take care of the young girl. But the boy had a soft spot when it came to females. He blamed his own daughter, Allorah. She had always been preaching about how women were treated in American society. Tano would sit with her for hours, nodding and agreeing with everything she said while she bashed men, and praised women for everything they had to overcome. Then the fucking bastard started putting females in his line.

Well, all of that was over now. Tano and his whole line would die as soon as they hit the Main Line at any of the state prisons. The ones who still remained free, he would use this botched hit as an excuse to green light them all.

Now that he knew his daughter was safe, he could finish up with Tano and his trash. Then go back to the rich, gangsta lifestyle that he was used to. It would just be icing on the cake that he would confiscate everything that Tano's line owned.

The ceasefire brought him back to the present situation. One glance out the window told him all he needed to know. Plastering a huge smile on his face, he walked out of the front door to greet his unwelcomed guest.

Separated from the threat by a small army of his soldiers, he tried to bait her into showing herself. "So, the little slut wants to play Big Gangster!" he yelled. "What? You come back for some more of what you got last time I saw you? All you had to do was ask. Me and the crew would had run the freight train on your yellow ass!"

A few of the men chuckled, but most stayed stoic, waiting for a piece of the woman to show itself. "What was your plan, Little CiCi? You thought you could kill us all with one gun? I hope you know this little stunt will be the reason why Tano and the rest of your people die."

Finally getting a response, she hollered, "The only people who are gonna die will be yours!"

Laughing, he said, "Well, come on out and kill us. You a big bad Blood, right? What? You need some motivation? Yeah, I was the one who told the boys to fuck you! I figured, since that's how you were introduced to womanhood, you would really get off on it. I mean, they might have been a bit rougher than your uncles, but it was a nice stroll down memory lane, wasn't it?"

"Fuck you, you dirty bastard. If it's the last thing I do, I promise I'm gonna kill you!"

Calmly, he said, "No you won't. In fact, you're gonna love me." In a fake Asian accent, he said, "You gonna love me long time!" The men dissolved into laughter after that.

"Listen," Poppy yelled after everyone got control of themselves. "Ciera, we're gonna hurt you," he added in a mock sad tone. "Me and my boys are gonna use you in the most degrading way possible. After we're done with you, I'm gonna hide you in one of my stash houses. I'll tie you face down on a rack, rent your high yellow ass to all the little foot soldiers out working the blocks. And, only after you drop to your knees and beg me for death, will I put you out of your misery. Sound like a plan to you, CiCi?"

Two thoughts crossed his mind when she stayed silent. The first, the car was armored. He couldn't understand why she hadn't hopped in and tried to escape sure death. Obviously, she wouldn't be killing anyone else today. A bit of unease started to creep up his spine.

The second thought was, where was the police? This was Malibu, for God's sake, not South Central. He'd had the police called on him when his music was too loud. Hundreds of rounds had been fired, and not one siren could be heard in the distance. Yeah, something was definitely wrong with this scene.

For no reason he could see, faintly, he heard Ciera start to giggle. It morphed into a chuckle, then a full-on belly laugh.

His soldiers glanced at each other with confusion on their faces. To his far right, one of the Homies lowered his gun and pointed to the horizon. “What the hell is that?” he asked.

Everyone’s eyes tracked to an area about a half mile out, over the water. The sun’s reflection beaming off of the ocean made it difficult to see. On first glance, he thought he was seeing a space ship. Whatever it was, it was definitely getting closer by the second.

Looking around, he yelled, “Stay focused! Bring your guns back up!” Half of his soldiers followed his order, the other half lowered their weapons and started to backstep.

“What the fuck is wrong with ya’ll?” he demanded. “Get the fuck back in formation!”

Loudly, Ciera asked, “You remember that Syfy shit Tano was talking about? Well, you’re about to have an up close and personal encounter with it!”

Before he could formulate a response, something struck him in the chest and he stumbled to the ground, landing flat on his back. Pain laced his being as heat consumed his body. He wanted so badly to curl up and protect his body from further abuse, but no matter how hard he tried, he couldn’t move.

Then, while he lay totally unprotected, just staring up at the sky, the cease fire ended. Someone yelled, “OH SHIT! It’s three of them!” Those were the only intelligible words spoken before he watched a missile fly over his head and reduce his mansion, and everyone inside, to itty-bitty pieces.

But the assault didn’t stop there. Screams and pounding feet tried to compete with what sounded like multiple Gatlin guns. In less than a minute, everything was quiet. He laid in utter horror as one of the drones stopped directly over his head, floating about ten feet up. Now he could see how it had been so easy to murder all of his men.

The thing had the shape of a miniature fighter jet. Three rotating guns hung from the body, and he could make out the tips of two missiles encased in a central compartment. The color was a mixture of chrome and light blue, making it eerily hard to focus on it while in the sky. When he thought it couldn't get any stranger, a masculine voice, loud and clear, said, "Everything is clear. He's all yours."

Soft footfalls started up after the announcement. The bitch didn't walk on the grass and take a direct route. She walked around, taking her sweet time, using the driveway to get to the walkway he was stationed on.

Of course, he couldn't see her, but he listened intently and tracked every step she took. Then, just out of sight, she paused. He heard the sound of a gun cocking seconds before she stepped into view. She kept walking until she was straddling his body, only bringing her attention to him after she had surveyed her surroundings.

She flashed a stunning smile, then said, "I called Allorah before this was set in motion. She said that she'd called you yesterday to let you know she was safe. She said that you told her she had three days to say goodbye to her husband because you were gonna put a hit out on him at that time. When I explained what you had your boys do to me, and what I planned to do about it, you want to know what she said?"

The pause pissed him off royally. The stupid slut knew he couldn't answer. She went on after her rhetorical question. "She said, 'Good, my family will be safe, and you can get some revenge.' So, with your daughter's blessing, here we are."

She paused again as she looked around at the carnage. "Every one of your stash houses were blown up, too. Every person that was directly in your line, except for Tano, was killed this morning. All of your guys in prison, the ones who were hustling on the streets, even the ones who were at home sleeping. They are all dead now.

"To top it all off, Tano struck a deal with the man who set all this up, and he's being released today. Him and everyone else in our line." Leaning over so she could look directly into his eyes, she asked, "Any last words before I send you to hell with the rest of your punk ass soldiers? You want to plead for your life? Maybe apologize for what you put me through?"

At the end of the day, Poppy was a Gangster. A Godfather level Blood who'd known he would never have the honor of dying a natural death. Violence beget violence, and he'd spread more than his fair share of the contagious disease.

It had started way before he'd been named a Gangster. But it seemed all that was over now. He accepted it, and he would die the same way he lived.

Whatever was wrong with his body, he still had control over his eyes. So, he made them appear cold. Hard. The eyes of a man who wasn't afraid to die. His hope was that she was able to read the look for what it was, because death had always been his friend. His destiny. He would be greeted in hell with open arms, the devil welcoming home one of his own.

Smirking at his bravado, she locked her hate-filled gaze with his own, lining up her handgun with his forehead. She said, "Well, take this message to hell with you: Tano line forever, BITCH!"

A quick sound. A flicker of light. Then…Nothing.

Epilogue

"The fact that we can't find her solidifies in my mind her identity," Reggie told his little brother. The Mastermind had been missing for two weeks now. They had tracked her to Georgia, then the trail had gone ice cold. Every satellite, cellphone camera, computer, and drone on the planet was being piggy-backed into trying to locate her. So far, she'd proven that her nickname was well earned.

"We'll find her, or we won't. Don't worry so much. She'll turn up in Australia or Russia or somewhere on the other side of the world. We'll locate her, snatch her, then get all the answers we need." Daniel's confidence didn't buoy his spirits. While his brother thought she was on the far side of the globe, he had a sneaky suspicion she was closer than Daniel thought.

"Anyway," said Reggie, changing the subject. "Are you sure it's alright for him to come to your wedding? I don't want to stress you out on your sentencing day."

Hearing the eyeroll in his voice, Daniel said, "Not all marriages are death sentences. When you find the right one, it's more like a lifelong vacation. And, for the last time, I'm sure he can come. He can be a pain in the ass, but we're in a better place now. Just have his tuxedo ready when he gets here, and tell him to leave the attitude in Brazil."

"Will do," Reggie told him. "I'll call him in a bit to give him the good news about his status. That'll definitely put him in an accommodating mood."

"Alright, well, I'll let you go. And don't worry about The Mastermind. These situations have a way of working themselves out." He hung up and Reggie immediately called Delmas.

"Yo! What's up?"

"How about answering the phone with a little more dignity and respect?" admonished Reggie.

"What the fuck do you want, Reggie? Is that dignified enough for you?"

Chuckling, Reggie said, "I'm sending you a quick clip of a news story that will be fed to the public tomorrow." He sent the audio clip and they both listened as it played.

A melodic, female voice said, "After almost a month of hard work and dedication by the FBI, US Marshalls, and local police departments all over the world, the elusive Prison Guard Killer has been located. The nationwide manhunt came to an end this morning after an anonymous tip was called in about a possible sighting.

"When law enforcement approached the location, a gun battle ensued that resulted in the PGK barricading himself inside a rest area in rural North Carolina. All efforts to negotiate proved futile.

"In a bizarre twist, the PGK, AKA Tremayne Michaels, shot himself when he realized his recapture was imminent. The self-inflicted gunshot proved to be fatal.

"The disfigured body is now being safeguarded by the Raleigh Medical Examiner, and we've learned that no one has come forward to claim the killer. FYI, if no one claims the body, the county will hold him for one year, then perform a cremation to get rid of the remains.

"There are some who will mourn the fact that they didn't get the closure that a courtroom can sometimes provide. Others will be happy that this nightmare has finally come to an end. As always, this is Ashley Kirt, Channel Three News, bringing you this exclusive repot. Be sure to stay tuned as we will be bringing you updates at the top and bottom of every hour."

"She'll get the first opportunity to broadcast, but soon after, every station on the planet will run with it," said Reggie.

Delmas let the silence fill the air as he took in all of what he'd just heard. Finally, he scoffed, not impressed in the least. "So, first, he sets me up to take the fall for a series of crimes he committed. Then, he uses my capture to launch the careers of his people. And finally, he rides in to save the day by faking my death, which will clear my name and allow me to return to society. Did I miss anything?"

"Uh, two things, actually," said Reggie.

"Well, will you please enlighten me? I'm having a hard time feeling grateful right now."

"Alright," said Reggie. "First, he cleared the way for me to offer you your job back as Head of Mission Development." He paused, but his brother remained silent, waiting for the second thing. "And the other, you know Daniel is getting married in two weeks. Well, he wants you to be one of his groomsmen."

"Bullshit!" exclaimed Delmas. "His bride will shit a brick if I show my face. You remember, I did try to kidnap her and Gabby?"

"He's already talked it over with Alisha and she's cool with it," said Reggie. "And Gabby, well, once you meet her, you'll understand. If she has something to say about it, she'll damn sure let you know."

"And what about Walt, Ann, and Denise? You think they'll be thrilled to see me walking around free?"

"Delmas, you have to remember that they know you're not the PGK," stated Reggie. "If they can forgive and forget what Daniel put them through, I don't think they'll stay mad at you for long. Plus, once you accept the job offer, you'll be untouchable, anyway. I used a lot of the WRA's muscle to get that storyline to fly with law enforcement. They're even setting up a fake shootout for tomorrow morning."

His brother was silent for a moment. "Reg, I don't want you to take this the wrong way, but fuck the WRA. Now that I'm finally free, I understand how oppressive it is working there. I think I'm gonna take a page out of Daniel's book and find something else to do. Who knows? I might find me a woman I can fall in love with."

Reggie was shocked. The WRA was pretty much Delmas' life. "You sure about this?"

Sighing, Delmas said, "Yeah, I'm sure. I think I need to settle down and start looking into the family thing. We're all getting too old for this warrior, always alone, shit."

"Okay," said Reggie, letting a little of his disbelief creep into his voice. "So, I already have your tuxedo, sized and all. I'll send you a text telling you the time and place. It's only gonna be a small, intimate ceremony with Daniel and Alisha's families and closest friends." After a slight pause, Reggie asked, "You're gonna be there for our little brother, right?"

Delmas remained silent. "Right?" Reggie asked again.

"I'll be there," he finally said. "But, I'm not putting up with anyone's shit. You tell Daniel to keep his people in check. That goes for Alisha and Gabby, too."

Reggie chuckled and said, "I don't even think Daniel could pull that one off." After a bit, he said, "I love you, bro. Mom could be tough on us sometimes, but she would be proud of how we're pulling together."

"Yeah," said Delmas. "I love you, too." Then he ended the call.

Reggie leaned back in his comfortable chair and let his eyes roam over the interior of his familiar office. When it came down to it, yeah, he could move to his mother's office. It was still vacant, along with her suite of rooms. But he didn't think he'd ever stop feeling like an intruder. So, he stayed in his old office and suite, where he'd been for the past 15 years.

While he studied his surroundings, he thought about what all his ancestors would feel about the current state of the WRA. He still had a littering of Burke, male cousins in the rank and file, but he was now the only man in a leadership role. His mother had wanted to situate her whole line so that the direction of the WRA could continue in her idea of perfection. But that path had only led to her destruction and ultimate death.

A family full of diabolical geniuses, Reggie thought, shaking his head. It seemed that, because there was no one to challenge them outside of the family, they were all doomed to turn on each other. Well, if Reggie had anything to say about it, that trend would now stop. All he had to do was find and exterminate The Mastermind, the last cancerous cell of the family's inner circle.

He knew he was up to the task, and he felt the rest of the WRA was, also. But time wasn't on their side. The longer The Mastermind remained free, the harder it would be to wrangle her in.

With that thought in mind, he focused on his computer screen and got to work. This mission would require everyone's attention and dedication. He just prayed those were the only requirements that this cold world demanded of the family he had left.

THE AUTHOR OF EVIL

HERE'S A SNEAK PEEK AT THE NEXT NOVEL IN THE MASTERMINDS SERIES

THE AUTHOR OF EVIL

Prologue

"Run!" the man commanded.

Anthony's body was frozen in shock, his mind befuddled as his eyes tracked from the dead woman at the man's feet up to the deadly expression spread across his face. What the man ordered made perfect sense, it's what Anthony wanted to do anyway. But he couldn't force his body and mind to get on the same page.

"RUN! you stupid son of a bitch!" the man screamed, as he bent down and snatched the knife out of the dead woman's chest. The moonlight glinting off of the polished steel did the trick that the commands couldn't. Anthony regained his mobility, turned, and hauled ass.

Wearing nothing but a pair of synthetic shorts and a pair of knockoff Nikes, both provided by the man who had just ordered him to run, Anthony never looked back. He didn't need to see if the man was stalking his headlong dash. Death would come if it came; he had no intentions of looking his murderer in the eyes.

Under the canopy of trees, everything was pitch-black, and the hot, night air had sweat dripping off of his body. His breaths heaved as he navigated the roots and foliage trying its best to trip him up. He would need about another two minutes to make it to the perimeter, then he would find out if he was truly free, or a dog still pinned in its cage.

Branches seemed to jump out and grab at his battered body, but despite the danger, he poured on the speed. New cuts and bruises started to blend with the old. He was weak, nearing the point of pure exhaustion, but nothing would stop or slow his progress. He needed to keep pushing onward.

THERE! he screamed in his mind. The gate that had been preventing him and the others from escaping their hellish prison. Thirty minutes ago, electricity had been flowing through it, making sure that the two remaining captives followed the rules of the game. Now, he was the last one left alive. But he was to the point where it wouldn't matter if the electricity was still on or not. One way or another, he was escaping this place.

Setting his course towards the twenty-foot barrier, he finally cast a backwards look over his shoulder. What he expected to see was a ghoulish sneer shining at him from the darkness, murderous intent projecting from a pair of coal-black eyes. He would have gladly taken his chances with the fence if his premonition proved to be reality, but nothing haunted his path. Focusing back on the goal, he prepared to launch his body at the only obstacle keeping him from breaking free.

He had watched someone try this days ago and the outcome had been brutal. The fucker holding them had set the current to a low enough level that the body stayed suspended on the fence until it was burned to a crisp. The victim had lived in agony for a very long time, their captor forcing the rest of them to watch as their fellow inmate suffered.

Now it was his turn to try. Doubts almost brought him to a stop, but he had to push on. There were people who were relying on him to return home. Not to mention the people who had died in this place who needed him to tell their story. Using all of the strength he had left in his being, he powered through two more steps, then jumped.

When his fingers locked onto the metal, all he felt was cold and relief. He took about a milli-second to celebrate his non-gruesome death, then he began to climb. He expected to feel a calloused hand grab his leg at any moment and yank him back to the ground, but he made it to the top without incident. And then he was over, a glimmer of hope giving him a boost of much needed energy.

Reaching the bottom, he paused. Suspicion causing his eyes to scan the side of the fence he'd just vacated. No way could the man afford to let him escape. What he had seen in the last eight days was enough to send the guy to Death Row. Shaking his head, not understanding what the man was playing at, he turned and continued his getaway.

Now that he was out from under the trees, moonlight illuminated his path as he sprinted across an open field. His legs were screaming for him to stop and take a break, but he knew, if he stopped, he might never start again. So, acre after acre, he ran. Not at all sure he was safe, but hoping the man would keep his word and let him live.

Just when he felt like he couldn't take another step, a glorious sound assaulted his ears; the high-pitched wail of tires rolling down an open road.

He made it out onto the pavement, arms waving wildly as his eyes made out a pair of headlights closing in on him. A screech of brakes, a door opening, and a man's voice asking, "Are you crazy? You tryna get ran over?" Then he collapsed, his body finally winning the battle over his will, which had been all that had gotten him this far.

He made it! He was safe. He was actually going to see his family again. After eight days of being in hell, he was never going to take his life for granted again.

With thoughts of another chance at life floating in his mind, and teardrops steadily streaming down his face, he allowed unconsciousness to claim him. Knowing that when he awakened, he would be surrounded by the ones he loved.

Chapter 1

Anthony 'Ant' Goodson had a good feeling about tonight, something his mother would call a premonition. He just knew that his life was about to change for the better. Since his marriage of three years was already starting to lose its gleam, he thought the first step in bringing about that change was to check out his other options in the romance department. And he couldn't think of a more appropriate venue than where he was headed.

A Charlotte, North Carolina native, Ant was used to the fast life. But, even though he was 24-years old, he had never been into the club scene. He had been too busy busting his ass, trying to make a name for himself in the welding world. He never had time to worry about who was fucking who, or who was wearing what. Tonight, though, he was gonna take his maiden voyage into that deep, dark ocean, hoping to catch a fish that was thick, rich, and satisfied with the role of a side-chick.

Anthony glided his matte-black Corvette ZR1 to a stop directly in front of the club. He figured, if he was gonna use tonight to consider his options, what better place than a club aptly named Choices. He glanced over at the line of people that stretched halfway down the block, took a deep, fortifying breath, then hopped out of the car.

The valet breezed over to him, studied him and his car for a few seconds, and deemed him worthy of his expertise. The young, white man peeked over at one of the bouncers and gave him a slight nod. Now all smiles, the valet handed him a ticket, hopped into his vacated seat, revved the powerful engine, and pulled off into the night. This left Ant facing off with a hundred spectators who were no doubt trying to figure out who and what he was.

Most of the gawkers instantly ruled out him being a professional athlete. Even though he was built solid from years of hard work, his 5'8", 150-pound body didn't scream basketball or football star. With his ropy muscles, he could have been a boxer or UFC fighter, but his lack of facial damage would make that option unlikely.

Others would deem him too short to be a model, even with his waist-length dreads, flawless, dark-chocolate skin-tone, and classic, African bone structure forcing all the women, and some of the men, to take a second, and third, look.

His attire would also be a topic of contention. With his Louis Vuitton button down, black, Purple-jeans, and all-black Jordan 5s, he could be a millionaire dressing down, or a broke man wearing his one good outfit. Anthony returned the stares for a few seconds, and then smiled as he took in all the curiosity. A murmur immediately started up within the female clicks. When the dimple made its appearance, they all decided he had to be an actor, though none of them were sure which movies he actually starred in.

Acting as if his heart wasn't about to pound out of his chest, and this was just a normal Friday night for him, he pulled out a couple of Big-faces, handing them to the bouncers as he confidently sauntered through. His wife, Sofia, would be laughing her ass off at the performance he was putting on. She would be the first one to point and proclaim, "He's nobody special! He's nothing but a welder!" That's one of the reasons he was out looking for a change, his wife never passed on the opportunity to remind him he was nothing more than a high-paid commoner.

Tonight, as he stopped in the world-renowned lobby of the club, he made up his mind to be whoever and whatever he needed to be. If that was a high-paid welder who'd recently relocated to Wheaton, Illinois, or an actor waiting to land his first big role, if it helped him reach his goal, that's who he would become. But first, he had to make a choice.

Club Choices was the newest hotspot in Chicago. A couple of big music stars had come together and formed one huge entertainment mecca. It contained six different clubs, each developed to cater to a patron's chosen atmosphere, restaurants, bars, and lounges for people to chill in after their night of partying.

The entryway was so famous because of its one-of-a-kind design. It was made of all-glass walls with openings that led into all-glass tunnels that directed you to each of the six clubs. From the spot he was now standing, he could see what was going on in each of the clubs, and could decide where he wanted to spend his night.

The good thing was, if you didn't like the mood in your first pick, you could switch areas as many times as you wanted. The doors didn't close until 3:00am, so it wasn't unusual for a customer to hit up all six clubs, then a restaurant and lounge to close out their night. At least that's what the internet reviews claimed.

Anthony had to bite the inside of his cheeks to keep the grin from splitting his face. Everywhere he looked were women in barely-there clothes, dancing to their flavor of music. His eyes locked onto a curvy, mixed chick, wearing a tight, leather, knee-length dress, rocking her hips from side to side.

Her long, straight hair, and beautiful, creamy skin-tone held his gaze hostage before she glanced up with mesmerizing, hazel eyes and saw him watching her. She added a bit more sway to her movements, her manicured fingers began to map out the contours of her shapely body. Brilliant, even teeth flashed in between plump, juicy, lips, the tip of her tongue making a quick appearance, the woman using erotic body language to broadcast her siren's song.

Because each section of the club was soundproofed, he had to glance at the sign hanging over the entrance to figure out which vibe it catered to: Reggae. Deciding that he wasn't in the mood for that, despite being very into the sexual display, he let his gaze travel to see what else Choices had to offer.

The R&B section contained a crowd that already looked boo'd up. Everyone was slow dancing, staring into their partner's eyes. That definitely wasn't what he was looking for, so he moved on to the next.

His pulse immediately kicked up a notch when he noticed what was going on inside the Hip-Hop area. He couldn't hear the sound, but he really didn't need to. On an elevated platform were five super-thick, super-sexy, black women, sporting different color thongs, twerking and shaking their asses. They were oiled up, thrown dollar bills were sticking to their undulating bodies. The sight was more strip club than he would have liked, but it was a scene that he couldn't pass up. He was all set to proceed through the opening, when a soft, angelic voice stopped him in his tracks.

"I'm so happy I caught you! I was prepared to search every section until I found you. Now, I don't have to!"

Anthony turned, and his mouth instantly went dry. Absolutely breathtaking. He was rendered speechless in the presence of such perfection. And it was effortless. Minimal makeup and a rose-gold watch her only accessories, other than a small Prada bag. Ant hated to admit it, but this Latina bombshell was totally out of his league.

Still, he gathered himself, smiled to flash his world-famous dimple, extended his hand, and said, "Hi! My name is Anthony. You have a beautiful accent. What's your name?"

She rewarded him with a sexy smile of her own, then said, "My name is Delianna, but my friends call me Deli. It is nice to meet you, Anthony. And thank you for the compliment."

"The pleasure is all mine," said Anthony, still latched on to her delicate, warm hand. His thumb brushed over her knuckles as he asked, "Brazilian?"

Showing no sign of discomfort with him holding her hand, she parted her smooth, glossy lips and blessed him with a mega-watt smile. “That’s right! No one ever guesses right on the first try! How did you know?”

“You want me to be honest?” he asked her. She nodded while taking a meniscal step towards him. He said, “Well, my job takes me to a lot of different places. I’ve been all over Central and South America. No other women in the world possess that perfect bronze skin-tone, those deep, chocolate eyes, and the curves of a goddess. The accent was just confirmation of what my eyes had already told me when I saw you out there in the line,” he added, letting her know that he had noticed her, also. They stood in the lobby area, staring into each other’s eyes like shy teenagers, until a crowd of rowdy patrons exited the Rave section, crushing their romantic introduction.

After the last person exited the building, Deli cleared her throat and asked, “So, which club are you going into?”

He pretended to think over her question, but his mind was now made up. No way was he about to share his time with her with anyone else. “I had been about to go into the Hip-Hop club, but that vibe isn’t gonna cut it for me anymore.”

A knowing expression flashed across her face. “What are you feeling now?”

He wished he was brave enough to say, “Nobody, other than you,” but he didn’t know if it was too early to make such a statement. He settled with, “I think somewhere a little bit quieter.” His eyes focused above her head for a second. “What do you say we go into the lounge area where we can talk and get to know each other?”

A slight blush caressed her cheeks. With lowered eyelashes, she said, “That’s fine with me, Anthony. That’s where I was on my way to, but I would have gone wherever you wanted to go.” Visions of dragging her from the building and finding the closest hotel floated in his mind, but she was worth more than a quick fuck. He actually wanted to learn who and what she was. This was a dangerous feeling to have when he had a wife waiting at home, but fuck it, if Sophia didn't want him around, it was time to find someone who did.

Ant glanced down at their still-linked right hands. Looking back up at her exotic face, he let his desire for her clearly show. He replaced his right hand with his left and said, "I can't risk you getting away from me. If you don't mind, I'd like to hold your hand until we find a suitable place to conversate." All she did was nod her permission before blessing him with another beautiful smile, then they were off.

The man stepped out of the shadows and a smile immediately lit his face. A woman, standing about ten feet to his left, dressed for a night of dancing, trembled and wrapped her arms protectively around herself. No one had noticed his emergence, but some were sensitive enough to have felt his presence as soon as he revealed himself. Some leftover ancestral instinct warning the possessor to the evil they were now being exposed to.

The woman who had briefly held his attention was safe for the night. She wouldn't do for what he had planned. Now, the pair that had just entered the Blue lounge, they were perfect for the last pieces he needed to place on the board. All the other players were secured and awaiting the games to start. He would do a little bit more research on the subjects, watch the interaction between Anthony Goodson and Delianna Cruz, then decide if they were suitable to play the needed roles.

Not one suspicious eye landed on him as he followed the newly introduced couple into the lounge. He was a master at blending in, and the shadowed atmosphere just made it that much easier. Keeping his movements as casual as possible, he used his dark skin and black clothing to become part of the scenery. A predator at the top of the food chain, possessing the ability to adapt to any environment.

He remained at the entrance until he spied the couple take a booth in the back of the purposely smoky interior of the room. Once they were completely engrossed in each other, he headed in their direction. Without slowing, he breezed pass them, flicking a small device on the floor between their feet. That accomplished, he made his way over to the other side of the area, claimed a booth of his own, and pulled out his cellphone.

The simple listening device would allow him to hear their whole conversation, and he could finish his research while he listened in. He was pretty sure that he had found his last two contestants, but he needed to make sure there would be no surprises.

If the police came looking for them too soon, the trail might be warm enough for them to find something. He wasn't particularly worried about being caught, he just didn't want his game to be interrupted until it reached a definite conclusion.

Getting comfortable on the leather cushion, he dug into his task. By tomorrow he wanted the game to commence. This was a new venture for him, he was stepping out into a new field of study that he hoped could hold his interest. Normally, he was satisfied with sitting around and coming up with inventive ways of killing people, but that was becoming repetitive. He now wanted to see how far a person would go to keep breathing.

Everyone would get a chance to survive, but anyone trying to break or circumvent the rules would die horribly. With that thought foremost in his mind, he tuned into the entertaining conversation taking place on the other side of the room, a satisfied smile casting a devious glint to his otherwise handsome face.

Chapter 2

"I'll be right back, Anthony. Promise that you won't run away while I visit the ladies' room," Delianna demanded.

He jerked back in surprise. "You're worried that I'll ditch you?" She shrugged as if anything could happen. "Deli, I'm not going anywhere. I want to learn everything there is to know about you. But, I promise to be here when you get back." She seemed satisfied with his answer, so she scooted out of the booth and made her way to the bathroom.

While they had been making their way into the lounge, he'd been a perfect gentleman and kept his eyes on her face. That hadn't been much of a hardship for him, God had definitely used his finest paintbrush to produce that masterpiece. He had the very dangerous thought that he could be happy waking up to it for the rest of his life.

The delicate symmetry, blended flawlessly with the strong, but feminine, features, spoke of divinity and humanity interacting on the highest level. Nothing fixed or fake, every millimeter natural and perfectly detailed to match seamlessly. But now that she was striding away from him, he could finally perform an unabashed study of all she had to offer.

Her hair was a curtain of black silk that ended a few inches above her prominent derriere. Bare shoulders and arms, fluidly muscled, but smooth, letting the world know that she was serious about every aspect of her body. The white, stretch top conformed to her shape, highlighting just how well-proportioned that body was. He couldn't begin to guess her measurements, but her tiny waist added emphasis to each of her ridiculous hills and valleys.

The top was tucked into a pair of loose-fitting, cream colored, designer sweatpants, but the area that captured his attention wasn't loose at all. As she sashayed away, his eyes lasered in on her flexing glutes. Mouth watering and head shaking at the absurdity of how much they shifted up and down with each step.

He didn't think she was putting on a show for his benefit, this was just the walk of a sexy woman who knew she could have any man she wanted. And she was absolutely sure that every male in the vicinity had their eyes glued to one of her stunning attributes.

But, a melancholy started to dampen his mood as soon as she disappeared from view. Thoughts of his wife floated, unwelcomed, into his mind. He loved her, and had felt that way since they first met in the seventh grade. He really wanted to spend the rest of his life with her. There was no doubt in his mind that she was his soulmate.

The problem was, lately, nothing he did for her was good enough. She felt that she had made the ultimate sacrifice by moving up from Charlotte last year because of his job. Now, if he used one minute of his free time to do anything that didn't include her, the accusations and insults started to fly.

It was bad enough that, whenever his boss sent him to foreign locales, she checked in with him damn near every hour. When he was home, she expected to be the center of his attention. And if she wasn't, if his concentration wavered for a second, there was hell to pay.

Flashes of their shared past almost made him slide out of the booth and rush home to be with Sophia, breaking the promise he had made a minute ago. And if Delianna hadn't chosen that exact moment to make her return, he might have been gone. But the vision of her full, succulent breasts, swaying unencumbered under her top, wiped all thought of leaving out of his mind.

It was crazy because, Sophia wasn't a slouch in the sex appeal department. If anything, the two women were cut from the same cloth. His wife wasn't as fit and compact as Deli, but most men preferred their women to have that extra layer of comfort. Until he had spent the last hour staring at all of her Brazilian magnificence, he was convinced he felt that way himself. Now, he wasn't so sure. There was just something about that tightly packed thickness that changed his whole outlook on what was actually sexy.

Deli smiled as she slid back into the seat across from him. "Did you miss me?" she asked, flirtatiously.

"Of course, I did," he replied. "How could I not? You're such an interesting person! I really just have one more question and then my interrogation will cease."

Throwing her hands up carelessly, she said, "Ask away. I'm an open book."

"Where is your man in all of this?" A shadow passed over her face, warning him that this wasn't a good direction to take, but he decided to press on. "I mean…I'm not suggesting that you need a man to get by, but you are a gorgeous woman. Why hasn't some guy given you the world to make you his?"

"Well," she said, reaching for her bag. "I actually have a confession to make." His heart fell to his feet as she rummaged around, looking for something in her small clutch. His fears became reality when she pulled her hand free and the gold glinted in the light. "I'm married," she proclaimed, then threw the ring back into the bag.

The sense of betrayal was foolish, he was also married and hadn't said a word. But her confession made their union a bit more complicated. Before they would have gone anywhere, he would have revealed his status and gave her the option to proceed or not. Now, with two different spouses in the mix, he didn't see how it could work.

She took in his devastated expression, and continued the conversation. "I've been separated for the last three years, but we've both been too busy to initiate the divorce process."

His hope soared once again, but he did start to glance around the lounge with worry etched on his face. She laughed and said, "You don't have anything to worry about. I haven't seen him in over a year. Plus, he moved back to

Philadelphia to be near his family. I guess the reason we didn't work was my fault. He just couldn't stomach the thought of men ogling my pictures anytime they wanted. So, he left me."

Within minutes of them sitting down, Delianna had told him that she was a successful Instagram model. She had millions of followers and was constantly offered modeling and acting jobs all over the world. Her home base was in Chicago, but she spent most of her time on the road. He had no problem believing that people would pay her huge sums of money to see her in skimpy attire.

When she pulled out her phone and showed him her page, his mouth had hit the floor. She really was perfectly put together. The fact that her body was natural, the result of hours spent in the gym, only deepened his attraction to her. Delianna was a shining example of an independent woman, determined to make her mark on the world.

Ant leaned back in his seat and huffed out a breath. "I can see how some men could be intimidated by a woman of your caliber, but I don't have any confidence problems. My opinion probably doesn't matter much at this point, but any man that would leave his woman for something so small, didn't deserve the woman in the first place."

She reached her hand out to him and he placed his in hers. "Your opinion does matter. And thank you for being so kind. I know that my career can get to be a lot for most guys, but I never thought he would leave me because of it. Anyway, our relationship is done, I just wanted to let you know what you would be signing up for."

Ant tilted his head and met her eyes. "Are you feeling like this could go beyond tonight?"

Deli's eyebrows shot up in response to his question. "Don't you? I mean, I don't expect a proposal by the time we leave, but I thought everything was going pretty good."

He deflated and pulled his hand from her grasp. "Deli, you are a one-of-a-kind woman that any man would be happy to call his own. But," he said, reaching into his pocket, "I have a confession to make, also." He pulled out his ring and placed it on his finger. "I'm also married. And I have no intention of leaving my wife."

For a minute, the words just hung between them. She slumped back in her seat, probably feeling the same sense of betrayal he'd felt after her announcement. He figured that he owed her more of an explanation than he'd already given.

"When I came out tonight, it was because my wife, Sophia, was harping on me about spending so much time away from her. She can get clingy at times, and when I don't give in to her demands, anger takes over her being. The insults start to fly, along with anything she can get her hands on. And, to be honest, I'm getting sick of all the fighting. I love her with all my heart, but I don't think I like her anymore. I came out because I needed a break from her and all her bullshit."

Deli didn't respond at all, just sat staring at him like he was a complete stranger to her. It wasn't far from the truth, but he didn't want her thinking badly of him.

"I've never cheated on my wife before," he explained. "I've never been on a date with another woman. Hell, I've never been with another woman, period. I fell in love with Sophia in the seventh grade, and it's been her and only her, ever since. I guess I just wanted to see what else life has to offer. Maybe there's something more I can get out of life."

Quietly, she sat. Her frown was just as exquisite as her smile, but he hated that he was the reason behind the expression. All of a sudden, she sighed, grabbed up her belongings, and started sliding out of the seat.

"Deli, please don't leave!" She stood up and turned to walk away from him. "Please! Delianna, just talk to me!"

"Why?" she yelled, spinning on him. "You want to feel like a big man before you head back to the little lady? Well, find somebody else to stroke your ego! I'm out of here!"

"Wait!" he exclaimed, jumping up and throwing money onto the table. All they'd had was coffee, but he tossed two twenties for holding the table for so long. "Hold on! Let me explain!" Delianna wasn't even listening, she was determined to escape as fast as her cream-colored sneakers would allow.

He followed her as she shot across the lobby and exited through the main entrance. She turned left and he stayed on her heels, ignoring the valet and bouncers who asked if everything was alright. Since it was so late, or depending on how you looked at it, so early, no more people were in the line. They were halfway down the street before she'd had enough and spun on him.

"What the hell is your problem? Why are you following me?" she asked.

"Deli, just give me a second to explain. I swear that I'm not trying to play games with you."

"Anthony, I'm not the kind of woman you're looking for. I'm not into one-nighters, okay. And I'm not a home-wreaker. Sure, I still think you're a good guy, but this isn't gonna happen. Please, just leave me alone and go home to your wife."

When she spun back around this time, he let her go. Slowly, he made his way back towards the club, his mind thinking over his actions during the past couple of hours. He had fucked up. And it was sad that it had taken another beautiful and independent woman to force his thoughts towards where they should have been all along: His wife.

Handing the ticket to the valet, he stood there with shame coursing through his blood. If Delianna had been a weaker woman, they would be on their way to her place, or a hotel, by now. He really needed to be thanking God that He hadn't stopped with her perfect outer shell. He had also given her strong morals and sense enough not to get tangled up in his bullshit.

Anyway, he had about a 45-minute drive to get back home and he didn't think he had the strength to make it. He would go to a hotel, call Sophia from there, then get some sleep. He was ready for this stupid fucking day to be over with.

Finally, the valet returned with his car. Anthony handed him a twenty and then climbed into the seat. Slamming the door, he zoomed off, his eyelids already starting to droop. He started to pull up his navigation, but saw a Hyatt at the end of the block. Steering the car into the parking lot, he was ready to take whatever accommodations they had available.

Ten minutes later, he was in a second-floor room, washing the stink of the day away. Shower out of the way, naked, he padded over to the window and shut the blinds tight. His next stop, face down on the Queen-sized bed. Before he even remembered he was supposed to be calling his wife, he was out like a light, dreaming of a Brazilian goddess telling him he wasn't getting anywhere near her ample assets.

When the morning came, he yawned and stretched, turning his face away from the punishing sunrays. Wait! Sunrays? Hadn't he closed the curtains last night. Focusing his eyes in that direction, he felt his whole world turn on its head. The view out of the window had made a drastic change.

Trees? In the middle of Chicago? "What the hell?" he murmured. Then he felt a shift beside him. He turned and then leaped up out of the bed. He had to rub his eyes a few times to make sure he was seeing what he was really seeing. He was standing there staring into the shocked, dark-chocolate eyes of Delianna Cruz.

Looking down at his body, he was now wearing a pair of shorts that he'd never seen a day in his life. He glanced back up at Deli, who had pulled the sheets up to cover all but her face, and angrily asked, "What the hell did you do to me?"

ABOUT THE AUTHOR

L. A. Burch is a Philly native who now resides in North Carolina. Burch attended Temple University, where he majored in Criminal Justice. You can learn more about him and keep up with his work on Goodreads, Barnes & Noble, Amazon Books, and Google Books. He can be reached at authorlaburch@gmail.com.

www.ingramcontent.com/pod-product-compliance
Lightning Source LLC
LaVergne TN
LVHW090557110826
845146LV00001B/166

* 9 7 9 8 9 9 0 2 4 7 2 6 0 *